HOUSE OF
TEMPTATIONS

By the same author:

HOUSE OF ANGELS
HOUSE OF INTRIGUE

HOUSE OF TEMPTATIONS

Yvonne Strickland

This book is a work of fiction.
In real life, make sure you practise safe sex.

First published in 1996 by
Nexus
332 Ladbroke Grove
London W10 5AH

Copyright © Yvonne Strickland 1996

Typeset by TW Typesetting, Plymouth, Devon

Printed and bound by
BPC Paperbacks Ltd, Aylesbury, Bucks

ISBN 0 352 33109 7

Contents

Contents

1

A Morning Passion

The soft morning air was sweet on her face and the sun, still low to the east, spread a gentle warmth. Reaching the shallow rise between the house and the valley, she stopped and turned. Gently easing a whisp of pale amber hair from her cheek and shading her hazel eyes, she looked back to the house; its white painted arches, terracotta roof, surrounding gardens and trees basked in the peaceful glow. Beyond the house, the tennis court lay deserted and a little sad. Between the front of the house and the curving driveway, the pool shimmered invitingly, its cluster of tables, chairs and bright sunshades accenting the background greenery with splashes of colour. The steady chirping of insects served to broaden the feeling of peace and tranquility which enveloped the land. Beyond the gardens lay the main road, backed by the vineyards of Languedoc, which stretched into the distance as far as her eye could see. Reaching the shallow rise between the house and the valley, she stopped. She felt the world might have been deserted.

Karen did not expect to find anybody else up and about at so early an hour but she had awakened at daybreak, showered, and with no special goal in mind, set out for a walk.

She thought about how her life had been altered during the months she had been at the house, recalling how she had applied for the secretarial job and remembering, too, the rainy day when she first met Sonia at the interview in England. She remembered her initial misgivings when she had found out that Sonia and her girls were involved in the SM and fetish scene on a commercial scale, and the initial loneliness she had experienced because her situation excluded her from the esoteric and bizarre activities with which the others there were so familiar. How could she have foreseen that in spite of her upbringing and attitude, she would have made such good friends amongst them? And how could she have known that the one whom she had regarded as devious and manipulative would draw her so deeply into her web of sensuality? For everyone at the house must by now have suspected, without the slightest hint of disapproval, that she and Sonia were more than just friends. Though perhaps they did not realise, for discretion was all, that Sonia had introduced her privately into some of the most voluptuous and devious of practices.

Karen placed her fingers upon the silver locket where it sat above her breasts. The locket was precious to Sonia, but Sonia had given it to her as a token of their intimacy, to keep secretly so that no one else should know. Even when she had returned to England, to consider the direction her life was taking, she had kept the locket. But Karen saw no point in pretending, for some, including Valerie, surely knew of that which had never been spoken.

This place was her home, these people her friends; perhaps the truest friends she had ever had. And though she had seen video movies of how they fulfilled their roles within and without the house, she had not judged them harshly, despite her less than liberal views on the pleasures of the flesh. But this world had its own frame of references, its own perspectives and meanings. They were just as real and relevant as those which she had been brought up with and had once taken for granted as being the norm. In her wildest imaginings, she could not have envisaged some of the things that had happened to her since her arrival.

If, at first, she had felt deep shame and guilt at what seemed to be the most improper acts of carnality, she had not, even in her most introspective moments, caught the sulphurous whiff of hellfire. If the demons were stalking her for what she had done, then at least she was in good

2

company. There was a demon, of course, and she was getting to know it well, for it was the demon of lust which had been allowed too little freedom for too long. And having tasted freedom, it wanted more, even more than she had so far ventured to permit it, for she had not yet dared to acknowledge that it might one day be given full rein. She still carried the guilt within, of course. Sometimes it spoke to her in silent disapproval, catching her at the oddest moments, often when she was alone at night. But it was only the shade of guilt which stalked her now, and not the granite ogre which had once so readily stood in her path.

Karen turned and continued to walk over the grassy rise until the house was out of sight and she could see across the wooded valley to the distant sea. There to her right was the wooden bench where she often sat, sometimes alone, sometimes with Angela, the one who had shown her understanding and helped so often in her times of doubt. The seat, empty now in the sunlight, stood beneath the pine tree which provided it with welcome shade when the sun was higher in the sky and the day hotter. Perhaps, before then, Angela would join her in this idyllic little place. If not, she would read for a while and then take a swim before breakfast, for under the loose-fitting purple and white beach dress, was the little gold and blue striped swim slip she had bought late last summer in Beziers. It was the auburn-haired, mischievous, Annette who had talked her into buying it from the boutique, for such an audaciously brief garment was not one she would have cared to be seen in until that day. She was aware of the cord passing down between the cheeks of her behind and of the small, elasticated front cupping her shaven sex and caressing it like a soft hand. Her hair had been removed permanently in the beauty parlour. She had been held down, unable to speak or to prevent them from doing it. Afterwards, they had served her voluptuously. It had almost driven her wild. The very memory of it made her heart beat faster.

She placed her white shoulder bag down and sat on the bench. With eyes closed, she listened to the insects for a time, then reached into the bag to pull out her cigarettes and lighter. Smoking was her little concession to another sin, for it was forbidden in the house.

The blue smoke drifted and coiled lazily upward into the air. Karen browsed through a paperback novel then laid it aside. She was not in the mood to read when the morning was hers to savour like a good wine.

She delighted in the gentle warmth and remained quite at ease until the cigarette was finished. Kicking off her shoes, she arose, and looking about to confirm that she was indeed as alone as she wished to be, she lifted up and removed her dress. She placed the dress over the wooden back rest, turned to face the sun and stretched out her limbs. It was good and sensual to feel the morning heat caress her body. She ran her fingers down over her firm breasts, over the pink nipples, down her sides and over the curve of her thighs. Sitting down, she leant back against the dress and closed her eyes, telling herself that this was the first morning ever and that she was quite alone in the world.

Her thoughts began to drift like a fallen petal upon a lazy stream, touching upon the things she had done and enjoyed doing, and the secrets that had been revealed in the new life she had embarked upon. Slowly, her hand moved over her stomach until her fingers rested against the smooth flesh a little above her sex. For a time, she hesitated, listening to the birds and hearing the whine of jet engines above. Opening her eyes, she pushed down the G-string slip, and laid it aside. Spreading her legs, she watched as the airliner, coming in from the west, banked and began its descent towards Montpellier. Her fingers found the focus of pleasure and she began to stroke, slowly at first. As she watched the passing jet, she thought that if it came down low enough, they might all see and know what she was doing to herself.

But, of course, the plane was too far away. Even so, the thought of being observed by all those passers-by, people who would never know or see her again, amused her and urged her on. Her fingers moved more quickly and entered

4

further into her inflamed sex, stroking with the rhythm of her heartbeat. The heat she was feeling now was greater, much greater, than that from the morning sun. She closed the world out and let her head fall back, feeling the effervescence welling up from her loins and spreading throughout her body. With her mouth opened a little, she began to sigh, quietly at first but, as unmeasured time drifted by, her breathing grew louder. When the tide of pleasure overwhelmed her, she let out a long, low cry, and her body went as rigid as crystal glass with the flames of pleasure glowing through it.

When she opened her eyes, the light was dazzling and she raised a hand to shield out the glare. The wide blue sky was empty, the airliner gone. She was reaching out for the sun slip when a voice from behind called, 'Hi Karen!'

She twisted about, startled. 'Oh, Angie! I – What are you –?'

Angela, with smiling blue-grey eyes and long, silver-blonde hair wound about her head and fastened at the side with a blue clasp, stood but a few paces away. 'I'm sorry, sweetie. I didn't mean to creep up on you. I was strolling along the ridge. I thought I heard someone call out just now. Didn't you hear anything?'

Karen felt her face redden. 'No – no, I've been dozing in the sun. Look – er, I'm sorry –' she reached behind for her dress – 'I didn't expect anyone about so early. I just thought I'd . . .'

Angela began to laugh. 'There's no need to be embarrassed, silly! I sunbathe in the nude here myself sometimes. Who cares!'

Karen smiled sheepishly, got up and pulled on the dress. She regarded Angela for a moment, in her white, sleeveless cotton top and flared, blue satin mini-skirt. Angela was in her early twenties, perhaps a year or two, at the most, younger than Karen. And like Karen and all the other girls at the house, she was beautiful. 'There's no need to get dressed on my account,' she continued. 'I'm sure we're the only ones out here.'

'No, I think I will anyway. The seat's a bit uncomfortable.'

5

She moved along to make space. 'Are you staying for a bit? D'you fancy a cigarette?'

'Yes, I will, if you don't mind; if you didn't want to be left alone, that is.'

'Angie, of course I don't mind. I always like your company, you know that.'

Angela sat beside her. 'It's a lovely time of the day, isn't it? I always think so, anyway.'

'Yes, gorgeous.'

'How come you're up and about so early on a Saturday?'

Karen held out a cigarette and smiled. 'It's one of those things I always thought I should do, but never managed until now. How about you?'

'Oh, I usually get up early. I always have since I was at school. The only time I have a lie-in is when we have visitors to entertain or put on a show. Well, you know . . .'

Karen did know. Sonia had made that clear at the interview. She knew about the erotic theatre that was played out and recorded for the ever-demanding market, and about the wealthy visitors who appeared at the house from time to time. And she was aware that Angela often played the submissive role in these fantasies, even though none of the girls ever broke the rules of discretion and discussed the details of their work openly.

'It doesn't seem possible that you've been here over a year,' said Angela, drawing on the cigarette.

'Well, I did have a few weeks break back in England didn't I? But I know what you mean. The time has gone by quickly – quicker than I could have imagined.'

'That must mean you're fairly happy now.'

'Yes,' replied Karen, 'I suppose I am.'

'But you're not terribly sure.'

'Well, it's not that . . .'

She looked into Angela's eyes, hoping that she might understand what was lurking inside the depths of her mind because Karen dared not express it openly, not even to her.

'Look,' said Karen, 'I was thinking I might go for a swim and then have breakfast. I'd be glad if you came along too. Unless you were planning something else, that is.'

6

'No, I wasn't,' Angela said with a gentle, knowing look. Karen sometimes wondered if Angela knew more than she let on.

They lay floating on their backs, the crystal water glistening about their slim bodies like two goddesses under a blissful sun and cobalt sky. They circled slowly around, their hair swarming out beneath their shoulders, their eyes closed.

Someone watched them with studied enthusiasm, eyes resting on each of their bodies in turn, seeing their breasts with their pink and prominent nipples break the water, noting the little string slip which adorned Karen and the equally minimal garment in deep blue satin worn by Angela. He leant on his spade and let out a long sigh.

Angela opened her eyes. 'Hey, look at that pervert staring at us!' she cried with mock indignation.

Karen looked about and grinned. 'Hi Mike!'

His face moulded to a broad smile, the sunlight glinted in his blue eyes. 'Me, a pervert? I'd have to be a pervert *not* to stare at you two!' He passed a hand across a suntanned forehead, and pushed the short, fair hair from his face. 'I might dive in and join you, if I thought I'd get out alive!'

'What?' replied Angela. 'In those dirty old things?'

He fingered his T-shirt and looked down at his jeans. 'Some of us have jobs to do!'

'On a Saturday?' said Karen.

'Yes!' He smiled. 'A man's work is never done!'

'That's because you take so long to get started!' responded Angela. 'Why don't you go and get us both an orange juice? You know where everything is. And wash that muck off your hands first!'

He scratched his head and affected a look of despair before laying down the spade. Then, strolling away from the pool, he made towards the French windows of the conservatory and bar, next to the main entrance to the house.

'Poor Mike,' said Karen, 'we do take advantage of him, don't we?'

7

'Not as much as Annette by any means. But he loves it really.'

They liked Mike, of course, for he had all the manners and discretion of a gentleman despite being barely into his thirties. Both Angela and Karen had experienced physical passion with him, neither disclosing the affair to the other. And he too was discreet, as much out of necessity as through good manners. They all knew that his present situation, as enviable as it might appear, had been born out of difficulty. It was no secret that his escape from the clutches of the British tax authorities had been in part due to Sonia's help, whilst he was still her financial adviser in London.

'I think we ought to get out and put something on before he comes back,' said Angela.

'You do?' responded Karen.

'Well, yes. If we're still like this, his hands will start shaking and he'll spill the drinks!'

Karen and Angela sat over a light breakfast in the conservatory. Through the window she could see Mike, digging over the flower beds at the sides of the driveway. From the direction of the bar, a figure approached. Karen turned to see Sonia nearing their table. 'Hello you two,' she said. 'I'm not butting in, am I?'

'No,' responded Karen, 'of course not.'

Angela smiled and said, 'Pull up a chair.'

Had they not been so familiar with Sonia, her intimidating appearance might have precluded such a casual greeting. For Sonia, with dark, slightly oriental features and black hair swept back from her face into a bun, had about her an aura of quiet authority, reinforced in no mean part by her attire of black leather biker jacket, heavy black lycra leggings and black, high-heeled ankle boots. Sonia normally wore black. It could seldom be otherwise. She sat down and peered through the windows, her gaze fixed on the far end of the curving driveway where it passed through the trees and joined the main road.

'Have you heard from them all yet?' asked Karen.

8

'All but one,' answered Sonia. 'Everything else is arranged.'

'Is there no way of finding out?'

'Apparently not,' replied Sonia. 'Trouble is, if she doesn't show up, the whole thing is a waste of time and money.'

'What's the problem?' Angela asked.

'It's the shots for our new London client,' answered Sonia. 'The studio people will be here with two of the models by eight thirty on Monday morning but the third model seems to have gone missing: whereabouts unknown.'

'Why don't you get one of us to stand in?' offered Angela.

'No, you couldn't,' responded Karen. 'They don't want anyone who's been in anything like this before.'

'Yes,' added Sonia, 'it has to be new faces but people familiar with the scene.'

'Shall I get you anything from the bar?' offered Angela.

Sonia glanced at her watch. 'If you wouldn't mind, please; a sandwich or something so I can get back to the office in case there's a phone call.'

She arose and without further comment, Angela followed.

'That's a bit odd, isn't it?' remarked Angela a little later. 'Surely nobody would know if it was one of us. Can it matter all that much?'

'Apparently it does,' replied Karen. 'It's the start of quite a big project too: international sales and all that.'

'What are they shooting?' asked Angela.

'Well, clothes for one thing and, er – all sorts of other bits and pieces. I'm not entirely sure.'

'Nothing dangerous, I hope.'

'I really wouldn't know,' replied Karen, picking up her coffee cup.

Angela picked up her cup too and regarded Karen. 'Why don't you have a go?'

'What, me?'

'Why not? Unless it's something you object to like, well you know.'

Karen stared back for a moment then looked down at the table. 'Em, well, I suppose Sonia did mention it to me once – modelling, that is. Nothing ever came of it.'

'You could hold your own with any model, anywhere,' said Angela with a smile.

'Thanks, but I've never been involved with anything like that. I mean, it might show if I haven't got the confidence.'

'You don't need all that much confidence with your looks and figure,' smiled Angela.

Karen swirled the coffee about in her cup and stared at it thoughtfully. 'Has anyone ever recognised you, Angie? All those things you and the others have been in. Somebody must have seen one of you at sometime or other.'

Angela smiled. 'Karen sweetie, I bet if you had just put down a copy of any well known fashion magazine and half the models from it walked by you in the street, you wouldn't realise it was them. None of us have had any problems that I'm aware of. I certainly haven't.'

'Oh well, I just wondered,' said Karen.

Karen left the bar and crossed the ground floor corridor to enter the main office opposite. Sonia was at her desk next to the window on the far side and about to finish a telephone conversation as Karen closed the door. She walked across the room towards Sonia, skirting about the group of green leather chairs arranged around the coffee table in the centre. Sonia replaced the telephone and looked up at her with a blank expression. Usually, Karen could expect a smile.

'No luck?'

'She's cleared off somewhere with her boyfriend. That's all anyone seems to know.'

'Well, I might be able to help out if – if you want, that is?'

Sonia leant back in the chair and held her with dark eyes. 'I don't see what you or anyone here can do. Anyway, you aren't supposed to be working today; it's Saturday.'

Karen pulled over a chair and sat down opposite. 'What I – what I mean is, if it would help out, I'll stand in for the other girl.'

'My dear,' replied Sonia, 'I do appreciate what you're saying, but none of this is your problem and it's not what I would expect of you. That has always been our understanding, since you accepted the situation here.'

'Yes, I know, but that was for my sake and I saw things a bit differently then. Anyway, you did once suggest that I could try a bit of modelling didn't you. And that's all it is, isn't it?'

Sonia looked at her for a moment, then smiled. 'Darling, there's no denying it would get me out of a mess. We have a contract with the publishers in London, but you are more important than –'

'Is it because you don't think I'd be good enough?' cut in Karen.

'Good enough! I think we both know there aren't any worries on that account.'

'All right,' continued Karen, 'I know all the outline details since I typed most of the letters. It's just an erotic fashion show isn't it? I mean, there's nothing else?'

Sonia placed clenched knuckles against her chin. 'Yes, there is I'm afraid. You've dealt with the letters and contracts but they don't go into all the details.'

'Oh, I see. Well, you could give me some idea anyway, couldn't you, seeing as we've got this far?'

Sonia relaxed further back into the chair. 'Look, do you want a drink? I opened a bottle of amontillado last night. It's in the fridge.'

'God, is it that bad?' smiled Karen.

'That is for you to decide. But it's me that needs the drink; I thought you might like to join me.'

'It's a bit early, but why not?'

Sonia proceeded to the kitchenette and reappeared moments later with the bottle and two glasses. 'All right,' she began, pouring the sherry, 'they are theme shots. The theme is a damsel in distress. The girl who plays her role is the one who seems to have cleared off.' Sonia looked at her over the sherry glass. 'The set-ups are bondage subjects, with all the props and appropriate backgrounds. That's the reason for them coming all the way here.'

'I see,' replied Karen, looking into her glass.

'There's no direct sex involved,' continued Sonia, 'but the two girls are complete strangers to everyone here. I haven't known them long myself. That is another reason why I don't expect you to concern yourself about it.'

Karen continued to stare into the glass. Silent moments drifted by. 'Sonia, some of the things I've done in this house – you and I, I mean – I don't think it's going to make much difference is it? And if I'm the only one who can help, well . . .'

Sonia smiled at her, knowing full well how Karen had been drawn ever deeper into the maze of sensuality since her arrival all those months ago. It was a maze she seemed to have no wish to find her way out of. 'I'd be very grateful, I really would. I did consider Rose, but she is still wanted by the police, so it doesn't seem like a good idea.'

'Yes,' replied Karen, 'I wondered about that myself. So, what's next?'

'Best if you talk to Cheryl about the details; she's responsible for outfits, and the rest. I've left everything to her, though she won't need to be around most of the time because everyone involved will know what they are supposed to do.'

'Hmm, perhaps it would be better if I didn't ask. I think I might leave things as they are and worry about it on Monday.'

'It's not being taped by James,' said Sonia. 'There's only the technician, and her female assistant, and they're used to it. They've worked for me all over Europe so you need not be concerned about them.'

'Why isn't it going on video?' asked Karen.

'Because there isn't a strong story line; it was never conceived as a movie. James isn't even here that day, though they will be using his cameras.'

'You mean they won't be in the room?'

Sonia smiled. 'No, they're processing the images as a

sequence of digitised stills. They'll be in the annexe. You don't have to meet them at all, my dear.'

Karen relaxed. 'God, I imagined tripods, flashguns and people dodging about all over the place to get the best angles.'

'Well, I'm glad to say it won't be quite like that. The images will even be modifed on computer. They will alter backgrounds, put in new features. But that's not our concern for now.'

Karen was glad about James, for all the people she knew at the house, Sonia was the only one she wished to see the images. Sonia could possess those, for Sonia already possessed her.

Karen thought of the tall and gaunt James; pale blue eyes peering magnified through thick spectacles beneath abundant white hair. James worked in the annexe gathering, recording and editing the images from the many discreet cameras positioned in those rooms of the house where they were required. He saw everything the girls and the visitors did in those special rooms with relative indifference. His emotional and physical inclinations were not towards members of the opposite sex. He was the perfect man for the job.

'There are only three set-ups being done here,' said Sonia. 'The rest will be shot in Paris in ten days time.'

Sonia held her gaze, hesitating for a moment. 'Look, if you're still keen and you fancy another trip to Paris, it will be purely fashion; indoor and outdoor location shots. You would be perfect for that too.'

'Well, yes, I'd love to have a go.'

'And,' continued Sonia, 'you can stay with Josephine again if you wish. I think she and Armand gave you a good time before, didn't they?'

'Yes,' answered Karen, feeling her heart quicken at the thought of what they had done together, 'they gave me a very good time.'

'Good,' said Sonia, 'then it's settled, and I can relax again. And you – what are you doing today?' Did you

13

know Lorna and a couple of the others are off to Narbonne soon? Why don't you go along with them?'

'No, I can't,' answered Karen, rising from the table. 'Val's doing my hair at eleven.'

'Oh, I see. Then perhaps I'll go myself, now that I don't have to sit by the phone any longer. I could do with a break from this office.'

Karen regarded this as unusual, for as she left, she recalled that Sonia rarely mixed socially with the others and usually went out alone in her own car. The offer of help had evidently removed a considerable weight from her shoulders.

After some time with Angela and Annette by the pool, Karen returned to the house, passed by the arched entrance to the bar and the door opposite the now empty office, then turned and hurried up the main stairs to her apartment on the second floor.

The apartment was cool, comfortable and self-contained. She pulled off her dress and gazed through the window across the gardens, at the shimmering pool and the sunlit landscape beyond. Her watch said ten forty. She began to wonder about the commitment she had made. In the warmth of the shower she wondered too about the events of earlier that morning. Had Angela been watching her? She recalled what she had seen Angela do in the gardens with those two men on the night of the party last year, and how she herself had been both shocked and aroused. It was possible that at that time she had begun to realise how her own sensuality was beginning to push out into the light, as a budding flower hidden beneath a stone needs to find the sun.

Once dried and in her small bedroom, she regarded herself in the long mirror. 'Can't delay,' she muttered, seeing the clock-radio display wink over to ten fifty-two. She stepped over to the wardrobe. Pulling open the door, she glanced over the profusion of dresses and outfits; some for everyday wear, some for occasions of a much more private nature. Most of them, including most of the shoes and underwear, had been put there on her return from London. No one had said anything about it since, and she had accepted that they were a gift from Sonia. There was no time to prevaricate. She opened the drawer beneath the dresser and lifted out her favourite style of bikini brief in sheerest black nylon, then selected and pulled on a close-fitting, sleeveless, high-necked top in white, ribbed nylon. It moulded perfectly to her body. Her chosen skirt was a denim blue flared mini and for her feet, high-heeled, sling-backed sandals in white leather with delicate braided straps and small gold buckles.

She closed the wardrobe door, looked at her reflection and pushed the hair back over her shoulders. She wanted to look good. Valerie and Kim always did in their own little domain, no matter what their duties involved. It was part of their image. It had to be part of Karen's.

Karen used the narrow back stairs to return to the ground floor. These were darker, windowless, and seldom used. She always tried to be discreet when visiting the beauty parlour, even when it was only for a hair-do. The guilt, like the thrill of that first visit had never entirely vanished.

When she reached the blue panelled door with the little APPOINTMENTS ONLY TODAY sign, she did not try the ornate brass handle for she knew the door would be locked. The fact that it was usually kept locked was a form of reassurance to others who used their services, as well as to Karen. She raised her hand and rang the brass doorbell. Seconds later, there was a click and the door swung inward. A smiling face appeared, a face with flashing gypsy eyes and long black crinkled hair held in place by a blue clasp. 'Hello lovey! Come inside.'

Karen followed, glancing briefly back about the corridor.

The door swung shut behind and they moved through the short passage to the inner door. The beauty parlour was welcoming, with soft pink cornice lights, deep blue tiled walls and rich mauve carpet. It could be regarded as a practical place, with a long wall-mirror above the two

15

sinks, the chrome and black leather chairs and the two hairdryers on stands further along, just before the bathroom. But Karen knew that it, like other parts of the house, had its tingling secrets. She was aware of the low bench extending out from the opposite wall, presently covered by fitted pink towelling, and the oddly shaped chair close to the hairdryers, its outline softened by the dark blue fabric cover. She knew well what they were meant for and why there were obscured.

Valerie and Kim did not fail her expectations. The contrast in their looks was obvious: Kim, in her early twenties, was a little younger than Valerie; her long hair was mid-brown, and her eyes were blue; her features were rounder and softer.

In attire they were identical, for both had on skin-tight, stretch-vinyl catsuits in deep metallic blue, with high collars and long sleeves. Their high-heeled ankle boots were metallic grey and the wide belt about their slim waists was the same colour. Whatever service Karen returned to this room for, she was always made to feel special. Perhaps Valerie and Kim made everyone feel special. Both smiled and chatted as they worked on her hair. Even the act of brushing was sensual. Karen sat with her eyes closed, wishing them never to stop.

She was, all the same, unable to dispel the anxiety from her mind. Had it been a mistake to offer herself for the photographic sessions? As time went by, the doubts were growing.

When they had finished brushing, Valerie said, 'You're tense, Karen. Is anything the matter?'

'Yes, I thought so too,' added Kim. 'You look a bit worried.'

'Do I? Well I suppose you might as well know. I've offered to help out with this photo shoot, because of the missing model.'

'Oh, so you're going to be the sacrificial victim.' Kim grinned from her reflection in the mirror. A look of concern passed over Karen's face. Valerie perceived it and said, 'Don't worry deary, it's nothing too heavy. Take no

16

notice of her. She's only jealous because she couldn't be in it!'

They sat on stools at either side of her and began to gently massage her face and neck. Karen relaxed and closed her eyes. They did their job well. Better than anyone Karen had ever encountered. Even styling and brushing hair was an act of sensuality in their hands and they well knew the effect it had upon her.

After a time, a voice close to her ear, Valerie's voice, whispered, 'We don't need to stop now. We can go on until all your tensions have vanished. It's all part of the service.'

'Yes, all part of the service,' added Kim, softly with a gentle smile.

Karen had heard those words before. She was well aware of what they implied.

'Don't say another word,' came the voice of Valerie in her other ear.

But while the words were familiar that did not mean there was a routine. She did not know exactly what to expect, and never had done. She had only come to know that she should keep her eyes closed and remain silent.

Two pairs of hands squeezed and caressed her neck, shoulders and arms. Soon, she was aware of them pulling up her nylon top. She raised her arms to allow it free passage as it slid over her head and was removed. Her heart began to beat faster beneath firm and naked breasts.

But no one spoke. Karen resisted the temptation to open her eyes a little in order to see what they were about to do, for she heard behind her a slight metallic chink: the now familar sound of a roller buckle. At last, something happened. She felt the harness as it was lowered into position over her head. She breathed in the pungent odour of latex as the soft pads pressed over her eyes and the rubber ball forced open and slid into her mouth. The buckles chinked and tightened as the rubber web was fitted securely about her face and head.

She knew they would deny her speech and possibly vision. Except for that first time, on the bench, they always had. They understood her very well. They understood that if she could not voice her objections, she need not feel guilt about what they did with her.

They helped her out of the chair and guided her a few unseeing and uncertain steps to what she guessed must be near to the centre of the room. Her wrists were taken simultaneously and both arms were pulled firmly up above her head. Each wrist was slipped quickly into the cool embrace of a leather cuff and each cuff was secured with its buckle until her arms were held up and apart, above her head. Now it was too late to wonder what they were going to do. No muffled protest, no tugging against the straps would make any difference. They were not the friends she knew outside the parlour, not the Val and Kim of the restaurant, the pool or the gardens. They were instruments of lust who held and controlled her body, though she knew that, in her case at least, it was not done without affection. The waistband loosened and her skirt was allowed to fall. Fingers and thumbs slipped down under the elastic of the little briefs, pushed them down and eased them over her shoes.

Something was being moved towards her across the carpet, a piece of furniture perhaps. It stopped close by. She gripped the connecting straps above her wrists as the unseen hands pulled her foot up from the floor and held it high, whilst the object they had brought over was slipped under her knee. The operation was repeated quickly with her other leg and Karen realised that they had placed the low bench beneath so that she was kneeling on the pink towelling which covered it. The hands took her legs and began to ease them apart. A cool strap was passed around each, just above the knee, and the pulling continued until her thighs were fixed wide and her arms and body were held rigid with the increased tension.

Moments after they moved away, another sound reached her ears. There was no mistaking the snap of the thin latex gloves they were adjusting on their hands. A cupboard door opened, and a glass stopper was removed from a bottle and placed down by the sink. She could hear them breathing and moving beside her. They dripped warm oil

18

about her shoulders and latex fingers smoothed it into her flesh. More followed and the oil, pleasantly burning, was spread and massaged about her back and over her breasts; hands squeezing about the nipples, making them sensitive and button hard. She did not know whose hands did what, for Valerie and Kim remained silent, but as electric fingers played further down her body, she ceased to consider the matter further.

Hands slipped and glided exquisitely about the base of her spine and stomach. Then they were about her thighs and behind, kneading and squeezing with gentle, tantalising sensuality, coursing over the smooth, hairless flesh above her vulva, following the burning trickle of oil which oozed remorselessly down between the cheeks of her behind. The smooth fingers moved close to the focus of her pleasure, but never quite reached the goal, each time making her jerk and take in her breath. Her nostrils flared as she breathed harder, and her heart beat faster. She felt her sex, moist and inflamed, circled by those maddening fingers; awaiting the final assault, the blue flames were already arcing through her body.

She moaned sharply through the gag as a finger and thumb squeezed the lips of her sex together whilst another stroked the clitoris. From behind, a hand slipped underneath and an oiled finger pushed into her anus. She tensed against the straps with a soft moan, twisting her head from side to side as the finger invaded her rear and pushed insistently up into the rectum. Her sex was entered too; this other finger stroking deeply into the core of her lust. They worked her gently enough, but they must have known how close was the crisis, and how she was starting to burn inside. Her moans passed about the rubber ball, louder and shorter as the flames engulfed her. She willed them to enter her more deeply, further than they could possibly go, until she threw back her head and her body heaved in its final, sobbing tumult of bliss.

After the shower, when her body was free of oil and she had wiped herself about with the big pink towel, the aroma

19

of fresh coffee drifted through the slightly open door. When she was dressed, Valerie and Kim greeted and kissed her, as if to offer her their congratulations on the successful passage through some unnamed ordeal. To Karen, the only ordeal might once have been her own shame. But, somehow, this act of affection as she entered the main room of the parlour underscored and finalised what had gone before, so that like a short play, it was ended, and their relationship could return to normal.

Karen left the beauty parlour intending to take a walk before lunch and, perhaps, to find Angela again. On passing from the air conditioned house, through the swing doors and on to the steps of the porch, she encountered two figures. Both were young, not yet twenty, and both had bristling punk hairstyles. It was the first time in many weeks that they had left the house without wigs for, as Karen knew, they had been deprived of their hair in an act of spite by the now departed Pauline. The very Pauline who had changed places with Cheryl and presently ran Sonia's establishment in London. The two girls, dressed in white T-shirts and blue denim mini skirts with designer frayed hems, were occupied with Valerie's ginger cat, Pancake, who stretched out on the step in purring contentment before them whilst they ran their fingers through his fur and scratched behind his ears.

'Hello you two!' said Karen.

Jackie turned first, a smile breaking out under her large brown eyes. Rose, her streetwise blue eyes set in slightly harder features, smiled too and mouthed a greeting.

'What d'you reckon?' asked Jackie, passing a hand across the top of her head. Both had once boasted long hair, Jackie's golden brown like Karen's, and Rose's straw blonde.

'It's coming along nicely,' Karen replied. 'You should both be able to go wherever you want now without worrying about it.'

'I'm not going nowhere –'

'Anywhere!' cut in Jackie.

'Right – anywhere, until mine gets longer. I wouldn't dare.'

Rose was a singular case. After eluding the police, who sought her as an accomplice in a jewel robbery in Lyon, she had been caught in the grounds of the house. Sonia had given her the opportunity of going on the run again, or joining her girls, provided she made the effort to cast off her east London coarseness and improve her presentation. It was considered that, like the beautiful and masochistic Jackie, she would prove to be an asset of no mean order in Sonia's exploitation of the male sex.

'At least we can get out more now and talk to the others,' continued Rose. 'It was like a concentration camp with that old cow around!'

Jackie returned her attentions to the cat and said nothing on the subject. Karen, as well as everyone else, was aware of the strong slave-to-mistress relationship that had existed between her and Pauline. It was a love-hate relationship which often left Jackie in tearful distress, but did not prevent her from falling foul of Pauline with remarkable ease and frequency. Since Rose's arrival, they had shared the same first floor apartment together, next to Pauline's old suite. During this time they had become closer, both emotionally and physically, than most people realised. Even so, neither would consider herself indifferent to members of the opposite sex and of that everyone was, in Jackie's case, well aware.

'How are you finding Cheryl?' asked Karen.

'She's fine.' Jackie smiled. 'I like her more now she's here for good and I know her better.'

'I wouldn't want to get on the wrong side of her,' commented Rose.

Karen smiled, knowing that getting on the wrong side of Cheryl was something Jackie was certain to do sooner rather than later. For it was now Cheryl's lot to oversee the day to day running of the house, to delegate domestic duties to the more submissive girls and to emphasise their roles through punishments when misbehaviour so required. Jackie was not unfamiliar with Cheryl's methods and Rose too had some experience of them from her early days at the house.

Karen would have chatted for longer but was aware that something was diverting their attention away from both herself and the cat. She looked up. Beyond the driveway, Mike had appeared at the poolside in his swimming shorts. He stood for a time, stretching his limbs in the midday sun before joining Annette in the crystal water.

They weaved and circled about beneath the cloudless sky, plunging and surfacing, their bodies shimmering against the blue tiles below. He broke the water, swept the hair from his eyes and stood, watching her pass close by in her diminutive blue swim slip, limbs moving gracefully, hair billowing over her shoulders.

She saw him waiting and surfaced, pushing back her auburn hair, darkened by the water, bright sun glistening in green eyes. 'You're still a bit sore at me, aren't you, Mike?' She approached him with pouting lips. 'That's not the grown-up boy I thought I knew.'

His eyes were fixed on hers but his attention was on her breasts, with swollen nipples shedding sapphire droplets of water. 'No, Annette, of course I'm not sore. Wary and suspicious maybe. That's different.'

He recalled the episode the previous summer, the culmination of their secret meetings, when she had set him up in one of the games rooms for a sexual escapade with herself and Cheryl, and caused him, as a consequence, to become fully involved in the activities of the house by having the whole episode recorded. She had exploited him with mischief, not malace, but their relationship had never reverted back to its earlier intimacy even though they remained on superficially amiable terms.

'Don't you think you're better off, now you're a star?' She grinned. 'You get paid for what other men would fall over themselves to pay for, if they could afford it!'

'God! You're so mercenary! There's got to be more to it than that.'

She started laughing.

'Well, I'm glad you think it's funny!' he remarked.

'Oh Mike, you get so serious sometimes! If I didn't think it was fun most of the time as well, I wouldn't be in it, money or no.'

'I see. So you did succumb to my charms a little bit? You didn't start out from the very beginning to set me up?'

'Of course I didn't. It just escalated over the weeks. It was as much your fault as mine, but I can't believe you didn't enjoy it.'

Mike considered the proposition, 'Well . . .'

'Come on, admit it!'

'Alright, yes. But I enjoyed it even more when it was you and I without all the damned lights and cameras.'

'Ooh, poor old Michael,' she said tantalisingly, pouting her lips at him and moving closer through the water. 'All those naughty ladies wanting to play with your body and not even the empire left to think about whilst they're doing it.'

'It would help me bear the strain if you'd come over and have a drink with me one day; the way we used to.'

'I'll consider it, maybe, if you say I'm totally forgiven.'

'OK,' he grinned, 'you're forgiven. Totally. I can't see that there's much else you can drop me into, so how about it?'

She regarded him with a hint of amusement in her eyes.

'Well, how about tomorrow?' he pressed.

'Tomorrow is Sunday,' she smiled. 'It's my day of rest.'

'That's fine,' he responded. 'You can come around and rest in my bed!'

'I think you're getting worse,' she replied. 'You know what they do with tomcats don't you?'

He screwed up his face in mock agony. 'Don't say things like that.'

'What time tomorrow did you have in mind, dear?' she grinned broadly.

'How about in the evening, after dinner?'

'Have you changed the bedding since I was last there?' she asked.

'No,' he said, 'I haven't actually. If you stand and watch, you can see it twitching.'

23

'It had better be fit for a lady, that's all, otherwise I'll turn around and –'

'Look, here's Karen,' he cut in.

Annette followed his gaze. Karen waved to them, still halfway between the house and the pool.

'About eight thirty then?' said Annette, waving towards Karen. 'We could meet here first.'

'Right, eight thirty. And I'll have a bottle of Chablis on ice.'

'Chablis! Mike, you tight sod! I expect champagne if I'm coming around to your place. And clean glasses!'

'You drive a tough bargain,' he beamed, dodging the water she threw up at him, 'but I'll sort something out.'

'Hi!' came the voice from the poolside. Karen stood smiling, her hand shading her eyes against the glare from the water.

'Coming in for a dip?' asked Mike.

'No, I was trying to find Angie. I thought I'd track her down and have lunch out here, it's so lovely.'

'Angie's on bar duty,' said Annette.

'Lunch out here seems a good idea,' put in Mike.

'I agree,' said Annette. 'You pop over and get some food and drinks while I chat to Karen.'

Mike, taken aback, looked from one to the other.

'No, don't get out,' smiled Karen. 'I'm dressed. I'll wander back and fetch a tray of goodies for all of us.'

Karen retraced her steps to the house. Mike said, 'You weren't trying to get rid of me, were you?'

'Of course not, but you're supposed to be a gentleman and look after us ladies with kindness, consideration and unquestioning obedience.'

'I'll be kind and considerate on Sunday, if not unquestioning!' he teased, then launched himself forward, gliding under the water towards the far end of the pool. Annette settled on to her back, and with eyes closed against the dazzling blue sky, swam slowly in the same direction.

'I hope neither of you considers me an easy touch after Pauline,' she said calmly.

24

'No,' answered Rose.

'No,' followed Jackie.

'I didn't altogether see eye to eye with her over some of her methods,' continued Cheryl, looking from one to the other with her sharp, blue eyes, 'and I don't intend to confine you both to your room. I'll just tell you to keep out of trouble and behave sensibly. I don't want any difficulties. If you agree to that, we'll get on fine. Is that understood?'

They nodded and answered, 'Yes.'

Cheryl, her face an image of cool Nordic beauty, looked younger than her thirty-two years. She regarded the girls intently. Jackie knew, in part from her own experience at Cheryl's hands, that she had trained as a nurse, and that she continued the theme of her earlier profession most successfully when dealing with Sonia's clients.

Cheryl was not emotionally expressive; she smiled even less than Pauline used to, but her manner and her looks, with her loosely permed blonde hair and sensual lips, Jackie and Rose found less intimidating.

'Rose,' she said, 'I'd appreciate it if you would go now and allow me a few minutes with Jackie.'

'Yes, OK,' answered Rose, looking at Jackie. 'I'll get off then and, er – see you later, Jackie.'

Cheryl watched her leave the room and close the door silently behind her. The room appeared much as Pauline had left it. To Jackie, standing in front of the desk where she had so often been called to account, but seeing a different person there, was an odd, mildly disquieting experience.

'Go and sit over there,' said Cheryl, indicating the green leather two seater and two single chairs by the window. Cheryl got up from behind the desk and followed her. 'Jackie, would you like a drink?'

'Er – no, no thanks,' replied Jackie with an unsure smile.

Cheryl sat down opposite and regarded her for a few seconds. Jackie looked down at the floor.

'Jackie, I do understand you. I know how it was with you and Pauline.'

'Yes all right!' responded a mildly flustered Jackie, looking up at her. 'I know I'm a bloody nympho and I know

25

perfectly well what a masochist is! And I know why it suits my old man to have me stay here, OK?'

'You don't have to worry about anything Jackie, that's all. You will come to this office for consultation on a regular basis. Your needs will be dealt with. Do you understand?'

Jackie nodded and answered almost inaudibly, 'If you say so.'

'If you say so,' repeated Cheryl. 'And I do say so, Jackie. I do say so!'

'That Cheryl,' said Rose, as they strolled away from the house along the drive, 'she doesn't seem a bad sort underneath.'

'Cheryl's OK,' agreed Jackie wistfully.

Rose gave her a questioning look. 'What did she want you to stay for? Something I'm not supposed to know?'

Jackie looked down with a faint smile. 'Oh, nothing special.'

'OK,' grinned Rose, 'I believe you. Tell you what, though, I reckon life is going to be a bit easier now, don't you?'

'Yes Rosie, you're probably right. A bit easier.'

They turned off the driveway and continued on towards the low rise which separated the house and gardens from the valley. To their right stood the stone chalet with the white painted wooden door and a pick-up truck parked at the rear. Rose regarded it for a moment then turned to Jackie. 'You been in there?'

'What in Mike's place? Well, I suppose I have. Why?'

'Just wondered, that's all,' answered Rose, nonchalantly.

They carried on a few steps further before Jackie asked, 'Why . . . have you?'

'Blimey, no! That doesn't mean I haven't thought about it, though. I mean, he's not bad looking is he?'

'I'm surprised you haven't let yourself in before now, Rose, knowing your ability with doors and locks.'

Rose looked back at the chalet. 'It's an idea, isn't it? What d'you think about us paying him a visit some time to cheer him up? Or d'you think he might get mad with us?'

'Get mad with us? Mike? No way! I'm sure he'd enjoy a visit from a couple of little lovebirds like us.'

'Right,' said Rose, 'so why don't we? Tonight maybe.'

'No, he's doing the poolside barbecue tonight. Sunday's are best. He usually has a few drinks in the bar then spends of the rest of the evening watching TV.'

'So we'll make it Sunday if you're game.'

'Why not?' smiled Jackie as they strolled on. 'He'll think it's his birthday!'

'Atta girl! We'll give him what for!'

'D'you know, Rosie, I'm beginning to wonder if you aren't worse than me!'

'I don't know. Maybe I just fancy letting myself go, now we don't have to look over our shoulders all the time. Don't you think?'

'Rosie,' said Jackie, stopping to face her friend, 'before you turned up, I was the joker in the pack, the one who messed up the order of things. I was the one Pauline always picked on. I know you thought she was a slag – I did often enough, but – but you've never really understood, have you?'

'Understood what?'

Jackie looked at her in despair for some moments. 'Oh, never mind!'

'But I do mind, love,' replied Rose, standing face to face with her. 'I know I've upset things a bit since I've been here but you and me are real pals, aren't we?' The sunlight glistened in her eyes as she spoke and the breeze from the distant sea caught her hair.

'Yes Rosie, we're pals all right. Real pals.'

They continued on towards the grassy rise, hand in hand.

2

An Unexpected Guest

'We don't want to be too obvious, do we?' said Jackie. 'I mean, we're not likely to be going anywhere special around here on a Sunday evening.'

'It should be all right if we go down the back stairs and out the back way,' answered Rose.

'But it's usually locked,' said Jackie. But then she realised, saying, 'Oh, of course, that's not a problem, is it?'

'No love, it isn't. I let myself in and out that way a few times before they caught up with me.'

'Let's get changed then,' said Jackie, 'and make ourselves irresistible.'

At eight o'clock, they were almost ready. Rose turned about before the long mirror and saw herself as she wished Mike to see her. She had chosen a long-sleeved chiffon blouse in gossamer black with a ruffle down the front, a mini-skirt in skin-tight metallic grey vinyl with a wide waist band and a large silver ring at the back proclaiming the top of the zip fastener. Her open body tights were of fine black lace, with back seams running down to the high, stiletto-heeled strap-on sandals in the same colour vinyl as her skirt. Her firm breasts, naked beneath the chiffon were easily discerned for the nipples protruded and defined themselves against the shadowy fabric. Like Jackie, Rose saw no reason to understate herself.

Jackie had opted for a shoestring top in white nylon, cut so low at the front as to almost reveal what it was intended to cover. Rose could see her in the mirror adjusting the elasticated tops of sheer black, stay-up stockings. Her shoes were of a similar style to Rose's but in pink vinyl. She adjusted the flared mini-skirt, made of shimmering deep pink satin with a wide belt in deeper pink, fastened tightly to emphasise a slim waist. Their lips glistened a deep pink. Their hair, still short, had been styled and tinted by Valerie to best effect. Both looked ready to pass through the stage door and enter the spotlights as a glamorous cabaret act in some intimate, back street theatre.

'I'll go first,' said Rose, dabbing perfume liberally about neck and arms. 'Give us about fifteen minutes; that back door lock is a bit stiff. Then you follow. If it looks like he's already in, I'll wait outside for you, right? If he isn't, I'll be inside, so you come up and knock.'

Rose pulled open the door and, after a brief glance each way, grinned at Jackie and headed off to the left.

'See you later, kid!' hissed Jackie before closing the door.

Rose continued on past the door of what was now Cheryl's apartment, and on to the dimly lit and little used back stairs. She continued downward past wall lamps with ornate brass fittings and, reaching the bottom of the stairs, stopped. Ahead and to the left was the ground floor passage. There were voices. After a few seconds, the voices died down. Rose moved on. Glancing along the passage to the front entrance, she caught sight of Annette in a black T-shirt and denim mini-skirt, her rich auburn hair swaying about her shoulders as she pushed through the swing doors and left the house to hurry down the steps and into the night.

Rose was tempted, almost, to forget about opening the lock and using the back entrance. Having seen the glamorous form of Annette, she wondered if her own appearance would attract undue attention. But a change of plan would mean retracing her steps to tell Jackie not to go this way. So she moved on to the end of the short hallway where the solid wooden door to her right stood opposite the cellar entrance.

She carefully slid the old iron bolts aside and bent down

to give her attention to the lock. Working quickly, with the advantage of much practice and a length of wire coathanger, she heard the mechanism give with a grating click. Seconds later, she was through and easing the door silently shut.

There was little illumination at the back of the house. The ground floor windows were higher, for the land fell away in that direction. It was familiar territory to Rose, nevertheless, for during several days of hiding out in the grounds, she had used this route to gain access to the kitchens in order to obtain food. She remembered too, that the ground was hard and would cause no problems for high-heeled shoes. From the end of the house and the annexe, she could pass directly in amongst the trees, with no need to cross the driveway until she had gone past the swimming pool on the other side.

The air was warm and carried the whirring of cicadas on a soft breeze. The stars arrayed themselves about the heavens even though the faint afterglow of the vanished day still hung in the west. Annette reached into her shoulder bag, fumbling for her cigarettes and lighter. As there was nobody else about, she had switched off the pool lights and sat waiting in the darkness amongst the sunshades and tables. She was about to light the cigarette when something attracted her attention.

A short way up the drive, a figure emerged from the wooded backdrop, easily seen as it crossed the driveway for the tall lamps there were not switched off until much later in the evening. Annette replaced the cigarette in its packet and arose quietly. She hurried along the poolside and around the bushes at the far end, going in the same direction as the figure which was, for the moment, out of sight. Her objective was the low embankment which obscured the drive further along where it curved towards the road. She only hesitated to remove her high heels, for the ground was softer here. Immediately over the rise, some distance beyond the driveway, stood the chalet.

The light in the small porch was switched on and illuminated the figure, now easily identifiable, as it stood waiting at the door. Annette saw her raise her hand and heard a tapping noise drift across on the night air. She continued to watch as Rose bent and occupied herself intently, close to the door. Annette wondered for a time what kept her so occupied, until the front door opened and Rose slipped inside.

'Hi!' came the voice from amongst the sunshades as Annette approached. 'I was beginning to wonder where you'd gone. I found your bag here.'

Mike, in a white T-shirt and blue jeans, sat in semi-obscurity at the small table.

'Just a little diversion, Mike; something unexpected, or so I assume.'

'Unexpected? What d'you mean?'

She smiled close to his face. 'I just saw somebody letting themselves into your place.'

'What!'

'Yes, I wondered if you had hired them to tidy it up at the last minute just to impress me.'

'Are you serious?' he asked, rising up and pushing back his chair.

'Oh, absolutely,' she answered with unnerving calmness.

'You're just standing there telling me I'm being broken into?'

'Don't fret, dear,' she continued. 'It's not a burglar and, you'll be glad to know, it's not the police either.'

'Well come on, who is it?'

Annette moved around the table to face him. 'Tell me,' she breathed, 'were you expecting company tonight?'

'Of course I was – you!'

'No, I mean anyone else?'

'Annette, you're winding me up! Why would I want anyone else coming around tonight of all nights? What the hell is going on?'

She leant forward and kissed him on the lips, her warm, perfumed breath caressing his face. 'Let's go back now. I think you may be in for a little surprise. At least I hope you are, dear!'

She stepped away towards the driveway and he followed, taking her hand, seeing that she was evidently in no mood to hurry. Further questions met with no more than a smile. They followed the curve of the driveway in silence until they reached the short, unlit path to the chalet.

Jackie eased the door shut. She too had glanced briefly along the corridor and seen no one. Uppermost in her mind was the thought of where Rose might now be, and if she had succeeded in gaining access to the chalet without being seen. She kept her eyes fixed on the carpet ahead and passed quietly by the arched doorways with the ornate lamps casting an amber glow upon the white walls. She did not glance at Cheryl's door, nor at any other. She had all but reached the rear stairs and placed her fingers upon the bannister when a voice behind called, 'And where do you think you are going?'

Jackie froze, her mouth half opened. She took a deep breath and turned.

'Well answer me!' said Cheryl, approaching with a coldly determined expression.

For that moment, Jackie's insides felt as though she was descending in a high-speed lift. 'Er, I'm going to meet Rose in the bar.'

'Oh really! And how long has she been waiting for you, do you think?'

'Em, not long – I'm not sure.'

'Well it can't be more than a few seconds, because that is where I have been for the last hour and she most certainly wasn't in evidence during that time!' Cheryl looked her up and down with slow and deliberate attentiveness, as if to question her glamorous attire.

Jackie stood in silence. Cheryl, dressed in a dark blue, close-fitting sleeveless dress, cut just above her knees, might not have looked intimidating, but Jackie was not reassured.

'She must have gone out then,' said Jackie weakly.

'Gone out where?'

'How should I know?'

'Because you share the same room,' replied Cheryl, 'and you are together for most of the time!'

Jackie shrugged, leant against the wall and folded her arms in resignation, her gaze fixed on the white skirting board by the top of the stairs.

'So,' continued Cheryl, 'we have established that she isn't waiting for you in the bar and, as you claim you don't know where she is, there isn't a lot of point in your going downstairs to see her, is there?'

'Suppose not,' answered Jackie, lifting her eyes to stare at the brass wall light opposite. Even that seemed to shine accusations at her.

'I think you had better come with me. I was looking for you anyway.'

Jackie followed back the way she had come, heart beating hard, a disturbing current passing through her belly.

Once inside the main room, Cheryl turned and ran a finger under the shoulder string of Jackie's white top. 'Let's have this off. And the skirt! And whatever you have on underneath!'

'What are you . . .?'

Cheryl continued to watch her. Jackie hesitated, then pulled the top up over her head to reveal naked breasts and hard, pink nipples. She began to loosen the belt as Cheryl said, 'You will spend the remainder of the evening under strict confinement. I'll talk to our friend Rose when she returns. I doubt if we're going to find her anywhere in the house though, are we?'

Jackie stood silently, in nothing but stockings and high-heeled sandals, biting her lip.

'Sit down and remove the sandals too,' ordered Cheryl.

Jackie obeyed and sat down on a green leather stool, her heart beating almost audibly, her body feeling a tremor of anticipation. She fumbled nervously with the ankle straps. The shoes were undone and laid aside. Cheryl walked to the far end of the room where, on the left side, stood the doorway with the black curtain, leading into the darkened chamber. It was a place with which Jackie was already acquainted. But the fact that Jackie had been obliged to experience what it had to offer did not mean that the immediate future was predictable. The small room and its fittings could, and had, been put to varying uses, as she could well testify.

When Cheryl reappeared, she had tucked under her arm a folded black object which held a glint of metal. Jackie recognised the nature of the garment even before Cheryl stopped close by her side and the pungent odour of latex drifted up to her face. Jackie felt the blood coursing through her veins and took a deep breath as Cheryl let it fall open before her to reveal the horizontal rubber sleeve running across the inside.

'You know what to do, Jackie! Now, arms in here!'

Jackie pushed first one arm and then the other into the sleeve until they crossed over inside. Cheryl moved behind, pulled the garment over her shoulders to enclose her arms and upper body completely, and at once began to fasten the row of heavy straps at the rear. Jackie, no stranger to this type of restraint, stood looking ahead, swaying on her feet as the straps were tightened and the straitjacket constricted. But on this occasion, she became aware of something which caused her to turn her head with an expression of wide-eyed surprise. 'Cheryl, I thought this was an ordinary . . .'

She had glanced down at the heavy, pouch-like object hanging below her chin. 'I won't be able to –'

'That's right,' cut in Cheryl, 'you won't!'

Most of the straps were secured and Jackie knew the futility of struggle. Cheryl reached over her shoulders and lifted up the flaccid rubber from beneath Jackie's chin, pulling it up over her face and down to enclose her head in a blank skin of heavy latex. As the visible world disappeared into darkness, Jackie felt and tasted the soft rubber bulb inside the helmet pushing insistently against her lower face. The bulb pressed ever harder as Cheryl secured the remaining straps at the neck and rear of the hood, until it eventually slipped inside her mouth. Cheryl took a second bulb which, via a short length of black tubing, she screwed on to the small valve at the front of the helmet. With a hand on the back of Jackie's head, she began to squeeze this bulb with a rapid movement of her fingers. Its lesser companion inflated quickly inside Jackie's mouth until it pressed hard against her cheeks.

'There,' breathed Cheryl, releasing the bulb. 'Nice and helpless, just the way we like it.'

Jackie stood motionless, sheathed from head to waist in gleaming black rubber, her only link with the outside world a small group of breathing holes under the nostrils and around the inflation valve. The hand, now on her shoulder, pushed and guided her along the room. She stepped cautiously, telling herself she could come to no harm, but she was filled with disquiet nevertheless. She wanted to ask Cheryl to stop the rubber bulb swinging from side to side on the end of its short tube beneath her chin, but any sound she might make would be stifled and meaningless.

She heard Cheryl push open a door ahead and switch on the light. It was obvious they were entering the bathroom and she knew what awaited her there. Cheryl manoeuvred her around and said, 'Sit down.'

She prepared for the chill of the hard blue porcelain bowl against the backs of her legs, but it always felt colder than expected. Cheryl had no need to fasten the leather strap about her chest to hold her firmly against the padded back rest, nor to fasten her legs wide apart over the bowl. But it was a part of the ritual and it was going to be done. It was intended to prove to Jackie how totally under control she was, and further proof was to follow. She could hear the rubber bottle being filled with soap solution and warm water, and sounds which would have been meaningless to others, but not to Jackie. Cheryl's dress brushed against her knee. In her mind's eye, Jackie could see her reaching up to the small bracket on the wall above to suspend the sagging bottle from it.

Anticipation stirred within her loins but Jackie remained outwardly relaxed. She recalled the first time they had done this to her and how she had resisted for a time. It had made no difference then and would make none now. When the blunt and lubricated end of the rubber nozzle touched against her anus, she tightened the muscles involuntarily. Cheryl heard her breathe in sharply through the helmet. But the instrument entered easily with cool insistence, moving remorselessly up inside, pushing into her rectum. Even though her eyes were covered by the thick rubber skin, she closed them and sighed, for she had absolved herself long ago of the guilt she had experienced when she first realised that this ordeal of humiliation was becoming a source of carnal pleasure.

Cheryl's latex-gloved hand touched under her thigh. The small valve at the base of the nozzle was turned. At once Jackie felt the surge inside her lower body as the rubber bottle above deflated and emptied. After a moment, the nozzle was withdrawn, slowly and sensually. The sound of water swirling in a vortex beneath was reassuring, for the murmuring within her bowels had already begun. Soon the murmuring became an uncontrollable urge. A hand took her chin and lifted it, pushing back the rubber-sheathed head as her body discharged itself in shameful, ecstatic relief.

The ritual was not quite finished. The flow of water inside the bowl was reduced. Jackie stiffened as the gloved fingers, slippery with soap, coursed about her most intimate and sensitive places in a final act of cleansing. Cheryl knew Jackie's threshold; knew for how long she should continue and knew how Jackie would silently beg her to go on. Before the crisis arrived, before Jackie lost control of herself in a different way, Cheryl stopped. What Cheryl did not do was going to be a part of the punishment.

Mike inserted the key into the lock carefully and quietly. The door swung open. The hallway was dark, except for a thin strip of light showing beneath the lounge door. He turned to Annette, close behind him, and placed a finger against his lips. She smiled and prodded him on. What she did not tell him was that she had seen a face and a pair of eyes staring briefly from the bedroom window with an expression of alarm as she and Mike walked up the pathway.

Cautiously, he pushed open the first door. They knew

that anyone inside the house would need to exit this way unless they escaped via a window or had unlocked the rear door. There was no intruder to be seen.

'Did you leave the light on?' asked Annette.

'Don't remember,' he answered quietly. 'Sometimes I do, sometimes I don't.'

'What about that glass on the table? There's still something in it.'

'Never mind that,' he hissed, moving forwards. 'I'm going to take a look in the kitchen. Don't you move.'

She watched him reach around the door and switch on the light. As he disappeared, Annette hurried over to the bedroom door, which stood ajar, pushed inside and quickly found the light switch. Her eyes darted about the room, behind the door and back over to the bed. She sniffed the air, knowing it was not the smell of aftershave which permeated the still air of the room. To her left stood a tall, pine wardrobe. She eyed this with a mischievous smile, for the door hung slightly open and a faint creaking reached her ear. Annette walked over and pulled the door wide. 'All right dear, you can come out now!'

There came a scratching and shuffling as the apprehensive Rose unbent and emerged awkwardly from the confined space. Mike entered the room, saying, 'There's a strong smell of perfume or something coming from . . .'

His expression at first was one of surprise, slowly turning to amused bewilderment as he watched her tugging down on the hem of the vinyl mini-skirt. It had ridden up as she struggled out of the wardrobe and was in danger of revealing what she did not have on beneath.

'I don't suppose this has anything to do with you, has it?' he asked Annette.

'No it hasn't. If it was anything to do with me, I wouldn't have had the poor girl stuffed inside your wardrobe. There's no telling what's in there!'

Rose let out a long breath. 'It's the only place I could find. There's an old case and other stuff shoved under the bed and I didn't have time to unlock the back door.'

'Yes, he's an untidy sod,' said Annette, glancing at the

bed and the open wardrobe. 'You must have noticed that as soon as you got in.'

'Er, excuse me!' Put in the indignant Mike. 'Never mind about my housekeeping.' Annette rolled her eyes and tutted as he continued. 'What I'd like to know is how you got into the place, and what you're up to!'

Rose was about to attempt an answer when Annette said, 'She comes from a family of lockpickers, don't you dear?'

'Yes,' stuttered Rose. 'I picked my first lock in primary school; it was just a bit of fun. Jackie and I were going to give you a surprise; just for a laugh.'

'And where might your little friend be hiding?' asked Mike.

'I don't know,' answered Rose. 'I thought it was her coming up the path when you turned up. She's not in here, honest.'

'She probably saw us and changed her mind,' said Annette.

Mike, a faint smile on his face, was regarding Rose with greater attention, noticing the way in which the chiffon blouse hung on her breasts and revealed so clearly her prominent nipples. His eyes moved down to the vinyl miniskirt stretched across the curve of her behind, as she turned with an anxious glance to Annette. 'Look, you won't say anything, will you? If Cheryl or Sonia find out we'll be for it again.'

'We won't say anything, will we?' responded Annette, shifting her attention to the preoccupied Mike, whose eyes were presently concentrated on Rose's long, shapely legs in their delicate black lace.

'Say anything? Oh, no, I'm sure neither of us will.'

'Thanks,' smiled Rose. 'You're a good sort you are Annette. And you Mike.' She folded her arms and glanced about the room. 'Well, I'll push off then and leave you both in peace, if that's OK?'

'Push off!' responded Annette. 'What for? You've taken all the trouble to get ready and come out here, and then ended up in his wardrobe with those smelly old clothes! You deserve a drink out of him at least.'

38

Mike raised a hand and opened his mouth to speak. No more than a croak had emerged before Annette placed an arm about Rose and continued, 'You spend the evening with us, dear. He's got a nice bottle of champagne in the fridge and probably a few more hidden away somewhere else.'

Mike opened his mouth and managed a weak, 'But . . .' before Annette looked at him pointedly and said, 'Go and get three glasses, Mike, and stick another bottle in to cool down while we polish off the first. You'll be able to entertain the two of us tonight instead of just me. You'll like that, won't you?'

The bemused Mike raised his hands in a gesture of despair and glanced up at the ceiling. He left the bedroom without further comment. Annette looked at Rose with mischief in her green eyes. Rose grinned at Annette. They burst out laughing and she said to Rose in a low voice, 'What were you and Jackie planning to do?'

Rose hesitated. 'Like I said, just have a bit of fun.'

'Well you still can if you want. You know what men are like. He won't mind.'

'But I thought you and him were —'

'We're just good friends,' said Annette. 'Mind you, he's not bad, you know. If he had stacks of money to spend the way he used to in London, I might consider him a serious proposition.'

'Right,' grinned Rose, 'so he's OK for a good time?'

'We'll see,' replied Annette. 'Let's find out who can get him to make the first move.'

'You mean tease him?'

'Yes, he loves it. You only have to —'

'Are you two still in there?' interrupted a voice from beyond.

Annette and Rose winked hard at each other before leaving the bedroom.

With the heavy curtains closed against the outside world, and only a couple of small lamps switched on, the lounge was welcoming and intimate. The pine two-seater, adorned

39

with plush maroon cushions, stood at right angles to the old, rustic fire grate. Before it stood the low pine table. The arrangement had been intended only for himself and Annette, but as they entered he was putting into place one of the two matching chairs so that it faced the two-seater across the table.

Annette and Rose moved around to the two seater and sat down to watch Mike ease the cork from the champagne bottle with a dull, hollow pop.

'Where's your ice bucket?' asked Annette, leaning back and slowly crossing her legs.

'Er, I forgot to make any ice,' he answered sheepishly.

'Champagne and no ice,' said Annette, turning to Rose with an expression of disgust.

'I don't mind . . .' Rose began to say.

Annette prodded her in the ribs with a finger and watched Mike carefully top-up the foaming glasses. 'If he's going to entertain ladies of class, he ought to think of things like that.'

'Yeah, ladies of class, we are,' added Rose as, following Annette's example, she too crossed her legs, slowly and provocatively. The distracted Mike overfilled the third glass so that its effervescent contents spilled over and formed a small, fizzing pool on the table top.

'Can you manage that all right dear?' asked Annette, sweetly.

With a glazed expression, he handed them each a glass and fought inwardly to regain a modest composure. 'So, cheers!' he grinned, sitting back in the chair and raising his drink.

'Cheers!' responded the two girls, re-crossing their legs.

He drank, hearing the swish of sheer nylon against sheer nylon but remained expressionless, though his mind was fixed entirely upon the two sensual figures opposite. Rose's breasts, with nipples pushing like fingers against the diaphanous blouse, demanded his attention, as did their gossamer skinned legs, for the skirts seemed to be riding ever higher up their thighs as from time to time they adjusted positions.

'Music?' suggested Annette.

'Oh yes,' responded Mike, clearing his throat and raising quickly from the chair.

'Something romantic?' suggested Rose.

'Utterly sleazy,' added Annette.

He passed by the two-seater, glancing down at them, feeling their warmth, mouthing to himself, 'Oh God,' as he carried on to the hi-fi unit. Moments later, the sound of a saxophone quartet coloured the perfumed air of the room. He refilled the champagne glasses, noticing as he leant forward, the expanse of stockinged thigh before him and Rose's high-heeled sandal swaying from side to side beneath his face, like a tantalising bait. When he looked up, Annette had her arm about Rose's shoulder. They were face to face and looking into each other's eyes. Rose stroked her fingers down Annette's cheek. They appeared to be on the verge of kissing.

He put down the bottle. 'Look, I'm going to have a nervous breakdown by the time you two have finished. You wouldn't mind letting me in on it would you? We could talk about it in the other room.'

They looked at him in surprise then back to each other. 'What's he suggesting?' asked Rose.

Annette glanced back at Mike. 'I really can't say but I hope it's nothing improper.'

Rose leant her head on Annette's shoulder and began to laugh. Mike gazed down at Rose's legs and saw the nakedness of her sex shadowed beneath the hem of the vinyl skirt. There was no mistaking his own arousal. Annette looked at his wide-eyed expression, saw his mouth set open. She leant forward and took his arm. 'Shall we finish the champagne first, dear; it's going to get warm. Or can't you wait that long?'

He shifted his gaze in surprise as though seeing her for the first time. 'Yes, you're right. We'll finish the champagne!'

Entering the bedroom, he felt both eagerness and trepidation. He and Annette knew each other as intimately as

41

two people could. They had played adult games together often, until things got out of hand and the secret meetings had stopped. Tonight he had expected to resume that relationship. Rose, he knew not at all. Though seeing her as an image, as sexually appealing as any of the other girls, he knew well how different were her background and attitude; certainly in the beginning. He considered it unlikely that Annette had connived in Rose's little adventure but could not entirely dispel doubts about it.

He slipped his arm about both waists and smiled at each in turn. Annette reached out and switched off the main light, leaving the sole source of illumination, a small bedside lamp, to bathe the room in a soft, cosy light. Rose smiled and kissed him. Mike, glad of her initiative, returned the kiss, breathed in her perfume and felt the stirring heat of her body as she gripped his arms. He was a little taken aback by her passion. He had not regarded her as being in any way sophisticated but as being on a different wavelength altogether from the likes of Annette or Angela.

Annette reached between them and, with an arm about Rose's waist, slipped open the top button of her blouse. She glanced at Mike with a fleeting smile and, without turning her eyes away from him, nodded towards Rose. He understood, and began to pluck at the buttons lower down. Rose looked from one to the other in mock surprise and continued to grip his arms, even as the blouse fell open to her waist. Annette moved behind and as he eased the gossamer black fabric away from her shoulders, she pulled down the zip at the rear of Rose's skirt by its metal ring. Rose showed no sign of concern and, as the blouse was tugged free of her arms, pressed her mouth hard against his with a soft moan and clasped her hands about his neck. Annette dragged down the little skirt and Rose needed no prompting to step out of it.

Standing there in just the open-body lace tights and vinyl high heels, Rose's enthusiasm increased. His hands slipped down over the nylon waistband and over the silk smooth orbs of her behind. Annette had moved around behind

Mike and he became aware of her hands on his waist, working slowly around him until they were at his front. They at once busied themselves in undoing the belt of his jeans. Annette's head was close to his. He disengaged himself from Rose and kissed her as the front of the jeans became unzipped and the hand slipped inside to squeeze the trapped and yearning erection within his blue cotton shorts.

He backed away from them both momentarily, loosening his sandals and kicking them off. While he pushed down the jeans to rid himself of these too, Annette took Rose's hand and led her over to the bed; the same bed where he and Annette had spent their passion together on several occasions. Mike approached them, the state of his arousal only too evident from the distended front of the shorts.

It seemed quite inappropriate that Annette should still be dressed. Smiling, he turned to her and reached down to take hold of the hem of her T-shirt. As though reading his thoughts, she at once pulled up the T-shirt and removed it without his assistance. The little denim skirt also slipped down before him, as did the small blue G-string briefs she wore beneath.

Annette stood naked, clad only in her garter-top black stockings and black high-heeled sandals. She looked at him in faint amusement, for he held his eyes upon her slim and beautiful body; a body which during the past few months had lived only in his imagination. For at the pool, in broad daylight, the form might be the same but the image was not.

Rose sat on the edge of the bed, leaning back on her arms and looking up at them. They stood before her and kissed, his hands on her thighs, his lips moving from her mouth, down her neck and on to her firm breasts where they sucked and teased about the nipples. Suddenly he tensed and drew in his breath. Rose had slid a hand inside the leg of his shorts and cool fingershad located the burgeoning penis. Annette smiled at her and both girls tugged on the shorts until his erection sprang free, reddened and swaggering before Rose's face. Her hand returned to the inflamed shaft, closed about the foreskin and began to work it slowly back and forth. Annette continued to occupy his attentions for only a few seconds longer, for the distraction was too much. He turned to face Rose who at once leant forward and took the head of the shaft into her mouth. He closed his eyes and groaned softly, placing his hands upon her head as she continued with enthusiasm, partly withdrawing him to twirl her tongue about the swollen head and causing the pelvis to shudder. Annette slipped an arm under his behind, caressed his testicles and watched intently, hearing him groan quietly. Rose emitted a long, 'Mmmm,' as though savouring a favorite dessert.

With a consummate demonstration of willpower he withdrew from Rose's burning lips, his organ glistening wet in the dim light, and fell down upon his knees between her legs. Annette climbed up on to the bed behind and pulled her down, Mike pushing her legs up and wide apart at the same time. At last he had access to her sex and his tongue lost no time in beginning its fiendish dialogue with her clitoris. He was not surprised to find her moist and aroused, but both he and Annette were taken aback by the short time it took her to reach a climax. For in less than a minute after he had begun to work upon the focus of her lust, she started to gasp repeatedly. Annette held her from behind, squeezing her breasts and teasing the reddened nipples. Rose stiffened for a moment, then her body shook as the currents of orgasm surged within, forcing a long, loud cry from her open mouth.

As she recovered and became calmer, she began to laugh, climbing up on to the bed and throwing her arms about Annette, who, with an expression of surprise exclaimed, 'God, there's no stopping you, is there?'

And there was not, for Rose only hesitated to reach out and grasp Mike's arm, pulling at him until he scrambled onto the bed to join them. There they knelt for a time, arms about each other in a tight little group, kissing, sucking and nibbling.

Mike let out a sharp, 'Oh!' as two hands descended upon

him simultaneously, one slipping under his testicles, the other closing with electrifying coolness about his erection. Rose and Annette laughed loudly and continued kissing each other. Mike felt that if he did not make a move very quickly, it would be all over, for the hand about his shaft was now working it vigorously. The currents in his loins were beginning to well up when he stayed the hand, finding it to be Rose's.

'Your turn,' he whispered into Annette's ear and pulled her around on her knees until she was facing along the bed with her back to the headboard. With one arm about her waist he supported himself with the other and, to the evident delight of Rose, leant downwards and brushed his lips across Annette's stomach. Rose joined him, face to face, as he reached the silkly smooth flesh above her sex, then down further until his tongue spread the lips open and found the pearl of love nestled within. Rose, eager not to lose her corner in the erotic triangle, once more closed her fingers about his shaft, watching intently and urging on his dialogue of lust with Annette. But she desired greater involvement and shifted about, running her free hand impatiently about Annette's thigh. Mike sensed this, as did Annette, and for a short time, he allowed Rose to take his place in the game of arousal. But this too was only transitional for the next move was Annette's.

'Always give way to experience,' she said, and disengaged herself from Rose.

She pushed Mike down on to his back and gestured for Rose to move aside as she straddled herself across his head with her face toward his erection. In a moment, lowering herself down, she had taken the head of his penis fully into her mouth and closed her eyes tightly as his tongue resumed its voluptuous discourse. If Rose considered herself excluded, she was soon to find out that it was not so, for Annette knelt upright, smiled at her and eyed the flushed and expectant organ. Rose read the signal instantly and climbed astride it to face Annette. Annette, feeling the currents of sensuality growing within herself, watched Rose position the head against the reddened lips of her own sex

45

and, with eyes half closed and mouth ajar, sink down to take in the lance to the hilt.

Rose and Annette fell into each other's arms for the final fling in this joust of lust. Mike, sheathed exquisitely within Rose's vagina, knew that it was the home run and gave his tongue full rein in its frenzied exploration of Annette's zone of pleasure, darting about her sex and anus, feeling her body respond to the parry and thrust as if touched by hot steel.

The fires within Rose, never completely extinguished, were building again as she moved rhythmically up and down on the burning lance. She and Annette gripped each other in lustful abandon. It was Annette, fired by the tactile dialogue of the remorseless tongue beneath, who lost control first, letting out a loud, 'Aaaaah!' Crying out, she arched her pelvis then sunk her nails into Rose's shoulders.

Mike held her thighs firmly as her body shook, revelling in the ecstasy of her climax. But the whirlpool of lust was drawing him in as well. He heard Rose begin to moan, felt her tighten her muscles about him and push down harder. Two sets of fingers gripped Annette's flesh as the electric surge of orgasm took them both and spun them about in abandoned joy, Rose's voice almost reaching a scream as he jetted and pulsed inside her body.

They kissed Rose warmly before she left the chalet then watched her move down the pathway and up the drive before vanishing into the night.

'Considering her age,' said Mike as the front door closed, 'she doesn't seem to have much to learn does she?'

'No,' answered Annette, 'but you might find Jackie has something to do with that.'

'Could be,' he grinned. 'I wonder what happened to her this evening.'

'Do you now?' responded Annette. 'Well I think three of us might have been too much even for you!'

'No, I didn't mean it like that, but, er, well, it's an interesting idea!'

'God, men!' breathed Annette, brushing her auburn hair

46

back from her cheeks. 'No wonder Sonia makes so much out of it all.'

'You don't do too badly from it either do you?' he asked.

She smiled at him with her green eyes. 'And nor do you, dear, when I consider what it costs some of Sonia's punters.'

He gazed at her for a moment, taken aback. 'Well, look, if there's anything I can give you. I wouldn't want you to feel that –'

'Oh, Mike!' she interrupted, putting her arms about his neck. 'Don't be silly. I came here because I wanted to, the way I used to. And,' she smiled, 'I thought you served us rather well. The way we ladies should be served.'

'Does that mean you're going to stay?'

'Mmm, I might. It'll cost you another bottle of champagne though!'

Rose soon found herself at the main entrance and, without hesitation, pushed open the swing door and walked through. Having passed the entrance to the bar room and reached the main stairs without incident, she walked as quickly as the high-heeled sandals would allow and reached the landing of the first floor corridor. Observing no-one, she reached Jackie's apartment and pushed open the door. The room was in darkness. Rose switched on the light and looked about. Seeing no sign of Jackie, she moved to the bedroom – which also proved to be in darkness. With the light on, she saw that the bed was unused and this room, too, was deserted.

It was when she sat on the bed to remove her shoes that she saw the envelope with her name on it. Picking it up, she assumed that it had been placed there for some reason by Jackie. Inside it was a sheet of notepaper with a message which read, 'Report to me at nine o'clock in the morning.' It was signed, 'Cheryl.'

3

Living Fantasies

'You're not having breakfast?' asked Angela, looking at her over the bar.

'No, I don't fancy anything,' replied Karen, stirring the coffee. She looked up at Angela. 'Except maybe a very large gin.'

'You mustn't be nervous, silly.' Anglea smiled. 'You don't really have to do much, do you?'

'I don't know; I didn't dare ask.' Karen looked at her watch. 'Actually, Angie, if it wasn't for getting Sonia out of a mess, I'm not all together sure I'd –'

'But I thought that's all it was anyway,' cut in Angela.

Karen held her eyes for a moment then drank the coffee in three gulps and pushed back her chair. 'See you later, Angie.'

Her first sight of them was in the main office. They were seated opposite Sonia with their backs to the door she had just entered through. She saw the long golden hair of one and the glossy, black waist-length hair of the other. They were early. It was only eight fifteen. Close to the house, the trees were still in shadow but through the window she could see the gardens beyond, bathed in morning sunlight.

Karen stopped short of the desk as both turned around. Sonia stood up and bade her come closer. 'This is Danielle,' she said, indicating the fair-haired girl.

Danielle held out her hand with a soft, 'Hello,' and a courteous smile. Her age was little more than Karen's; her eyes were the same hazel brown but her features were rounder.

48

'And this,' continued Sonia, 'is Sophie.'

Sophie, too, was in her mid-twenties, but her features were a little narrower, a little sharper than those of her companion; her expression was bordering on the sullen. She too offered her hand. Both wore plain summer dresses in cotton, low cut but not especially short. Both were, of course, slim and beautiful. But their initial friendliness, reassuring though it might be, was born of practised etiquette rather than of natural amicability.

There was not a spare chair in the immediate vicinity for Karen, but Sonia remained standing and said, 'I hope you will excuse me if I leave you to carry on.' She moved around to Karen. 'Danielle and Sophie are fully briefed and have already seen the first floor rooms. Everything is ready. Just be natural my dear, that's all. Be yourself but believe that each situation is real. Our looking-glass world, remember?'

Karen looked from Sonia to Danielle and Sophie, and back to Sonia, her heart beating hard. 'Yes, I'm sure we'll do fine. I'll be myself, just as you say.'

Karen had never before entered this room. Nor had she, until now, entered any of the first floor rooms on this side of the passageway. She knew about them, of course, or thought she did.

The truth for Karen, over the last year, had a habit of asserting itself over the image she still retained of herself. When she considered some of the things she had done since her arrival at the house, she persuaded herself that it was an alter ego to which these had happened. She imagined a Karen who stood aside from it and merely observed as a spectator. The illusion had been breached so many times that she had wondered how it could persist for so long. But it had. And, very soon, it was going to be shattered once more.

'OK,' said Sophie in a matter-of-fact manner, 'you know the brief, I think?'

'No, I don't,' answered Karen. 'I understand I go along with you two since I'm the dogsbody.'

'Excuse me?' asked Danielle, folding her arms. 'What is this about the dog?'

'Oh, sorry. What I mean is, I have to do as you say.'

'But of course!' replied Sophie. 'We are, what you say, in charge, yes?'

'I think that's the general idea,' replied Karen.

'OK,' said Danielle, 'so we get changed now. Everything is ready for us but we should not talk except to say those things which need to be said in our play, because it will not look right on the pictures. Also, we make expressions with our hands and faces so that people look at the pictures and know what we think, yes?'

'Perhaps I should have done my homework,' remarked Karen.

'Sorry?' queried Danielle.

'I should have practised.'

'Oh no,' put in Sophie, 'for you this is easy. You should look with surprise or alarm much of the time. Your part is *malchance*, er – misfortune, I think. You do not have anything to say if you do not wish.'

Although different in some details, the type of dress Karen was putting on with the help of Sophie, was not unlike the maids' dresses she had seen worn by some of the girls allocated domestic duties; those girls whose nature predisposed them to a role of subservience. Perhaps the obvious example was Jackie. Occasionally it had been Angela. Until Pauline went, it had also been Rose, although that had been a matter of obligation rather than of predisposition, as far as anyone knew.

Danielle helped her on with the dress. Karen was quite aware she could never have managed it alone. It stretched about her body like a rubber skin; black, sleek and very short. The collar was high about her neck but was cut away below in a circle which scooped down over her breasts and was positioned so as to just avoid exposing the nipples. The bodice fitted like a glove as did the skirt; they were so tight that Danielle had for some time struggled with the zip fastener at the back. With the sheer black tights and black patent leather high-heeled shoes of exaggerated height, Karen was, if not consumed by the spirit of the occasion, certainly prepared as planned.

'Now you will think and behave as our servant,' said Danielle without a trace of humour.

Karen regarded herself in the long mirror and ran her hands down the sleek rubber tunic. Behind, she observed the room. It was not as she had expected, not like the secret room which lay between the beauty parlour and Sonia's suite, with its sinister fittings and furniture. This room reminded her of a modern hotel suite. True, the chairs were familiar but would not have otherwise attracted her attention. They were set about a low table on the rich maroon carpet. There was also a large cupboard and a chest of drawers. There was, however, one feature of the room which compromised the appearance of normality. To one side of it stood a circle of heavy black curtain, completely closed and suspended from a circular track just beneath the ceiling. The pink cornice lights were switched on and so were a selected number of spotlights, giving the room a moody, contrasted feel, with some areas brightly lit and others in shadow.

'Please, we must keep the shine good,' said Danielle, wiping with a hasty, circular motion about Karen's shoulders and arms with a small white cloth.

'What is it?' asked Karen as Danielle continued down her sides and over her behind.

'It is treated with a special polish for latex. Your uniform must be shining and without marks.'

She moved around to Karen's front and began to wipe the area around her breasts and stomach, circling ever downward. Karen put out a hand and took her wrist. 'Look, let me finish this, OK?'

'Very good, if you wish,' replied the unsmiling Danielle.

Danielle's impersonal manner made her feel vulnerable. Karen was being treated like an object, not a person. 'In the sink, inside the little kitchen, you will find flowers,' said Danielle. 'These you will bring out to arrange in the vases and place them about the room. Much of the time you must try and face into the room and not to the wall. When we come in, we will require drinks to be served. The tray, glasses and the decanter are over there.' She indicated a glass-fronted cabinet at the far end. 'Now I must go for a short time and you must carry on with your job. Remember you should stand up straight and not allow the dress to crease.'

Danielle walked away without another word and left the room.

Karen wondered if the whole thing was being taken too seriously. Then, perhaps, if the photographs were to look convincing the participants must be convinced as well. That is what Sonia wanted.

She walked to the kitchenette and entered by one of the two doors at the far end of the room. There in the sink were bunches of fresh flowers and three glass vases. She filled the first vase and carried this carefully into the room. She thought of the others who played this role as part of their domestic duties, often in these outrageous little dresses, designed to emphasise their roles as submissives. Karen had wondered before what it must feel like to be seen by others dressed in what amounted to a statement of sexual servility. The dress felt odd as she moved, stretching and moulding warmly to her body, caressing her breasts and thighs in its elastic embrace.

She had placed down the last vase when she heard their voices and turned to face the door. The two figures entered, smiling into each other's faces. Both were dressed in full horseriding attire with tweed jackets, jodhpurs and riding boots of shiny brown leather. Each carried under her arm a riding crop. They walked over to the low table, ignoring Karen altogether until they were seated. Then Sophie raised her finger and called, 'We will have drinks now, please!'

Karen's initial misgivings were in no way lessened by their appearance. They were dressed against the elements, and looked both forceful and threatening. She felt more vulnerable still in the scanty and revealing dress which defined every curve of her body and seemed to openly advertise its accessibility.

Her hands shook a little as she placed the decanter of sherry and the two glasses on to the small brass tray. At least her limbs were free. If they had fettered her in the way Pauline used to do with the other girls as an additional humiliation, she believed she would have found it impossible to manage at all. Danielle and Sophie were sprawled in their chairs as they gestured and talked loudly and quickly in French. They ignored Karen as she placed the tray between them upon the table. She felt herself overly nervous and unsteady as she poured the sherry into the glasses.

Before she had moved her hand away from the second glass, Sophie, laughing and waving her arm, struck Karen's elbow. Her fingers rapped against the glass and it fell over, dashing its contents across the table top where they spilled over the edge on to Danielle's jodhpurs. The laughing ceased abruptly, and was replaced by a shattering silence. Danielle and Sophie looked aghast at the spreading pool as if they could not believe their own eyes. Time appeared to freeze for a moment until Danielle glared up at Karen and shrilled, 'You stupid fool!' at the top of her voice. Both stood up at once to confront her. Karen felt quite naked.

'Get a cloth!' shouted Sophie. 'Clean this away now!'

Danielle brought up the riding crop as if to strike Karen across the face. Karen instinctively raised a hand to protect herself.

As she crossed the room, the words passed through Karen's mind repeatedly, 'It's just a game! It's just a game!' But she could not prevent the fear and humiliation from welling up inside. The only alternative, that she should call a halt now, appeared to be even worse, for they would have beaten her psychologically and she in turn would have let Sonia down. The charade had to go on.

Danielle and Sophie stood with hands on hips, and watched her in concentrated silence as she mopped up the spilled sherry with a damp cloth. The hem of the dress had ridden up higher on her thighs but she dared not reach down to tug at it. She was about to turn away when Sophie rapped hard on the table with the riding crop. 'What about this?' she said with threatening coolness.

There remained a small spot which Karen had over-looked. She wiped it clean, staring only at her own hands. The two still stood at the table, watching her take away the cloth. Waiting. Frowning. They had not moved when she approached them once more with pounding heart.

Danielle stepped forward and seized her arm. 'You will bend over this chair!'

Karen pulled back but Sophie took hold of her on the other side and they propelled her forward, towards one of the black leather chairs.

'No! No! I won't!' Karen yelled. 'This has gone far enough!'

But she was forced over the back of the chair and as the first stinging blow fell across her behind, Sophie shouted, 'Not in any way far enough!'

Danielle hurried around the chair and pulled Karen's arms forward. Sophie, with one hand in the middle of her back, held her down and wielded the riding crop with the other. Struggle as she might, Karen was unable to pull free. Her squirming only served to make the dress ride up her thighs until the lower part of her behind was revealed. The sheer black tights gave no protection and she had been given nothing else to put on beneath. Kicking her legs only made matters worse as a second and a third swish cut the air and the riding crop found its mark.

Several more blows fell with a loud crack across the thin nylon. Then they stopped and allowed her up to face them in burning shame, barely able to hold back the tears. Karen bit her lip, feeling the angry pulsing in her flesh, as she tugged down on the hem. She straightened up and looked each of them in the eye. They remained thus for a few moments. Danielle looked at Sophie. Sophie looked back at Danielle. At once, their mouths creased into smiles, then laughter. They laughed into each other's faces, Sophie putting a hand on to Danielle's shoulder.

'You see,' said Danielle turning to Karen, 'it is only a game.'

'And now this one is finished,' added Sophie. 'Very soon, we can play the next!'

'I think it's far from bloody funny,' breathed Karen as they turned away from her.

As she showered away the perspiration and the aroma of the rubber, Karen wondered about what had happened. She had found the dress sensual, especially wearing it in front of two complete strangers. They had hurt her as part of the ritual but had done no harm. And the burning glow in her behind had passed into her loins and was proving no longer unpleasant. At one time she would have fled in terror at the prospect of such an experience. Now the dark stirring in her belly was not so much one of fear but of anticipation for what was yet to come. And that was the disturbing thing; she had no idea what had been contrived. She had declined the opportunity of being informed and found herself on the rollercoaster, unable to get off, unaware of how high she was to be taken and how deep might be the next breathtaking plunge. She looked at herself in the mirror and laughed softly.

The second venue was the room nearest to the front of the house. Danielle and Sophie were already there when Karen appeared in the first floor corridor. Like her, they each wore a bathrobe. Karen folded her arms and said nothing, but looked at them and waited.

'We are inside our time,' remarked Sophie, pushing open the door. 'There is no need to hurry.'

They stood aside until Karen had entered, as if to imply that she could not be trusted to follow them. Passing through the small ante-room, they entered an area surrounded by blue and green curtains which formed a passageway and concealed the rest of the room beyond. The closed-in feeling and the still, warm air had a quieting effect. If Karen had needed to speak, she would have done so in a low voice. It was not well lit, although there was evidence of potential light in abundance, for clusters of spotlights were visible on tracks above the curtains. Danielle and Sophie moved ahead and Karen followed until they reached a door at the far end. They opened this and again waited for Karen to pass inside.

The room she entered appeared similar to that which served the beauty parlour. It had a shower cubicle, a sink and a low-level bowl with padded back rest. In addition there was a large mirror over a work surface and before this, a chair. The lamps above the mirror sprang into life as Sophie pushed the switch. They illuminated the bottles, jars, tubes and other accoutrements of a hairdressing salon. Under the present circumstances, Karen found it all a little reassuring. Or she did, until she saw what lay folded and waiting upon the black leather chair.

'First we will do the dressing up,' said Danielle, tugging at the belt on Karen's bathrobe.

Karen pushed her hands away and undid the belt herself, letting the bathrobe fall open. Beneath it she had on dark purple nylon bikini briefs.

'Perhaps you do not like these games,' remarked Danielle. 'I think then, why do you take part?'

'Maybe you have not done this before,' added Sophie.

'No, I haven't,' replied Karen.

'You have the stiff upper lip of the English,' said Danielle, lifting up a garment from the chair and presenting it to her. 'Now, we must help you to put this on. You cannot do it on your own.'

Karen saw that it was a basque; black and heavily boned. The odour of latex was once again unmistakable. Without waiting for either of them to move, she let the bathrobe slip from her body and draped it over the back of the chair. Danielle and Sophie did not look at her face, nor at her naked breasts, but moved behind her without speaking. They pushed her arms out and passed the garment around her. It was cool and soft against her body at first but quickly began to tighten. It was not intended to conceal her breasts. On the contrary, the brief, wired cups fitted snugly underneath; they lifted and defined them, holding them slightly wider apart, presenting them as an offering to the onlooker. The basque was trimmed at the waist with red lace and hung with six thin, elasticated silk

56

suspenders which danced up and down against her thighs as the two occupied themselves behind her.

The basque tightened further as laces swished through brass eyelets. Danielle steadied Karen by the shoulders as Sophie tugged and tightened until the two edges met and she could fasten the laces into a bow at the bottom.

'We will help with these also,' said Danielle, indicating the other items on the chair.

'Perhaps she would rather put them on herself,' suggested Sophie. 'If so we will wait outside.'

'Yes, I'll manage on my own,' responded Karen.

'Very good,' answered Danielle, 'then that will only leave one thing more for you to have on.'

They turned and left in silence. Karen reached down to the items on the chair.

The shoes were obvious and she had expected the black, seamed stockings. At the sight of the smallest item, she opened her mouth in surprise. It was, for want of a better term, a G-string, but not quite in any style she had seen before. She looked over her shoulder and waited for a moment before easing down her briefs.

A short time later, she looked at herself in the mirror. The basque was constricting but comfortable and she decided she liked it, even though she had no intention of hinting at that to Danielle and Sophie. The sheer black stockings were held up tightly by the six glossy suspenders and the black patent leather sandals with red bows at the front and long stiletto heels made her legs appear long and elegant. Her only misgiving was for the garment which fitted under the suspenders and about her loins. The rubber waistband of some three centimetres width was comfortable enough, but the strap which passed down over her shaven sex, between her legs and under her behind was of the same material and width. It emphasised with its brevity what it barely concealed and as it softened, warmed and moulded over her sex, felt disturbingly pleasant. She called out, nervously, 'OK!'

The two reappeared in the doorway and regarded her without expression as they approached. Danielle muttered,

'Very good.' Sophie held in her hands a small black bundle from which hung a couple of swaying lengths of lace. They stood either side of her and Sophie let the heavy latex garment in her hands unroll. Karen looked at it, puzzled as to its purpose. It appeared to be a rubber sleeve, perhaps eighty centimetres long, fitted along most of its length, except for the middle section, with two rows of brass eyelets. Its outer sections would have opened out flat had not the eyelets been loosely threaded by the black laces. Sophie lifted one end of the sleeve, took Karen's arm and began to pull it over her hand and upward. Danielle reached down, caught up the other end of the sleeve and reached for Karen's free arm.

'Wait a minute!' cried Karen, pulling back. 'What is this?'

'Ah! You have not seen one of these before?' asked Danielle. 'Well, never mind, it is just the final part of the outfit. You will not find it uncomfortable, I think.'

She had a decision to make and she needed to make it quickly. It was obviously some kind of restraint and she was not sure that Danielle and Sophie were the two she cared to share this experience with. Meanwhile they renewed their efforts and lifted her arms up behind her back. She looked ahead, sighed quietly and allowed them to continue. It was not for their sake, or hers, she told herself.

Within seconds, both of her arms were eased fully into the sleeve, enclosed and folded behind her back. Danielle and Sophie worked quickly with the laces, tightening the sleeve upward at each side, forcing Karen's fingertips against her elbows and constricting her upper arms. Once the laces were knotted, Karen looked aside at the mirror and saw her arms encased in the smooth, gleaming rubber, from armpit to armpit, forming a squared letter 'U'. Sophie turned her around until the spotlights over the sink illuminated her face.

'One more thing only, now,' said Danielle, picking up a black leather stool and placing it behind Karen. 'Please sit down.'

As Karen sat, the rubber strap moved between her legs,

warm and intimate. Sophie unscrewed the cap from a small flat jar and brought it, with a large, soft brush, close to Karen's face. She dipped the brush into the jar, circled it rapidly about then reached forward and dabbed it about Karen's cheeks. Danielle, standing behind, started to brush her hair in long, sensuous strokes.

'I could have done this myself earlier,' remarked Karen.

'But not now. You can do nothing now,' replied the unsmiling Sophie.

Sophie replaced the jar and brush. Continuing her work with a small plastic palette in one hand and a fine, sable brush in the other, she applied shadow make-up above Karen's eyes. She stared intently at her work, much as an artist might regard the application of a delicate detail upon an inert canvas. The brushing of her hair had stopped but Danielle remained at her back, watching Sophie's hands reflected in the mirror as she worked. Karen was unable to see herself, for Sophie stood blocking her vision. Even when Sophie turned again to choose a third item from the counter, Karen's vision was obscured. She wanted to speak. She felt that sitting in silence was inappropriate, but if she said anything, she feared it would meet with little response. Danielle and Sophie appeared to regard her as a plaything rather than a person, unlike Valerie and Kim in the beauty parlour, who gave her love and friendship as well as intense physical pleasure.

Sophie had already uncapped the small tube when she turned to Karen again. The lipstick was red, vivid red. Karen opened her mouth slightly and closed her eyes whilst Sophie stroked the colour on to her lips, hesitated to regard her work, then added a little more.

For the final act of this miniature ritual, Sophie applied the mascara and eyeliner with the delicacy and precision of a professional. At last, she stood back and viewed the result, glancing briefly at Danielle. Through the mirror, Karen saw Danielle nod her approval.

'OK, we can stand now,' said Danielle, pushing up beneath Karen's folded and encased arms.

Karen arose with care because of the high-heeled shoes

and the latex crotch strap. She saw herself in the mirror as Sophie moved aside to let her see. Her eyes widened with surprise, for the face that had been the subject of Sophie's artistry was that of a whore, a participant in a backstreet cabaret in some dubious quarter of a big city. Karen saw herself as a painted doll, and for a moment her mind was numb. When a hand touched her elbow and a voice said, 'OK, we will go now,' she instinctively tried to flex her arms. But the rubber sleeve seemed to have set and moulded so closely about them, that even her fingers were immobile.

Danielle and Sophie walked over to the door and opened it. 'You must wait five minutes,' said Danielle. 'We will switch on the lights then you must follow. You will see a gap in the curtains. That is the way to enter.'

They were gone and Karen was alone. She stood before the mirror, seeing a harlot stare back at her, seeing her body packaged and restrained in a manner which made her heart beat harder. She imagined herself walking before an audience as she was now, or perhaps acting out with others some blatant, voluptuous role in which she, the helpless victim, was displayed in an act of lust for all to see.

She looked about the room. There was no clock to be seen. The five minutes would have to be a guess. She looked back into the mirror. What was going to happen next? Why had they left her alone to follow later? Was she going to do as Danielle had told her? There was no alternative. After what she considered an appropriate length of time, Karen walked to the open and waiting door.

When she passed through there was no one to be seen. Ahead of her lay the narrow, curtained-off area with the door at its far end where they had entered. But about half way along, light spilled through the curtains and lit up a patch of carpet in front of the gap. She approached the light and stopped a little way short of it, listening. The silence was absolute.

On passing through the curtains Karen found herself in a strange, synthetic world. She had entered a short passage, lit from above by the spotlights, its walls lined with crumpled, sparkling aluminium foil. Not two metres in front, it ended where another passage crossed at right angles. The wall ahead was jet black. Reaching this, she turned to her right and froze with a sharp intake of breath. Directly in front stood a figure on a small plinth set back in an alcove. The figure wore long leather boots, a leather body harness and a small mask. It was otherwise naked except for the bright steel cuffs on its hands and feet. Despite the life-like appearance, with realistic breasts and genitals, Karen soon recognised it to be a life-sized mannequin. But the shock had been real and she wished her arms were free. Behind the model the alcove wall was partly mirrored but just beyond it, the black walls turned abruptly around a corner. She looked back the other way. The other wall was a full-length mirror and she had a full view of herself with the figure standing behind. That way appeared to be a dead end.

She moved on past the figure and around the corner. This short passage opened out on each side to reveal more mannequins; two in each alcove. The walls behind these were also mirrored so that the figures were multiplied. One of them, to her right, was dressed in a shining black vinyl catsuit, and her long golden hair cascaded over her shoulders. In her hand was held a short, black whip in braided leather. The others were dressed in fetish clothing and lingerie, and wore restraints of varying strictness. One of them, dressed in a manner not very different to her own but with its arms contained at the rear in a leather sheath, was obviously male.

She wondered if the entire room was partitioned and set up like this. If so, it must be a bizarre maze. She was aware of how close and intimate it had become and thought how anyone suffering from claustrophobia might react. With the familiar odour of leather and latex in her nose, she moved on to the next junction. This time, very close, a mirror faced her on each side, though to her left, another exit appeared a little way along. She moved on cautiously and around this next turn, finding ahead another mirrored wall with a passage off to its right. Whoever had designed this labyrinth obviously intended that she should repeatedly see herself as she went.

This next change of direction led into a chamber with six figures. On the other side was yet another mirrored passage with a side exit. Karen became still and looked about in awe. The figures were very real and threatening, and seemed to be crowding in on her. All were bizarrely adorned; one was in a blank helmet, straitjacket and harness, and was suspended some twenty centimetres above the floor by two chains. To its side stood a figure wearing a half mask and a long black gown, its hand resting upon a white plaster pedestal. She moved on; seeing the multiplied images under the glare of the lights, and felt that the world had become totally unreal. She could swear that some of the eyes watched her. She hesitated to look at a figure dressed in lace lingerie and wearing steel cuffs at its back; its wrists were connected by a short chain to a steel collar. At that moment, reflected in the mirror behind it, one of the figures moved. She spun about, frantically tugged at her imprisoned arms and screamed as the figure in the black gown stepped silently towards her. It loomed menacingly, closing in.

They stood face to face. Karen trembled uncontrollably, wide-eyed and transfixed by the eyes which stared through the small holes in the black mask. 'You are enjoying our little game, I hope,' came the voice of Danielle.

'For Christ's sake what are you trying to do?' shouted Karen.

Danielle did not reply but Karen started and cried out again as a hand fell upon her shoulder from behind. She twisted around to see the figure in the black vinyl catsuit, the black whip tucked into its belt. She opened her mouth to speak again but at once, a hand came up before her face and a rubber ball was thrust into her mouth. Danielle held it there whilst Sophie took the strap and buckled it tightly and securely behind Karen's neck. Rendered speechless, she ceased to struggle. Through her turbulent mind rushed the words she could not speak: 'Any moment now! Any moment now, I'm going to wake up!'

They took her inside the alcove opposite to where the gowned figure had stood. By the figure in the lace lingerie was an empty space. Above this space hung a steel chain.

From behind one of the plinths, Danielle withdrew a black leather harness. They fitted this quickly over her body, passing the straps about her waist, her chest and finally about her neck. Connecting straps ran down from collar to waist, between her breasts and over her enclosed arms at the rear. She felt a tug behind then heard a click, and knew at once that they had linked the harness to the hanging chain. Karen tried to move forward but the chain was fully stretched and she found herself losing her balance, only to be kept upright by the chain. The two figures knelt either side of her. Each seized an ankle, ignoring her muffled protests. They pulled apart her legs until the chain took some of her weight and prevented her from falling. She felt the cool leather bands fitted around her ankles, heard the rasp of the buckles and knew that no protest or action was possible, regardless of what they intended to do with her.

But they did no more. The figure in the catsuit left the chamber without speaking. The figure in the gown moved back to the plinth and stood beside it, placing her hand back in position as Karen had first seen it.

Karen gave out a muffled moan and looked around. Everything was still and silent. Regarding the figures grouped about her, for she could see them arrayed kaleidoscopically in the mirrors, she noticed for the first time how like their faces had her own been made to look. Even one of the male figures, in its frozen pose nearby, had been so treated and she had at first, because of its attire, not recognised its gender.

She saw herself reflected clearly, her naked breasts held firmly by the basque, the rubber strap passing down between her legs where it stretched over her sex and through the cleavage of her behind. She was barely able to move and could only sway a little and turn her head. And in the silence, it occurred to her that if she remained completely still, she might be indistinguishable from the mannequins, for that was what she had become. It was surely what they had intended. But why?

Suddenly there were sounds and voices. They were coming from the same direction as the one from which she had entered. She let out a stifled exclamation and stared hard at the motionless figure in the black gown.

'Stay absolutely still!' hissed the voice. 'They will pass by this way.'

The sounds of conversation grew louder. The terrified Karen fixed her eyes on one of the angled spotlights some three metres away. Breathing in and out hard, she let the harness and chain take a little more of the weight from her outspread legs. The voices were only around the corner, mere seconds away. She wanted to close her eyes and felt a tremor in her belly. Four faces appeared on the far side of the chamber. They emerged fully into the room, their faces bathed in bright light. They looked about at the standing figures with wide-eyed amusement.

At the front of the group stood Cheryl in a denim blue dress with white belt and sandals. The two men, both pale skinned and clean shaven, wore business suits; one light grey, the other pale ochre. One had brushed back dark hair, the other was fairer but receding. Both were in their forties but the fourth member of the party was younger. She was slim and blonde, her long hair hanging down behind over her vivid red two-piece suit with its short skirt and black trimmings. As her head turned from side to side the reflections glinted from her gold-framed sunglasses; the large gold rings in her ears glistened in the harsh light. Her high-heeled shoes in gold leather made her appear tall and elegant. 'Ah, this is very good!' she said with obvious pleasure.

'*Ja*,' agreed one of the men, 'we can take much of this for our showrooms.'

'They are all so real,' said the blonde girl, turning about. 'Any moment I expect that one of them will reach down and touch me!'

She approached a figure close to Karen and raised her arm out towards it. It was a female mannequin in a maroon satin corset with black lace trim, and maroon leather, high-heeled thigh boots; its arms were held to its sides by a black leather belt and steel cuffs. She stared closely at its face. 'This is wonderful! This one we must have, complete with its outfit, *ja*?'

'We'll send you the photographs in a few days,' said Cheryl. 'You'll see them long before the brochure is produced.'

The blonde girl moved along and stood before Karen, smiling. 'This one too – so real.' She turned to one of the men. 'See Klaus, they even have shown a little wetness about the gag!'

The men glanced at her but turned their attention to one of the figures opposite. 'But this is even more real,' commented one of them. 'Even more perfect!'

'OK,' said Cheryl, glancing at Karen's eyes, 'we have time to see another room before lunch if you wish.'

'*Ja*, good, we should do this,' agreed the man in the ochre suit.

They continued by, but the other male hesitated to touch the basque about Karen's middle. She held her breath, feeling the blood pumping through her bound body. Then they carried on and disappeared around the corner.

Karen closed her eyes, let out a long sigh of relief under the gag and swayed gently on the chain. The gowned figure opposite stepped away from the pedestal and the figure in the catsuit appeared at the entrance to the chamber.

'Better make it a large one,' said Karen, as Angela uncapped the whisky bottle.

'Are you sure about this? You haven't even had any lunch.'

'Quite sure,' replied Karen. 'And no ice.'

'No, I know you don't take ice,' said Angela. 'Was it really that bad?'

Karen eased herself up on to the bar stool and rested her elbows on the counter. 'I'm not sure Angie, I think it might have all been a dream.'

'I thought you looked a bit flustered when you came in just now. You did volunteer though, didn't you?

'Yes,' agreed Karen pensively, 'I did, didn't I?'

She took a gulp from the glass and watched Angela move the bottles and wipe over the shelves. She looked glamorous in her short, silver sequinned dress with its shoestring top and her matching thong sandals with their high stiletto heels. Glamorous enough to walk right on to a cabaret stage or a movie set. No doubt to Angela, the roles she had played that morning would have been part of the job. Karen could not deny to herself that it had been exciting in an odd way now this part, at least, was over.

'Angie,' she said at length. Angela turned to look at her, a gentle smile passing across her face and her blue-grey eyes.

'Angie, er - don't say anything to the others, will you? I mean, about . . .'

'Of course I won't. But the publication might be seen here; you know that.'

'God,' said Karen. 'I didn't think of the obvious, did I?'

'Well, I wouldn't let it bother you any,' reassured Angela. 'This is the one place where it doesn't matter in the least. Look, I really think you should have a bite to eat. You've got another session, haven't you?'

'Yes, at two thirty. Perhaps I'll have a cheese and tomato sandwich.'

'OK lovey, I'll sort it out. It'll fortify you for the afternoon. Is it something easy you're doing?'

'I don't know,' replied Karen. 'I - I thought it would be better if I just jumped in.'

'God, you're braver than I am then. I wouldn't . . .'

'Hi!' cut in a voice from behind.

Karen turned to see Mike entering from the conservatory, and wiping his forehead with a blue handkerchief.

'Looks like a large beer might be needed,' suggested Angela.

'Spot on!' replied Mike, sitting down on the bar stool next to Karen. 'It's too hot to be working out there today. I'm going to cheat if Sonia isn't looking and go for a swim.'

'She's not in today,' said Karen.

'Then d'you fancy coming out for a dip? There's nobody else around.' He smiled.

'I'd love to, Mike, but I've got work to do.'

He looked into her soft brown eyes and sighed, 'Ah, such devotion.' Then he noticed the half finished glass of scotch. 'I suppose if I was cooped up in that office all day, I'd take to the booze as well!'

On leaving her room Karen was trembling more now than when she had begun. She had no idea what the strangely indifferent Danielle and Sophie were going to do with her other than that it would be quite different from what had already transpired. Clutching the belt of her bathrobe, she hurried once more down the back stairs to join the two who she knew would be waiting.

They were there. But they waited not outside either of the rooms they had previously used, but at a doorway closer to the middle of the corridor and opposite to Cheryl's apartment. This door was already partly opened and Sophie entered as Karen approached. Karen passed through without a word. Danielle closed the door behind them.

There was no ante-room or short passage, but what appeared to be a well-appointed lounge. It was totally unlike the first two rooms. It fascinated Karen, for though she knew about these first floor rooms, no one discussed them. She had heard them referred to as playrooms or guest rooms, on the very rare occasions when they were mentioned at all.

In the centre, around a low rectangular table were arranged two chairs and a two-seater, familiar enough in their chrome and black leather. The whole area was softly lit by rose pink cornice lights and its air of modern luxury was accentuated by the deep maroon carpet. To the left there were two doors. One was ajar and the room, lit from within, was a bathroom. On the right a large cupboard with mirrored doors was set into the wall. But what attracted Karen's attention was the wide archway at the far end, and the ominous black curtain which hung directly behind it to hide the chamber beyond.

Danielle touched Karen's arm and indicated towards the bathroom. 'Your things are in there.'

Without a word, Karen walked across and entered the smaller room. At least here was familiar, for it was again in all essentials, the same as the bathroom in the beauty parlour with its rich blue tiles and luxurious pink rugs. And there, on the seat next to the shower cubicle were set out the things she was to wear.

She regarded these for a short time, with some misgivings. Not because of what was there but because of what was not. But it had gone this far. There was no point in being concerned now. This was to be the last show.

She pulled on the black latex stockings first. They were well powdered and slid over her flesh with a sensual coolness. They fitted up to the tops of her thighs and had discreet little straps around the tops to secure them tightly. She recalled seeing Jackie wear such stockings at the party the previous year. She was not surprised to find the shoes fitted perfectly, nor were the exaggerated stiletto heels any longer a novelty, though she would not have cared to walk any great distance in them. They were of black patent leather and fitted with thin but strong ankle straps. The black latex gloves were a little more difficult but she teased, snapped and stroked them up her arms until they fitted almost to her shoulders. The only item left was a black, patent leather choker which fastened with a small stud at the back of her neck. She looked beneath the seat and to either side of it in case what she sought had slipped on to the floor. She had been left nothing with which to cover her most intimate place.

As she moved with caution towards the door, she hesitated before the long mirror and saw her body with its limbs encased in smooth black latex, reflecting the warm lights with a dull sheen. The rubber was moulded to her arms and legs; warm, intimate and oddly reassuring. On reaching the door, she was tempted to take the bathrobe down from its hook, to cover her nakedness, but realised this to be pointless and left it where it hung.

* * *

Two figures awaited her when she entered the main room. Both wore long, belted gowns in deep purple with gold trimmings at the collar and cuffs. As they approached, she could see their black, high-heeled knee boots of gleaming patent leather. Karen, faced with these well-attired and intimidating individuals, instinctively tried to cover her sex and breasts. But they at once seized her arms, pulled them behind her back and, before she could begin to struggle, snapped steel bracelets about her wrists. She gasped loudly and looked at them in turn but said nothing. She twisted about to look at her hands. The bracelets glared hard against the soft latex.

Danielle picked up a garment from the floor and opened it out. She passed it about Karen's body and fastened it with a small button at the neck. Karen found herself enclosed from neck to ankles in the black satin cloak. When she felt a hand on the back of her head, Karen knew what to expect. The black rubber ball was slipped easily into her mouth and secured firmly in position as the strap was tightened.

'This way now,' said Sophie, though they had already begun to guide her towards the black curtain.

Danielle pulled the curtain aside and Karen, with Sophie close behind, passed through. She had entered not a room, but an enclosed space surrounded by more black curtains. To her left, against the suspended blackness, stood a high-backed, gothic wooden chair, raised from the floor on a wooden plinth. The chair, with its triangular wooden head embellished with crockets, finials and quatrefoil cut-outs, stood empty. Against the wall beyond it, stood an iron cage and on this wall, as far as the curtains to her right, hung numerous restraints and devices which Karen had not the time nor the inclination to study closely. The curtain to her right obviously closed off the other half of the room, for light could be seen spilling over the top. Against this curtain, facing the high chair at a distance of some six metres, there stood a long table or bench of padded black leather. Karen knew such an item of furniture from the beauty parlour, but this one was not horizontal. Instead, it was propped up on tubular steel supports at an angle of forty-five degrees. Both the high chair, the bench and the area of carpet in between were illuminated by lamps, angled down on ceiling tracks. Karen looked from Danielle to Sophie, willing them to answer the questions she could not ask.

Something moved in the corner of her vision. Karen turned her gaze to the high chair. To the side of it nearest to them, a figure emerged and glided silently from between the curtains. It was a sinister figure, robed and masked in the manner of a medieval inquisitor or the officiator of some nameless, dark ritual. The figure stepped upon the plinth and turned slowly to seat itself in the chair as one enthroned for the passing of dire judgement. It remained still and silent, its masked face pointing directly ahead. Karen was aware of hands upon her, moving her forward towards the dark form, before she could even attempt to resist. She let out a stifled cry through the gag and pushed back with her body. It made no difference. She was moved inexorably onward until she found herself shivering beneath its gaze.

No sound was made, but the seated figure raised its right hand in the parody of a greeting. At this gesture, the cloak was pulled away from Karen's body to reveal her nakedness and she was pushed forward until she stood before the throne. She knew the figure was feasting its eyes upon her and she desired nothing more than to shout at it, to make it answer her unspoken question: 'Who are you?'

Karen was pushed downward. She resisted for a time but found her knees giving way until she sank to the floor. Her manacled wrists were grasped from both sides and her arms were pulled over in an arc, forcing her lower until her forehead touched the carpet.

There was no warning of what was to come. The swish, crack and biting sting of the leather strap against her behind brought a sharp cry of surprise. The next stroke followed immediately, from the other side. Despite her muffled cries of protest and her frantic squirming, the punishment continued, each stroke finding its mark, biting and

70

burning her flesh long after she had lost count of their number and her eyes had filled with tears.

When, eventually, they stopped she was lifted to her feet and found her eyes being dabbed to dry up the tears, and the area about her gagged mouth being wiped clean of saliva. She stood, breathing hard and bent forward before the masked figure. For a second time, the hand was raised. Karen was turned around and forcibly walked towards the angled bench, as the dull throbbing heat in her behind spread throughout her loins.

Once before the bench, her wrists were grasped and her arms held tightly. There was a metallic click and she felt her right arm freed of the steel bracelet. But at once she was pulled around and, though struggling to prevent it, found her wrists manacled again, but at the front. She had no time to think, for her arms were held aloft and at the same instant, she was forced against the lower edge of the bench so that she fell back against its inclined surface. Her arms were pulled up hard above her head, as far as they would go. A strap was passed quickly between her wrists and looped around the short chain joining the bracelets. She heard it rasping through the buckle above, felt her rubber-gloved arms being pulled tighter and knew the strap was secured.

Danielle and Sophie did not look at her, and did not speak as they knelt at each side of the bench. Hands took each of Karen's black sheathed legs. Pulling them outward, they then forced them back in underneath until her thighs were held wide apart by the bench's width. The cool embrace of leather took her ankles and secured them firmly to the underside, holding her spread and immobile. Karen watched them raise up slowly. They moved away from the bench and stood to face the seated figure. Karen, splayed out and helpless before it, watched, giving out a quiet moan, as it arose with deliberate but menacing slowness, stepped down from the plinth and moved towards them. It passed between her and a cluster of spotlights and she part-closed her eyes against the glare. She could see the figure as a sinister drifting form, getting ever closer, and moving in ominous silence.

Danielle, at her right, stepped aside and the figure passed as a shadow between them. Karen could make nothing of its identity but knew it had moved around and now stood above her at the head of the bench. Danielle and Sophie had turned and stood facing each other like sentinels across the prostrate form. Above her head, something swished like a breeze stirring dead leaves. At first, Karen could see nothing, then a glint caught her eye. She stared upward in dread, seeing clearly what the hands grasped and held poised above her chest.

The long blade came fully into view; its bright steel surface glinted with deadly harshness. It started to move down, slowly and deliberately, until the needle tip hovered between her breasts. Her eyes widened in terror as she watched the leather-gloved hands adjust themselves and tighten about the hilt. An electric tide flooded through her loins. She heaved and tried to cry out but the rubber ball only embedded itself deeper into her mouth, allowing no more than a plaintive, subdued moan to pass forth. The point of the blade touched her flesh, the searing anguish of its caress passing instantly through every fibre of her body. All of her senses were concentrated in that tiny spot. She closed her eyes and felt herself slip into a turmoil of chaos. Lights flashed about and meaningless forms darted by.

Her eyes were still closed tightly when she became aware of her breath rasping about the gag, and the coolness of her own saliva trickling down her neck. She allowed her eyes to open.

The purple-gowned figures were gone. Only the dark figure remained, standing at her side and looking down at her. She could see the light reflected in the eyes behind the mask and see, too, that the hands were empty.

The figure moved to the lower end of the bench and stood for a moment. It appeared smaller, less threatening than before, and moved in a more natural manner. She sensed that they were alone in the room and that the theatre had ended. The harsh glare of the lights was gone and the enclosed area was bathed only in the pink warmth of the cornice lights. The figure leant forward, resting its hands on the sides of the bench above her thighs; it moved closer until Karen could see the eyes staring at her intently. The leather cloak brushed against her body, settling cool and sensual against her sex. 'I believe you were truly afraid, my dear,' came the voice. 'Or perhaps you are a born actress.'

Karen closed her eyes and gave a long sigh. She was again aware of the burning within, as well as without, her body where the straps had played their game of torment. The warmth of Sonia's breath, and then her lips, touched between her chest where the point of the sword had been set to pierce her. The lips moved about, closing in turn upon the teats of her breasts and aroused them to full firmness. Karen sighed again as the masked face zig-zagged, slowly down her stomach, as softly as a butterfly upon a flower, to the flesh above her vulva.

After the ordeal of fear, the pendulum was swinging the other way, and swinging quickly, for it had gone altogether too far into the deep shadows and the balance had to be redressed. She relaxed against her unyielding bonds, feeling the warmth flood over her body, only tensing a little and exclaiming a soft, 'Aaah!' as the tongue breached her temple of pleasure and found the pearl nestled within.

For a while the tongue teased and tormented, leading her towards the void of sensuality; it had her spread her wings ready for flight but at the last moment left her to stumble in despair. But Sonia knew how far to taunt her before final release. When the tongue invaded her fully and the mouth enclosed her, Karen's body tensed like a spring and it was not a moan but a long, loud cry which burst forth from her helpless form. Sonia felt her quiver in lustful submission and tasted the nectar of her orgasm.

'I thought I   I thought I was going to die.'

'No harm will come to you in this house.'

They lay in the darkness with the moonlight filtering through the blinds.

'I didn't know what was going to happen,' sighed Karen. 'I didn't want to know.'

'Cheryl should have told you, or those two girls, then you wouldn't have been upset.'

'Then I wouldn't have been so convincing. I couldn't have, not if I didn't believe it.'

'Well,' said Sonia, squeezing her hand, 'it's over and done with now. Forget about it. Go to sleep and think of your trip to Paris next week.'

'Yes, I'll think of Paris.'

They turned to each other and kissed, and after kissing, lay back in silence. But Karen did not sleep at first. The events of the day passed through her mind until she relived that final drama of fear and carnality, spread naked and helpless before her tormentor.

It had seemed so very real.

4

Pleasures and Penalties

'And how is our new star this morning?'

Cheryl, wearing a mauve and white beach dress, slipped into the chair beneath the sunshade. Karen looked up, adjusting her sunglasses and lowering the magazine. 'I don't regard myself as a star at all,' she answered. 'I was the only one able to help out and that's all there is to it.'

'If you say so.' Cheryl smiled. Someone jumped into the swimming pool with a resounding splash. A cascade of water arched up against the blue sky, hung glittering in the air for a moment, then collapsed. Cheryl glanced at the water and at Kim rolling over on to her back with the sun catching her naked breasts. 'I know where I'm going in a minute and that's for a nice cool swim. How about you?'

Karen regarded her cool Nordic beauty and clear blue eyes. 'No, not yet. I have work to do.'

Cheryl pushed back the chair and smiled. 'Perhaps I'll see you later.'

Karen rolled up the magazine and clutched it nervously. 'Cheryl!'

Cheryl turned. 'Yes?'

'How much was recorded yesterday?'

Cheryl looked into her eyes for a moment. 'All of it, of course.'

'All of it? How far – I mean, when did it end?'

'At the sacrificial scene, as soon as the lights went off. Why?'

'Nothing, I just wondered.'

'We don't spy on people you know,' said Cheryl. 'When the show's over, it's over.'

75

She turned again to leave but hesitated, looking across the pool. 'Oh dear, there's trouble!'

Karen followed her gaze. Along the driveway walked Rose, her little blue lurex skirt stretched tightly across her behind, her sleeveless white T-shirt moulded over her nipples and breasts. She cut off the driveway and on to the path, crossing some distance beyond the end of the pool until her progress was obscured by the intervening bushes.

'I hope she hasn't borrowed those high heels from the store room,' remarked Cheryl, shading her eyes from the sun.

'Well, they won't be hers,' replied Karen. 'She didn't have anything when she came here that was worth keeping.'

'We do pay her,' said Cheryl, 'and she has been given a wardrobe.'

'Oh, I know,' continued Karen, 'but I don't suppose she's going to spoil them.'

'She will if she's going where I think she's going.'

'Oh? Where?'

Cheryl looked at Karen with amused concern. 'She's off to the chalet to find Mike. I know he's not in because Sonia asked him to smarten up those seats between here and the main road.'

'Does it matter if she has something going with Mike?' asked Karen.

'I'm not sure she has,' replied Cheryl. 'She's an opportunist just like the other one. But it can cause problems if we're not careful and that is something we cannot have. There are ways of dealing with Jackie but our Rose is a little more independent and stronger willed.'

'Where is Jackie?' asked Karen, wondering at the same instant if the question was not an imprudent one.

'Domestic duties,' replied Cheryl, nonchalantly. 'It seems to suit her as much now as it did when Pauline was in charge of things. And it keeps her out of trouble.'

In her mind's eye, Karen could see Jackie in the black latex maid's uniform, going about her duties, possibly manacled and hobbled, knowing that if her duties were not

76

carried out properly, Cheryl had ways of expressing her disapproval; ways which were more disagreeable to some than they were to others.

'Anyone care for refreshments?' cut in a voice.

'Not for me thanks, Angie,' responded Cheryl, 'I have other things to do.'

'Hi, Angie!' greeted Karen. 'Are you on bar duty?'

'Yes,' she sighed, 'but there's nobody around; I'm bored.'

'Come and sit here for a while. They can help themselves if anyone wants a drink. I'm OK for the moment.'

'You're not working today?' queried Angela, taking Cheryl's place.

'Sonia said not to bother but I have a few things to sort out. Maybe I'll go in fifteen minutes or so.'

'Oh, don't, if she's given you the time off. She probably thinks you deserve it after yesterday.'

'Yes, well . . .'

'Well what?' asked Angela with a grin. 'You've obviously come through it in one piece. Are you glad you agreed to it or just plain disgusted? I'm bursting to know, sweetie!'

Karen rummaged around in her shoulder bag and pulled out a packet of cigarettes. 'Want one?' she asked.

'Yes, OK.' Angela drew out the cigarette without taking her eyes off Karen.

'I think I'm going to need one before I answer your question.' She flicked the cigarette lighter and offered it to Angela. 'Look, Angie,' she said, leaning forward and resting her chin on the palm of her hand, 'I've always felt I could confide in you; you've always been a real friend to me. You know more about me than almost anyone else.'

She drew hard on the cigarette and exhaled a long wisp of blue smoke up into the sunshade. 'If anyone had asked me to do anything like that last year, I'd have run a bloody mile, you know that. I'll say it to you because you understand. It gave me a buzz. What I mean is, if the chance came up again I wouldn't say no. And – er, I was really scared at times. That's what worries me – what I wanted to tell you – that being scared made it exciting.'

'There's nothing wrong with that is there, sweetie? It's why people go to see horror movies or take rides on the big dipper.'

'Don't talk to me about horror movies, Angie. At one point I thought it was the real thing.'

Angela smiled and squeezed her hand.

'It sounds to me as though you were thrown in at the deep end. Still, here you are fresh as a daisy. Perhaps next time we have visitors you can muck in again.'

'Quite, yes. Talking about visitors,' said Karen stubbing out the cigarette, 'do you know who's back here in a couple of days?'

'No, I've heard nothing. Who?'

'Carlene and Rodolfo.'

'That's great! I didn't think we'd be seeing them until the fashion show in September. Sonia must have something planned. Who knows, you might get another chance sooner than you thought!'

'Yes,' answered Karen, 'I might, mightn't I?'

Rose did not approach the chalet, she simply took a short cut and rejoined the main drive further along on its curve towards the road. She already knew where Mike was. Keeping her eyes and ears open was a habit which had long ago become second nature.

He saw Rose leave the driveway and pause to remove her shoes. Her slim figure approached him and he leant back in the wooden seat, putting aside the magazine and moving away his discarded shirt to leave an empty space. He recalled the first time he had seen her, the night when she had been caught swimming in the pool whilst she was on the run from the police. Her hair had been long then; almost down to her waist. Now it was short and boyish but he found her no less appealing. 'What's brought you here?' He smiled.

'I was out for a walk,' she answered, folding her arms before him. 'I saw you down here. I wondered what you were doing.'

'I'm supposed to be painting these seats as it happens.'

She looked down at the two wooden benches and smiled. 'But as it happens, you haven't got around to it yet.' She sat down close beside him, crossed her legs and tugged down the hem of the lurex mini-skirt. 'Well I'm not wanting to hold you up. I'll sit here for a couple of minutes and then shove off. Er, you don't happen to have a cigarette do you?'

'I've given up,' he answered, slipping his arm along the back of the seat behind her. He could smell her perfume and feel the heat of her body despite the warmth of the sun.

She clasped her hands about her knee and though she remained gazing ahead, was aware of his eyes glancing at her breasts and legs. She smiled up at him as his hand touched her shoulder. 'Shall I be off then, as you're so busy?'

'There's no hurry.' He smiled back. His hand moved over her shoulder and squeezed the top of her arm.

She turned her face to him and her eyes widened. 'I think there's a creepy crawly in your hair,' she said, reaching up and stroking with her fingers above and around his ear.

'You could be right,' he breathed, as their lips met. He pulled her around with his other arm. She uncrossed her legs and twisted about to face him, circling an arm about his neck.

'You're a good bloke you are, Mike,' she whispered. 'I like you.'

'You're a lovely lady, Rose,' he breathed in her ear. 'I like you too.'

'Nobody ever called me one of them before; a lady, I mean.'

With both arms around him, she ran her fingers about his neck and the base of his spine. He held her tightly, his lips moving from her mouth to her ear, his hand discovering its inevitable way inside her T-shirt. He felt her warm hard nipples. Rose moved her hand down over his jeans and squeezed his thigh but kept her thumb hard against the root of his penis. She felt his arousal through the coarse material. Their lips moved apart and he looked aside.

'What's the matter?' she whispered, pulling him back.

'Rose, we're on full view here. We can't –'

'Never mind Mike, there's no one about.'

Since their encounter at the chalet, he had come to appreciate that a lack of initiative was not one of Rose's faults. She began to pull on his belt and released its buckle.

'Rose!' he hissed. 'Not here!'

He got to his feet and helped her up. With their arms tightly about each other they walked around the group of trees to the far side. There, the grass was cool and soft, and the ground shaded from the bright sun. They kissed for a moment before he pulled up the T-shirt and eased it over her head, releasing her breasts into the warm air. Her hands at once fell to the front of his jeans, where the top button offered little resistance and the zip fastener even less. He had already kicked off his shoes when the jeans were pushed down about his knees, so their complete removal was, if a little undignified as such acts are, at least rapidly accomplished. The thin material of his cotton shorts proved no obstacle to his burgeoning erection, nor did the elasticated waist to the entry of her hand; the voltage of her cool touch as the fingers closed about him, caused a sharp intake of breath. He at once reached around her waist to find the zip fastener at the rear of the skirt, but this eluded him as she fell to her knees, dragging down the shorts as she went until they were about his ankles. He was hardly able to rid himself of them before her lips enveloped the head of his engorged penis, one hand circling the root of the shaft whilst the other held his testicles in their cool embrace. For a time, he stood with his legs a little apart and his hands on her hair, watching each ecstatic back and forth movement of her head, feeling the currents raging in his loins. He closed his eyes, not wishing anything to cause him the slightest distraction.

'Rosie,' he groaned. 'Rosie, I'm going to . . .'

But she knew his orgasm was near and pulled back to leave him glistening and eager, like an arrow about to spring from a steel bow. She stood up quickly; smiling, she turned aside and released her skirt. Mike, aware that she had so far taken the initiative moved quickly to her and, slipping his fingers beneath the elastic of her small black briefs, lost no time in removing them from her and casting them aside. He turned her around, not to face him, but so that he held her from the rear, with his lips upon her neck and his hands cupping her breasts. The head of his penis reared and thrust hotly into the softness of her behind, pushing forward beneath her anus until it reached the moist and inviting prize of her sex. She closed her eyes and pushed herself back against him so that he partially entered her, chafing and butting between the inflamed lips with frenzied impatience. He squeezed her as in a vice, attempting to penetrate her where they stood, his pelvis moving back and forth against the yielding softness.

Neither of them cared for anything other than their lust. She twisted about in his arms and squeezed her thighs upon the aching shaft, then they both fell upon the grass. He thrust deep into her, as she pushed up her knees and crossed her legs over his back. He raised himself up to strike more deeply and vigorously, lifting her behind clear of the grass. Both were determined to triumph in this joust of love and the world beyond their own bodies had ceased to exist. The circuits closed for them both at the same time and the currents surged through their loins. Rose let out a sobbing cry as her body shook and his groans signalled his own release.

'I don't want to move,' she sighed. 'I could stay here all day.'

'Well, I can't,' he said, leaning over and kissing her.

'Not even for a few minutes?'

'If you want to talk,' he said, pulling on his jeans, 'come around to the other side and chat whilst I get on with my work.'

She got up and began to pull on her own clothes, bending down to kiss him as he knelt to fix his shoes.

'I think I'm getting a bit soft Mike, if you know what I mean.'

'No Rosie, I don't,' he answered.

'Well, I mean, we get on all right don't we? You like me, don't you?'

'Rosie, of course I do. I like everyone here.'

They walked back into the sunlight and Rose began, 'No, I didn't mean it like that. I mean you . . .'

Her words trailed off into silence. On the seat, browsing through his magazine, sat Cheryl, and on her lap, curled into a ginger ball was Pancake, the cat.

'Ah-ha,' breathed Mike.

'Oh, bloody hell,' groaned Rose behind him.

Cheryl laid aside the magazine and tickled the cat behind the ear, causing him to push back his head, squeeze shut his eyes and lift up a paw.

'Well now, Pancake,' she said glancing up without expression at Mike and Rose, then returning her attentions to the cat, 'look at these wicked people. What are we going to do with them?'

The cat yawned and regarded the two with its yellow eyes for a moment before closing them once more.

'I suppose we're in trouble,' said Mike.

'We haven't done nothing,' muttered Rose. 'Tell her, we haven't!'

'Don't bother,' said Cheryl coolly. 'It really isn't worth it.'

'Look,' said Mike, 'it's not doing anybody any harm, is it? There's no need to tell Sonia.'

'Mike,' replied Cheryl with austere self control. 'If you want her to move in with you and she agrees, we'll put it to Sonia. Until then there are rules. And if you are going to break the rules, at least don't be stupid enough to make it this obvious!'

'What are you going to do?' asked Rose.

'We won't discuss that now,' replied Cheryl, lifting up and putting aside the cat, 'but just consider yourself very fortunate that Pauline is no longer with us. If she was, you wouldn't be sitting down again for a week or having your hair grow back!'

'Well,' said Rose, pushing her arm into Mike's, 'if it's going to solve all the problem, I don't mind moving in with him. What d'you say, Mike?'

He looked from Rose to Cheryl with an expression of amused disquiet, then back to Rose. 'Now, wait! Let's not starting making plans about anything concerning me. I don't want to rock the boat with Sonia.'

Rose pulled her arm away and fixed her eyes on the ground. Cheryl stood up and regarded her. Mike regarded Cheryl. Only two of the girls resident at the house had so far not fallen prey to his attentions. One was Valerie and the other stood before him. He was not entirely sure about Valerie's attitude towards men. In the case of Cheryl, he had fewer doubts, though the prospect of her being able to ascertain his thoughts through his expression caused him to quickly shift his gaze to the wooden seat and the two unopened cans of paint on the grass next to it.

'Be at my door by two fifteen,' said Cheryl, eyeing Rose.

Rose remained silent.

'Rose! Have you gone deaf?'

'No, I haven't,' mumbled Rose. 'Two fifteen.'

'Prompt!' added Cheryl. 'Now off you go!'

Rose picked up her shoes and walked away; not towards the driveway but across the fields and directly towards the house. She did not look back.

'Try to show a bit of responsibility will you, Mike,' said Cheryl. 'You know what a tearaway she was when she arrived here. Well, she's got a home base now and made friends with people. If she gets involved with you it's going to cause problems.'

'Cheryl!' he protested. 'It wasn't my fault, was it? I didn't know she was going to head this way. Anyhow, I'm only human like the rest of you.'

'Oh yes, I know that, Mike,' she said coolly. 'I know that only too well.'

He looked into her eyes for a few seconds. She seemed to read his thoughts. 'You'd better carry on with your job, hadn't you Mike. I'm sure Sonia will be around at some point to check your handiwork.'

'Why are you looking so serious?' asked Jackie, pausing over a glass of orange.

'Oh, I'm in the shit again,' answered Rose.

'Tut, tut, Rosie: language,' said Jackie with more than a hint of disapproval and a brief glance about the conservatory to see if any of the half a dozen or so people about them had overheard.

'Sorry,' answered Rose, looking down at the untouched tuna and lettuce sandwich in front of her, 'but I'm in it anyway.'

'Want to tell me about it?'

Rose leant forward and lowered her voice. 'It was Cheryl this morning. She caught me and Mike together.'

'So what's wrong with being caught together,' asked Jackie, putting the straw to her lips.

'No stupid,' hissed Rose, glancing about furtively. 'We was at it!'

The liquid in the glass was still diminishing as Jackie's eyes blinked wide open. Suddenly her cheeks bulged and she grabbed for a serviette. At the same time she rattled the glass down upon the table and coughed uncontrollably. A quantity of orange juice spluttered from her mouth and spattered across the table before she could get the tissue up to prevent it. Everyone in the room turned around as Jackie, her face close to the table and burning red, continued to cough and convulse with uncontrollable laughter, the tears, mixing with the orange juice, streaming down her cheeks and nose. Rose watched as Valerie got up from nearby and hurried over to put an arm about Jackie's shoulders. 'Are you all right deary?' she asked, lifting Jackie upright.

Jackie gasped, still red in the face, and tried to catch her breath.

With some effort she managed to compose herself and stared for a moment with watery eyes at the bewildered Rose before snorting with laughter again. Jackie's laughter had become infectious and several others had begun to laugh as well.

'You wouldn't like to share the joke, would you?' asked Valerie.

'Don't you dare!' responded Rose.

'No, no it's nothing really,' said Jackie as she wiped her eyes with the damp serviette.

'I didn't think it was funny at all!' Rose glared as Valerie left them.

'Rose,' answered Jackie, pressing her hands to the sides of her face and sniffing, 'it's the funniest thing I've heard for ages! What did Cheryl say?'

'Not a lot,' answered Rose, 'except I have to go and see her at quarter past two. I suppose I'm in for it now.'

'That makes two of us,' said Jackie. 'I have to be up there dead on two.'

'What d'you mean? Why?'

'Well I was playing at being maid this morning and knocked that poxy old imitation Greek vase over. I know she didn't like it, otherwise I'd have been more careful, but it went all over the place and took me ages to clear up the mess.'

'You ought to be more careful,' chided Rose.

'Listen who's talking!' responded Jackie. 'At least I haven't been caught at it with Mike yet.'

'No, you haven't, but it was probably more fun than breaking an old vase. What's she going to do with us?'

'Your guess is as good as mine, Rosie. Probably keep us confined for the rest of the afternoon I suppose. But something you'd better do whilst you've still got time is to use the toilet and the bidet, unless you don't mind it being done for you!'

'You're quite a girl, aren't you Rose?' said Cheryl.

Rose stood before the desk with her arms by her sides. 'I don't see what you mean.'

'Of course you do! You've been involved in a robbery and goodness knows what else. You were living off our supplies before we caught you and you have shown quite a lot of initiative since, including letting yourself in and out through locked doors and –'

'Here, how did you know?' cut in Rose

'Never mind how, Rose; I just do. Let's say you're not as careful as you ought to be – like this morning. You have to learn to be discrete. That is very important! Even Jackie manages that a lot of the time. And when she doesn't, she knows what she could be in for.'

'So, what about this morning?'

'That must not happen again, Rose; never!'

'But it's not just me that's – '

'No Rose, I'm sure it isn't; life is not like that. The difference is that you were found out, you were that obvious.'

'Cheryl, look, I'm sorry; honest,' said Rose quietly. 'I, er, fancy Mike a bit, that's all.'

'Rose, I'm sure he'd be very flattered to hear you say it. But be realistic, he's almost twice your age and you're no doubt influenced by the fact that he's the only man available here most of the time.' Cheryl arose from the chair. 'Go and sit down over there,' she said, indicating the green leather easy chairs and two-seater by the window. Rose stepped across the room and eased herself into one of the chairs.

'Do you want a glass of sherry?' asked Cheryl.

'Yes, but I thought I – '

'I know what you thought Rose, but never mind for now. We have to talk.'

She returned from the drinks cabinet holding two glasses of amontillado and sat opposite Rose. 'Now,' she said, handing the glass over. 'You have been here long enough to know everyone and to understand fully what we are about. I know how upset you were over your hair and I know that should not have happened to you and Jackie. But it's growing back nicely and you don't need to hide or wear a wig. Meanwhile you've had plenty of fun and been paid for it. And here's the point of all this, Rose; we need to decide where we go from here. You were given a similar decision once before, when we first met you; now you have it again.'

Rose did not speak, but sipped from the glass and looked intently at Cheryl.

'You need a job, Rose. You need to be one of us: one of the girls. It means playing roles. You've done it before, whether you realised it or not, so I'm not suggesting anything frighteningly new. The difference will be that what you do will be more regulated and planned ahead. If you feel that is not acceptable then nobody will force you to remain with us. Do you want to say anything at this point?'

86

Rose looked into the amber contents of the glass. 'I don't want to leave,' she said quietly. 'I like the people, the house and, what you said is true, I've had a lot of fun. Perhaps, if you just go on with what you were saying.'

'All right. You and Jackie: I know you're good friends and you make a good pair. But you're quite different in important ways. You have initiative and aggression. Jackie isn't like that. I know she likes to show off, and you'll see that clearly enough when Carlene and Rodolfo turn up –'

'Who?' interrupted Rose.

'Oh, if she hasn't mentioned them to you yet, ask Jackie. As I was saying, you're different. Jackie is a born submissive. You must know that. She's a masochist. Do you know what a masochist is, Rose?'

Rose shuffled self-consciously in the seat. 'It's someone who likes – er, being whipped?'

'Well, that can be part of it. To some people that's all of it. It generally applies to people who get pleasure out of pain, humiliation or both. There are many in positions of power and authority to whom this type of treatment appeals greatly. For them, it is the other side of the coin, the side they wish to be kept secret. For people in the public eye, politicians for instance, it can be risky and that risk can add to the excitement. However, they need to find people they can trust in order to fulfil their desires. That costs a lot of money. That is in part how Sonia, and others here and in various European cities, make the money that pays for all this. We don't just sell what these people like to have done to them, Rose. We sell reliability and discretion. You see, occasionally, one of them gets found out. And of course, all their pals and associates distance themselves from them, as though they've got the plague, even though they might be at it themselves, or worse.'

'That's why Pauline's in London,' said Rose.

'Yes. Look here. I might be going over things you already understand. I appreciate you're young in years Rose but you've got an older head on your shoulders and you pick things up quickly.'

'Well,' answered Rose thoughtfully, 'I put two and two

together a while back. But what goes on here Cheryl, that's not too secret, is it? I found out without much trouble, didn't I?'

'Yes Rose. But this is a private house and we're in a more tolerant country. The sort of people I'm talking about don't even know it exists, except maybe through hearsay, and they wouldn't dare be seen near the place even if they had our address.'

'You wouldn't want me going over there like you and Annette and some of the others, would you?'

'Oh no, Rose. That would be far too risky. But of course that doesn't mean you can't go to some other parts of Europe. There are glamorous people, interesting places . . .'

Rose considered for a moment. 'Jackie never goes away, does she? She's here all the time.'

'Yes, well, I assumed you might know about that. She's not the most discrete of people.'

'No, she's told me all sorts of things but - well, you tell me.'

'It's her father, Rose. He's an acquaintance, a client if you want the truth, of Sonia's. Jackie is not the best person to have running around loose if you're in public life as he is. You already know her physical needs, I'm sure.'

Rose looked at Cheryl and a flush of embarrassment shaded her face. Cheryl continued. 'He regarded her as a liability and felt it a good idea to keep her out of the way. At the same time her needs could be catered for in full. She was the only one sorry to see Pauline go; you must have realised that. I think almost everyone else has.'

'Yes,' said Rose, 'it wasn't too difficult to figure that one out. But I like her Cheryl. She's a good pal to me and we have a good laugh together.'

'Yes, a good laugh,' said Cheryl. 'That's very important. Never take anything too seriously even if you have to appear to. That was Pauline's problem. Even if you keep a straight face, always see the funny side. You will need to, believe me!'

Rose drank the remains of her sherry. 'Is Jackie -?'

'She's over the corridor, Rose. In the room you first broke in to.' Cheryl looked at her watch. Rose kept her eyes on Cheryl, waiting. 'It's time I attended to her, Rose. You may join me if you wish in our little ritual.'

'What are you going to do?'

'I'm going to punish her in the way she expects. But what she won't expect is that you will be joining me. She thinks you are going to be punished too, as indeed you should be. Do you wish to do it? Do you wish to take part?'

Rose considered for a moment, recalling that she had already played this role with Jackie but that Cheryl could not know of it unless Jackie had told her. This, she considered unlikely. 'All right, I'll join in. But I won't harm her, Cheryl!'

'No Rose, we're not going to harm her,' answered Cheryl, getting up from the chair. 'It is not my intention to harm anybody. It will be recorded, of course. You must take that for granted on all such occasions.'

Rose did not reply but followed her to the door. They crossed the corridor and entered the room, passing directly into the softly lit area with its black leather suite and low table.

'We'll get changed first,' said Cheryl, pulling open the large mirrored door of the walk-in cupboard. 'What do you think we should wear, Rose? What do you feel would be suitable?'

Rose looked inside the cupboard and pondered for a time. Her eye fell upon something hanging from one of the racks and she turned to Cheryl. 'It should be plain and black; like those catsuits hanging up behind.'

'Very well,' said Cheryl, looking over Rose's shoulder, 'we'll go for those. That's what we'll wear. We'll make ourselves appear very intimidating, won't we?'

It was some ten minutes later that they stood before the big mirror. For a moment, as they remained motionless, they were as black marble statues in the rose pink light. The satin lycra catsuits covered each of them like a skin.

Only their heads and hands remained exposed. On their feet were black, patent leather sandals with high stiletto heels. Rose ran her hands down over her breasts and thighs, the thin material detracting little from the feel of her fingers.

'One more thing to put on,' said Cheryl, reaching into the cupboard where she pulled down a small box from one of the shelves. She withdrew two pairs of short, black latex gloves, before replacing the box. She handed one pair without further comment to Rose. Both stood and eased on the gloves, snapping them and flexing their fingers until their hands, like their bodies, reflected the light in a dull, eerie sheen. Rose smiled. Cheryl looked satisfied. Rose watched her place a number of items into a plastic bag but could not ascertain what they were.

She stepped back out into the room and said, 'One of our little black bags, Rose.'

Rose regarded the bag as Cheryl let it swing in her hand for a few moments. She did not know what it contained but did not doubt that whatever it had inside was intended for Jackie.

'Shall we go?' asked Cheryl, indicating the big archway with its heavy black curtain.

'Ready when you are,' replied Rose.

'Remember,' added Cheryl, 'keep conversation to a minimum. Concentrate on what you are doing and look business-like. Let all the emotional expression come from our subject. It is the effect it has on her that is important. Understand?'

Rose nodded dutifully. 'Yes, I understand.'

Cheryl pushed aside the curtain and entered the next room with Rose close behind. Rose had forgotten what Cheryl had said about recording and expected to find the room bathed in the same soft light as when she had first seen it. But it was not. The spotlights glared down from their tracks, illuminating with stark crispness the sinister contents of the chamber; the black leather gleaming, the chromium and steel, harsh and bright. Rose glanced about the room.

In a steel cage to her left, stood what Cheryl had described as their subject. Her legs were clad in stockings of sheer black lace with gold glitter-patterned and lace garter tops to hold them up. On her feet were gold vinyl stiletto-heeled shoes. From neck to waist Jackie was encased in an envelope of sleek, black vinyl, her arms held securely within it, and folded across her front. She stared wide-eyed through the bars at Rose. Cheryl placed the bag on the floor by a padded leather table. 'She'll keep the straitjacket on, of course,' said Cheryl as they moved towards the cage. 'There'll be no problem in controlling her whilst she's wearing it.'

'Rosie!' came the voice from within the cage. 'This isn't just a – I mean, you're not supposed to!'

Cheryl ignored her and taking the key from its wall hook, inserted it into the cage door. Rose remained silent and watched Cheryl intently. The steel door swung open with a metallic sigh.

'Out!' ordered Cheryl.

Jackie obeyed, looking sideways at Rose in bewilderment. Rose overcame with some difficulty the temptation to smile and speak. Cheryl propelled Jackie towards the table but as soon as it was obvious that this was their destination, she pulled back and turned, opening her mouth in protest. 'No! Wait!'

But Cheryl indicated to Rose that she must help and Rose responded quickly, stepping to the opposite side of Jackie and assisting her in her efforts. Jackie was unable to prevent them from moving her on. Rose was aware as to the reasons for Jackie's concern. Their relationship had, up until now, been equal and one to one. Even when Rose had rendered her helpless and teased and tormented her, it had only been a game. They had suffered ordeals and humiliation together at the hands of Pauline. Always it had been together. Now, Rose had changed sides without warning, and left Jackie uncertain, insecure and helpless.

The table stood some seventy-five centimetres high. It was under a metre wide, and its length was that of an average person. Its tubular steel legs were set well back from the edges and formed a cluster of supports near the centre. At its head, spaced a short distance on either side, were fixed two steel poles running from floor to ceiling, each bearing a leather cuff attached to a point less than a metre above the surface of the table. Jackie made a token resistance as they eased her back and on to the table but, without the use of her arms, she could not expect to achieve anything.

Rose stood next to the table, supporting Jackie with her arm. Out of the corner of her eye, she saw Cheryl reach into the bag and also saw what was taken from it. She looked into Jackie's eyes and, with a fleeting smile, kissed her on the lips, winking discreetly as she pulled away. Cheryl showed no reaction but passed the red rubber ball in front of Jackie's mouth and forced it between her lips. Rose held it in position with finger and thumb, her other hand behind Jackie's head, whilst Cheryl tightened and secured the strap behind her neck. They let her head down and Jackie, keeping her legs together, lay on her back and looked from side to side. Cheryl leant over her, and from pockets inside the leather padding of the table, drew out a strap on each side of Jackie's waist. In a moment, this was fastened about her body, just below the straitjacket. The action was repeated, but this time the straps passed around her chest to secure her upper body completely. Cheryl tugged at one of the straps hanging from the poles and said to Rose, 'Ankles in these.'

At once, both of Jackie's ankles were seized and her legs pulled upward, apart and back. The cool and firm embrace of the leather cuffs about them was followed by the rasp of buckles as each ankle was secured firmly to its steel post. Rose watched Cheryl move to the end of the table and reach underneath. There was a sharp click and a section of the table came away in her hands, leaving the new edge under Jackie's exposed behind. The next stage was done just as quickly for the sides of the remaining length of the table were hinged down to leave Jackie supported on a surface of only thirty centimetres in width.

Cheryl looked at Rose across the splayed out legs. 'We

can begin her treatment now, but you may care to notice that she is already beginning to show signs of arousal.'

Rose continued to watch as Cheryl emptied the contents of the bag on to a nearby chair. Rose could see clearly what the helpless Jackie could not.

Cheryl busied herself for a moment before turning to face Rose. In her hand she held an object which Rose had seen depicted but never before encountered. It at first appeared to be a male-shaped, pink rubber vibrator, and though of normal thickness was only some twelve centimetres long. One end was rounded and blunt but it narrowed abruptly at the other end to flare out again into a disc. Cheryl held it blunt end upward in her hand, and Rose saw it glisten as clear jelly flowed slowly down the sides.

'Are you familiar with these?' asked Cheryl, bringing the object down between Jackie's legs.

'No, I don't think so,' answered Rose.

'You'd know if you were,' remarked Cheryl, as she brought the head into contact with Jackie's anus.

Jackie tensed visibly and let out a muffled moan as it was forced harder against her.

'There,' said Cheryl. 'She can't resist it · not with the lubricant. Now, we do it slowly so that it slides up into the rectum. Once it goes far enough her muscle will close over the narrow neck and hold it in place.'

Jackie gasped about the gag as the probe entered her coolly, feeling larger by far than it really was. When Cheryl removed her fingers, all that could be seen was a flat latex disc just below Jackie's visibly moistened sex.

'She is very sensitive there, you know. As she struggles, it will move about inside her. She won't be able to stop it.'

'I bet,' muttered Rose, imagining that she felt the sensual invader moving within her own body too.

Cheryl reached back to the chair and picked up two items; she handed one of them to Rose. Jackie saw the black school strap, its three tails swinging against the lights, as Cheryl held it deliberately in full view of her before handing it to Rose. She saw, too, that Cheryl held a similar strap of her own. She let out a loud but muffled protest, her eyes shifting with alarm from one to the other, her lips sealed about the rubber ball.

'As you are right handed,' said Cheryl, 'you work on her right. I'll use my left hand; I'm used to it.'

Jackie protested again. This time she writhed against the restraints, the heels of her shoes squeaking against the steel posts at either side.

'Will you begin or shall I?' asked Cheryl.

The answer was a sharp crack as Rose brought the strap down against the right side of Jackie's behind. The next stroke followed quickly from Cheryl, who placed her free arm around Jackie's left thigh. Rose did likewise with the right thigh for her second stroke; she could feel the flesh twitch hard as the blow fell.

The protests become longer and louder with successive strokes, the legs jerking alternately against the restraints as each crack echoed about the chamber. The tears filled Jackie's eyes and ran copiously down her cheeks to form a damp patch at either side of her head. Her behind showed irregular markings of deep pink where the straps had played their game of torment across her flesh. Before the next stroke, Cheryl took her hand from the thigh and brought her fingers down to the rubber disc which covered Jackie's anus. She pressed and moved it with a small circular motion as the strap was applied, then nodded to Rose and mouthed silently, 'Go on.' Rose understood.

She had seen, as must have Cheryl, how inflamed and wet Jackie's sex had become. She too released the thigh and, applying the strap once more, slid her fingers down the shaven skin above the vulva until they rested against the quivering heat. As Cheryl applied the next stroke, Rose's fingers lighted upon the pearl of voluptuousness and slid into Jackie with tentacle-like ease. Jackie gasped about the latex ball and both Cheryl and Rose, feeling her body become rigid, knew her time was very close.

With the tailed straps put aside and the two hands working on her, Jackie's protests became moans; moans which soon became more urgent. Rose could almost feel relief herself as the currents of lust surged through Jackie's body and she heaved against the restraints. It seemed as though she would burst them, crying out through the gag as though the life was passing from her.

Each of them released one of Jackie's ankles and undid the straps about her body. Jackie closed her eyes, drew up her knees and sighed.

'This isn't altogether new to you, is it?' asked Cheryl softly.

Rose looked into her eyes and opened her mouth but no reply came.

'I thought not,' breathed Cheryl. 'Come on, let's get her undone and clear up.'

Cheryl reached under Jackie's behind and slowly withdrew the anal plug. Rose reached behind her head and undid the strap, pulling the rubber ball glistening with saliva, out of Jackie's mouth.

'Cheryl,' said Rose. 'I'll sort everything out if you like. I think Jackie might be a bit annoyed.'

Cheryl looked from Rose to Jackie. Jackie smiled weakly. 'I don't mind.'

'OK,' agreed Cheryl, 'I'll do a couple of things and leave you to it.'

They sat on the edge of the bed in the darkness, Rose's arm about Jackie's shoulder. 'If you're mad at me Jackie, I'm sorry. I thought it might be more fun for you, because we're pals, see.'

'I'm not mad at you, Rosie. It's just that I didn't expect it. You see, it's different with Cheryl. She's not a friend like you; it's not the same.'

'Then I won't do it again Jackie, honest I won't. And I'll make it up to you.'

'Will you, Rose?'

'Yes, I said I will.'

'Then promise me something.'

'All right,' answered Rose, 'go on.'

'OK, you've had your fun with Mike. I know you fancy

him. When Carlene and Rodolfo get here, it's my pitch with him, yes?'

'Yes love, I promise.'

'Then it's OK, I'm not mad with you, Rosie.'

They sat in silence for a time, hearing the chirp of insects drift through the window on the warm night air.

'Are you still comfortable?' asked Rose.

'Yes, I'll survive.'

'Because,' continued Rose, 'I'm not going to undo you until the morning, you know that.'

'It's not the first time I've slept in a straitjacket, Rosie. When Pauline was here –'

'Sod Pauline!' cut in Rose. 'It's us now, right?'

'Right.'

'In that case,' said Rose, 'are you tired?'

'Not particularly,' answered Jackie.

'Then that little toy we played with once, the double-ended job. Where is it?'

'God!' sighed Jackie. 'I thought you'd never ask. It's in the top draw right ahead. You don't need the light.'

5

The Stars Return

By Thursday everyone knew they were coming back for a few days. The nearest anyone could say about their time of arrival was that it should be during lunch time. They had left Marseilles earlier that morning. Karen had learnt from their stay the previous autumn what effect Carlene and Rodolfo had upon almost everyone. Gone were jeans and T-shirts, all relegated to the darkness of the cupboards, out came the more stylish and glamorous clothes worn on special occasions. The two who remained least affected were Jackie and Rose, whose inclination to appear out of the ordinary had never required a pretext.

Sonia had said earlier, 'When they arrive, let me see them to say hello, then take them into the bar for a bite to eat. And, by the way, they'll have someone with them who's never been here before. Someone none of you will have met.'

Nothing more was mentioned about the third person but it would not be long before Karen's curiosity was satisfied. She was sharing a light lunch with Annette and Valerie in the bar. They sat close to the archway which separated the bar room from the conservatory. From beyond the archway, a voice called, 'I think it's them!'

'Rodolfo must be something special,' remarked Valerie. 'He seems to have outlasted the rest.'

'He's from a fairly wealthy family, isn't he?' commented Annette. 'He doesn't have to sponge off her. In fact,' she continued, smiling at Karen and Valerie, 'I might get her to let me know when she's finished with him.'

'I'd better go and meet them,' said Karen.

'They're coming in here, aren't they?' asked Valerie.

'Oh yes,' answered Karen, getting up from the chair, 'but Sonia has to see them first.'

When Karen pulled open the front door, the red sports car had already glided up and stopped by the portico and the three passengers were lifting out their bags.

'Karen baby – hi!' Carlene beamed. Her dark eyes flashed, and her voice was resonant with enthusiasm.

'*Buongiorno!*' Rodolfo smiled, and waved his hand in a grand operatic manner. The third member of the party glanced up but said nothing.

Like everyone else, Karen had foregone too casual an appearance for the occasion. She wore a short, form-fitting sleeveless cotton dress in deep blue and with a black chiffon panel forming a deep V between her full breasts. About her waist was a braided gold leather belt and on her feet were matching gold sandals. It was as formal as she wished to be, though it was obvious as they walked the short distance towards her, that in the manner of attire, as in almost everything else, Carlene was not in the habit of making concessions, even in the warmth of this day. For the sun stood high in the azure blue and the heat of its embrace was not to be ignored. Karen felt relieved on her behalf that the house was effectively air conditioned. The stunning, wide-eyed Carlene, whose African father and Caucasian mother had bestowed upon her the beauty of both races in full measure, entered and put down her travel bag. She turned, took Karen enthusiastically by the arms and looked searchingly into her eyes. 'Well, it's just great to see you again, kid! How are you doing?'

They kissed each other on the cheeks. 'I'm fine,' said Karen with a smile.

Rodolfo moved up to her and she smiled into his blue eyes. 'Hello Roddy.'

Rodolfo at once took her hand. He held it with both of his own and pressed it hard to his lips. 'Ah, *signorina*, how often your image has passed before my eyes since we last met.'

'OK Roddy, quit crawlin' up to the kid and shift your-self!' Carlene grinned as the third member of the party approached.

She was slim and of average height, her skin a soft brown, her age no more than twenty. With her high cheek-bones and eyes as dark as Carlene's she held a countenance of striking beauty. She smiled gently, and with practised grace, held out her hand to Karen. Karen took the hand. Carlene said, 'Karen meet Indrani Indrani, Karen.'

The girl smiled and gave a hint of a curtsey. Karen at once felt that Indrani was different to anyone else she had ever met. It was as though she was in the presence of one whose breeding and charm had been nurtured over gener-ations.

Sonia was already waiting at the door as they reached the main office; she was wearing her black leather biker's jacket and black, satin lycra leggings with high-heeled ankle boots. Sonia always did as she wished. She did not need to make any concessions.

'Oh! Sonny.' Carlene laughed as she seized and kissed her. 'It's great to be back with you and all these wonderful ladies again!'

Sonia returned her kisses and turned to Rodolfo. 'And it's nice to see you again, Roddy.'

'Ah, *signorina*,' he said with a look of exaggerated con-cern, 'all of the pleasure is mine.'

The hand kissing was repeated, but with considerably more reserve than had been experienced by Karen.

'Indrani,' said Sonia, holding out her hand, 'I'm so happy to meet you at last.' Indrani mouthed an inaudible greeting.

'Shall I tell the others they're coming through?' asked Karen.

'Yes, my dear,' answered Sonia. 'Just give us five minutes.'

'Do they all look mega-glamorous?' asked Annette.

'Carlene certainly does,' replied Karen. 'She's a real eye-opener this time. You should see her outfit.'

'This other girl,' said Valerie, 'what's she like?'

'She looks Indian,' answered Karen. 'She's a bit younger than Carlene and really lovely.'

'Quick – look at him,' whispered Annette with a giggle. 'Be casual about it. Don't let him see you staring.'

Valerie and Karen glanced aside. Across the room, a little way from the entrance, sat Mike, wearing a denim shirt and fawn slacks. He held a newspaper in his hands and studied it with silent concentration. Before him on the table stood a half finished glass of beer.

'He's pretending to read the paper,' said Annette, 'so it doesn't look as though he's waiting to see Carlene. His eyes haven't moved at all in the last five minutes, I'll swear.'

I can't wait to see his face when they walk in,' said Karen trying hard to contain her laughter.

'I think you're just about to,' commented Valerie, looking towards the door.

Carlene entered the bar room like a film star. Her eyes flashed and she beamed a broad smile around the room. 'Hi babes!' She grinned, raising her arms. 'How are you all today?'

There was a unanimous response of smiles and waves. Rodolfo followed her into the room, pushing back his sleek black hair; he bowed elegantly and threw out his arms as if in expectation of a round of applause. Indrani followed, smiling gently but did no more than raise her hand a little. Nobody could fail to be impressed by the image of Carlene. The little furry grey beret which topped her glossy black, shoulder-length hair was fixed at a cheeky angle. Her suit, in light-weight cotton, bore a fine black and white checked pattern. The jacket was cut away and open at the front to reveal a high-necked satin blouse in vivid crimson with a black satin bow at the neck. The skirt was tight and conspicuously short, with a high waist and a wide, glossy black vinyl belt. Her sandals, in similar material were poised on high stiletto heels. The ensemble showed one feature off more than any other: her legs. They were beautifully formed, and sheathed in sheer gossamer nylon. Her large pendant earrings sparkled as a counterpoint, as they swung about and flashed above her shoulders.

'I bet she didn't drive here in those shoes,' muttered Karen.

'Just look at him' said Valerie, nodding towards the seated figure at the table opposite.

Mike had lowered the paper and, with mouth slightly open, had his gaze frozen upon the lower part of Carlene's anatomy.

'I think he's dribbling,' remarked Annette.

The grinning Rodolfo, his clean shaven jaw jutting out, wore a tan-coloured chamois shirt, open low enough to reveal a large medallion. 'Looks like a bloody dinner gong,' mused Valerie.

His deep blue slacks were ornamented with numerous brass studs and were held about his slim waist by a braided leather belt sporting a large and ornate brass buckle. But all eyes had moved to their companion. She was more simply adorned in a plain, close-fitting, sleeveless white dress, which finished below her knees but had a split side which ended well up on her thigh. About her neck was a wide choker of braided gold wire set with gleaming black stones. On her feet were white, wedge-heeled open sandals. The dress might not have been as showy as Carlene's outfit but it did nothing to disguise the firm and curvaceous figure which lay beneath.

'OK kids!' announced Carlene, putting her arm lightly about the girl's shoulder and easing her forward. 'This gorgeous and innocent little lady is Indrani! She's here for our show, but she can't stay for now because she has to talk to Sonny. But at least you've all met her!'

Indrani smiled and raised her hand but only hesitated for a moment before turning to leave the room, her glossy black hair swinging down almost as far as her trim waist.

'She's a real cutie, isn't she?' remarked Annette. 'I wonder what she's into.'

'I'm told she practises yoga,' answered Karen. 'As part of her work, that is.'

'That sounds interesting.' Annette grinned.

Carlene was already chatting and laughing with Angela and Lorna at the bar, when Valerie asked, 'Is he all right?'

They looked at Mike, who had evidently still not moved.

'I think he's gone into shock,' said Annette. 'I'd better do something before Carlene gets closer or he'll stop breathing and we'll lose him.'

Annette dipped her fingers into her glass of orange juice and retrieved two ice cubes. Holding them on the palm of her hand, she rose from the chair and quickly crossed the buzzing room to stand behind the seated figure, who showed no sign of being aware of her presence. All conversation stopped abruptly as a cry cut through the air.

Everyone except Annette, who was returning to the table with an expression of plain nonchalance, turned to look at Mike. He had risen suddenly and knocked over his chair as he struggled with the back of his shirt and tugged at the rear of his belt.

'Oh, you poor guy!' proclaimed Carlene, stepping towards the tormented figure. Suddenly, he stood upright and yanked hard at the seat of his slacks. An expression of alarm crossed his face as be began to shake his left foot. Carlene put out a hand to support him as the room looked on; two glittering ice cubes were expelled from his trouser leg and jumped across the carpet to come to rest in the middle of the floor. There was an immediate and enthusiastic round of applause. The outraged victim glared at Annette. Annette winked demurely.

'Oh my,' said Carlene, putting her arm about the embarrassed Mike, 'who would do such a terrible thing to a nice guy like you? Come and sit down, baby. Take it easy.'

He sat down, grinning sheepishly. He glanced at the hem of Carlene's mini-skirt and the enticing thighs which were uncomfortably close to his face. Carlene bent forward, squeezed his shoulder and kissed him on the forehead with a deliberately loud sucking noise.

'I think he's going to have a seizure,' hissed Annette.

Carlene turned about with her hands on her waist and wiggled her behind in front of his face with a shrill, 'How's that, baby!' Mike's eyes widened, but the smile remained.

'Poor Mike,' said Karen, 'he really does get teased, doesn't he?'

'Poor Mike!' exclaimed Valerie. 'I'll bet you couldn't persuade him away from here with a kilo of gelignite!'

'I think we have another floor show coming up,' said Annette. 'Look at Hot Roddy!'

Whilst Carlene laughed loudly and chatted with Angela and Kim, Rodolfo had strolled casually across the room to where Jackie and Rose sat.

'He's taking the bait,' added Valerie.

'Ah, Madonna,' said Rodolfo as Jackie got up to greet him, her firm breasts barely covered by the black nylon shoestring top. She circled his waist with her arms and they kissed, Rodolfo slipping his hands down over the back of her blue denim mini-skirt. Rodolfo, looking over her shoulder said, 'And the signorina, I think we have not met before.'

'This is Rose,' said Jackie. Rose held out her hand but remained seated.

'Ah, *la bella Rosa*,' sighed Rodolfo. As he bent to kiss her hand he gazed hard into her eyes.

Rose remained impassive apart from a fleeting smile, then she got up and said, 'I'm going to talk to Mike for a while if you want my chair.'

Rodolfo stepped aside to let her pass and smiled. '*Mille grazie, signorina*.'

Jackie and Rodolfo sat opposite each other at the small table. Almost at once, their voices became soft and inaudible.

'You very busy?'

Mike looked up to see Rose standing by him in her translucent, cobalt blue blouse and black, skin-like, satin lycra tights.

'Me busy?' He smiled. 'No, not really – not since the ice cubes that is.'

'Fancy a walk, then? Everyone else seems to be occupied with something except for you and me.'

He put the newspaper aside, finished the remains of the lager and stood up. 'OK Rosie, I wouldn't mind a walk.'

'Can't go out in the fields wearing these, though,'

grinned Rose, indicating her black leather, stiletto-heeled ankle boots.

'Perhaps just as well,' muttered Mike as they crossed the room to the sound of whooping laughter from the effervescent Carlene. He was unable to resist a final glance at her legs as they passed by. Annette watched Rose tuck her arm into Mike's as they left via the conservatory, then glanced over her shoulder to see Rodolfo and Jackie, hands held across the table, in close and hushed conversation. She smiled to herself.

'No more entertainment after all,' said Karen.

'Not yet,' replied Annette, 'but I think we're working up to it.'

Moments later, Cheryl entered from the main corridor, followed closely by Indrani and Sonia. Everyone, except for the preoccupied Rodolfo and Jackie, had cause to notice; not only because of the new arrival, but because Sonia herself was not a frequent visitor to the bar room. They passed through and into the now unoccupied conservatory, Cheryl watching the pair at the far end of the room as they did so. As they pulled back the chairs by the French windows, she also observed the two strolling along the driveway towards the swimming pool.

'Looks like a cabinet meeting,' remarked Valerie.

'I think they're still planning for tomorrow,' said Annette.

'Sonia wants to do some kind of deal with Indrani as well,' added Karen. 'I don't know what.'

'I'm doing that lovely hair of hers before dinner,' said Valerie. 'Maybe I'll sound her out then.'

Had Karen entered the first floor room that afternoon, she would have been aware of some changes since that first scene with Sophie and Danielle. The dining table and chairs were gone and the lighting had been altered. The main feature still remained; the circular black curtain, hanging from its curved track and enclosing an area of somewhat less than three metres across.

Before the curtain stood two figures, bare breasted and

positioned as sentinels. Both Angela's silver blonde and Kim's light brown hair were swept back and hung as pony tails down their backs. Each wore an ornate bronze pectoral about her neck and, below the waist, a skirt made of brown leather straps, embellished with brass studs and held high about the waist by a wide, scroll-decorated leather belt with an ornate bronze buckle. Their laced brown boots fitted tightly up to the middle of the thigh, to just beneath the hem of the skirt, where they flared out slightly. Each stood still, posing with hands upon hips, waiting.

The only sound within the room came from the left of the two figures and the curtain. Against the wall stood a steel cage, brightly illuminated from above. Within the cage was enclosed Indrani, standing with her hands manacled to the bars of the cage roof. As she twisted about, the metallic creak of the chains broke the silence. Apart from a jewelled leather choker about her neck, Indrani was naked. Her raven hair had been wound into a tight spiral above her head and was held in place by ornate clips. Her eyeshadow was of fine gold dust and her lips were crimson. Around the nipples of her firm breasts glittered small gold rings. Her body, totally devoid of hair, gleamed with the oil which had so recently been applied. She turned her head aside; there were voices.

Three figures entered from the ante-room and moved slowly across the thick maroon carpet towards Angela and Kim. Two of the group, Annette and Lorna, were attired in the same manner as Angela and Kim, but the third presented an altogether different image. Carlene wore a Cossack-style tunic with large brass buttons and trousers in heavy black satin. The fur hat upon her head was adorned with small gilt chains, as were the high collar and the cuffs of her suit. The black newly polished leather of her high-heeled knee boots glistened. In the wide, red belt about the tunic was coiled the unambiguous form of a leather whip.

Carlene stopped before the sentinel forms of Angela and Kim, withdrew the whip from her belt and stood with one arm by her side, the other holding the coiled whip against her waist. Annette and Lorna proceeded on to the cage; Annette paused only to pluck up a small bunch of keys from an ornate table by the wall, before they took up positions on each side of Indrani's steel prison.

Carlene waited for a long while, then held up the coiled whip and gestured in the direction of the hanging circle of curtain. Angela and Kim turned; each taking hold of an edge of the curtain, they drew it aside. They moved away from each other in ceremonial manner, slowly opening the black drapes to reveal the hidden area within. At the far side, they met and released the bunched up curtain. Directly before them stood a square wooden pillar, rising from floor to ceiling. Angela reached up behind this. There was a click and at once the whole area, formally obscured, was flooded with bright light from the ring of spotlights above.

Within, standing upon the floor of polished wood, was a circular bed almost two and a half metres in diameter and covered in deep purple satin. Upon the bed lay Rodolfo, stretched out on his back, with his arms and legs spread out to form a human cross. Each wrist and each ankle was held by a bright steel bracelet, and each bracelet by a steel chain which passed tightly over the edge of the bed and down beneath to a hidden fixing point. His head, with eyes closed and twisted aside to avoid the glare of the lights, rested upon a small black leather pillow. He was naked, unless the scant little pouch in sheer black nylon which barely contained his penis could be regarded as an item of clothing. As Angela and Kim moved to face each other on either side of him, he opened his eyes.

Carlene walked around the bed and stopped to face the cage. At the signal of the raised whip, Annette reached up to the top of the cage with the keys poised in her fingers. In a moment, one of Indrani's arms was freed; seconds later, the other. She at once seized the bars of the door and glared between them at Carlene, who turned again to face the bed. As if on cue, Angela and Kim each placed a knee upon the bed and leant towards each other over the helpless Rodolfo. The effects of their proximity, the potential of the situation and his own helplessness had not left

Rodolfo unmoved. His arousal was very evident even though it was held in check by the straining pouch. Angela and Kim each passed a cool finger into the gaping sides of the pouch and stroked against the base of his ample penis, feeling him twitch; a soft groan passed from his lips.

'He's definitely interested,' said Kim.

'I agree,' replied Angela.

'How are we all looking, kids?' asked Carlene.

'We're looking fine!' replied Angela.

'OK then ladies! Let the little guy out!'

Angela and Kim reached down to the cord at Rodolfo's waist and tugged. The pouch at once flew back and the penis sprang up as though released from a trap. Kim pulled the diminutive garment from under him and cast it down by the side of the wooden pillar. Angela slipped her fingers about the generously proportioned organ and began to work it slowly up and down. Rodolfo caught his breath and sighed. A loud click caught her attention and she looked up to see Annette unlocking the cage door. Carlene stepped back close to the wall, midway between the cage and the bed. As the door swung open Angela and Kim left Rodolfo and took up positions facing the head of the bed. Annette and Lorna remained at either side of the cage.

Indrani did not wait for the door to open fully, but sprang out on to the carpet with eyes flashing. She at once turned to face Carlene and crouched, like an angry cat, as if she meant to leap up at her. Carlene shook out the whip and cracked it loudly, hissing it by Indrani's face almost faster than the eye could see. Indrani recoiled as the whip cracked again and Carlene gestured with it towards the bed. Indrani affected a snarl and spun about. Without hesitation she threw herself forward and cartwheeled once, before leaping up on to the bed to end up standing with her back to Rodolfo, her legs either side of his spread-eagled body. For a time, she stood motionless as though in contemplation, then raised up her arms, reaching out horizontally to each side. Slowly she stretched back her right leg and bent her left, lowering her body and twisting sideways so that her left hand rested on the bed and her right was thrust up at an angle. Rodolfo, mouth partly open, watched intently. She sank further until the head of his penis pushed against the softness of her stomach. There she remained for some seconds then slowly eased forward, allowing the head of his organ to slip towards her sex. Rodolfo tensed expectantly against the chains, his mouth opening wider. But Indrani stood up and resumed her former position.

She remained expressionless and placed her hands behind her back with fingers touching and pointing downward. Her next move was to twist her hands inward and upward until they were positioned prayer-like between her shoulder blades. Rodolfo let out a gasp of surprise as she jumped to place her left leg back and her right leg forward with the foot pressed against his outstretched leg. Slowly, very slowly, she lowered her body down from the waist until her face was directly above the flushed and aching shaft. She continued downward. Rodolfo tried to push up his pelvis and let out a soft groan as her lips opened and slipped warmly down over the head. This pose she held for twenty seconds, remaining quite still despite Rodolfo arching his back to enter her mouth further. When at last she lifted up, the shaft was reddened and glistening wet. Rodolfo groaned in despair.

Indrani moved backward and knelt astride Rodolfo's head with her feet resting on his chained arms. If her intentions were obvious to anybody they must have been more so to Rodolfo, who stared transfixed as her behind settled a tongue's length above his face. She fell forward over her knees and stretched her arms out directly in front, allowing the head of his engorged penis once again deep into her mouth; she squatted sphinx-like above his helpless form. Because of her weight, he was unable to move his pelvis upward, but his tongue, hidden by her thighs, was evidently playing its voluptuous role upon the stage of her sex, for after some thirty seconds, she began to moan quietly and spread her legs even further. After another minute, she lifted her head, withdrawing the engorged and wet shaft from her mouth and enclosing it in her hand.

With her eyes closed and her head pushed back, she moaned louder still. When her mouth fell open her moans became cries. Suddenly, her body stiffened and she pushed her pelvis down hard against him as she let out a final loud, high-pitched cry. And so, for a moment, she remained.

The whip cracked. Indrani started and looked wide-eyed at Carlene. Without warning she sprang forward and back-flipped up on to her feet. She spun around and faced Rodolfo for the first time, with hands on hips and legs spread wide. Keeping her legs straight, she arched her body downward until she stood on all fours above him. With her eyes fixed hard upon his, she bent her legs slowly until the lips of her sex stroked against the moistened head of his craving erection. He arched his pelvis to push into her but she only fuelled his desperation by pulling away momentarily. Twice more she did this, feeling the head twitch hotly against her. After the third time, with her eyes still gazing down at his, she allowed him to enter her a short way, once more hesitating to increase the tension and torment yet further. Then she sank down, straightening up her body and taking the whole of the inflamed and burning shaft up to the root. With her hands clasped behind her head, she moved her pelvis rapidly until the stiffening of his body told her that his orgasm was close. As his mouth opened to cry out, she pulled upward and withdrew him, but just as quickly, seized the pulsating shaft in her hand and worked it rapidly. He jerked hard against the chains; ejaculating vigorously and copiously over her upper body, he gasped desperately as though he was on the point of expiration.

Indrani released him and let her head fall back. Then she splayed her fingers about the front of her body and slowly spread the running semen about her breasts and stomach. Then she remained still, with her eyes closed, as Angela and Kim moved around the bed, pulling the black curtain behind them on each side until they met again where they had begun. The tableau was now hidden from view.

One by one, the lights went out until the room was in darkness.

* * *

'Gone?' exclaimed Angela. 'But she's only just got here.'

'I know,' said Carlene, turning over on the sunbed and propping herself up on her elbows, 'but Indrani's one busy lady. She doesn't hang around nowhere for long.'

'I saw Kim drive off early this morning,' said Lorna, smoothing back her raven hair. She reached for the sun cream.

'Yes,' answered Carlene, 'that was her. Kim dropped her off at Béziers and she got herself on the TGV, straight to Paris.'

'Pity we didn't get to know her,' said Angela, swishing her feet around in the crystal water.

'Well, I don't think so,' replied Carlene. 'I've known her some time but I don't think she rates friendship too highly. I've met with more conversational people at an autopsy. I still don't know if she comes from India, east Africa or Bradford; she never said!'

'Anybody want the cream?' asked Lorna, rubbing her shoulders and breasts, then recapping the tube.

'No thanks,' replied Angela, closing her eyes against the morning sun.

'I'm OK,' said Carlene. 'I came packaged with a built-in suntan so I don't –'

She was interrupted by a shriek from the far end of the pool. They looked about and saw Jackie leaping up and down in the pool, rapidly hurling cascade after cascade of glittering water at Rodolfo. He swung about, one hand gripping the curved rail of the steps, the other reaching out to grab at her each time she came close. At each pass he laughed and shouted, '*Cattiva ragazza!*'

Jackie had on no more or less than the other girls at the pool; just a small, backless swimslip with the cord passing down between the orbs of her behind. Angela noted Rodolfo's sleek nylon bikini trunks in fine gold and blue diagonal stripes. 'He seems to have recovered from the trauma of yesterday,' she commented.

'You bet he has!' replied Carlene as Rodolfo raised himself to dive into the pool. 'It looks like somebody shoved a polony down the front of his briefs.' She raised herself up and shouted, 'Hey Roddy!'

Rodolfo stepped back from the edge and, pushing the hair back from his forehead with both hands, looked over to Carlene.

'Don't jump in with that medallion round your neck!' she called. 'You'll never surface!'

'Oh Carlene!' he called back, sticking out his jaw and raising both hands palm upward. 'I am having only a little sport!'

'Like hell!' she responded, much to the amusement of Angela and Lorna. Carlene relaxed and turned back to them. 'The only sport he wants is to get inside her G-string.'

'He's a good looking guy,' said Lorna.

'Oh, sure he is. But there are plenty more around,' grinned Carlene, glancing back at Rodolfo, who stood by the pool edge with hands on his waist and jaw thrust out. 'See that pose?' she said. 'He's been trying to impress people with it ever since he saw an old movie about Mussolini!'

'You can't blame him,' said Angela. 'Jackie's a real teaser. She used to be the same with Mike but I think Rose has taken over there.'

'Yes, well,' said Carlene, 'I have more than just a notion Cheryl has plans for those two little ladies before long.'

'Has anyone seen Rose about, as a matter of interest?' asked Angela.

'I served her in the bar last night,' replied Lorna. 'She'd had rather a lot to drink too. I haven't seen her today, though.'

'How about Mike?' enquired Angela.

'Oh, he's around,' answered Lorna. 'I saw him pruning the bushes near the tennis court after breakfast. He didn't look terribly happy.'

'Mmm, do I sense intrigue in the air?' asked Carlene.

'Could be,' replied Angela. 'Anyway, I'm going for a swim. I'll keep an eye on Hot Roddy for you!'

'And you recall nothing which might give us an idea where she's gone?' asked Sonia.

'Er, no,' answered Mike nervously. 'After I made it clear

that I didn't want her moving in with me, she walked off. I stayed away from the bar and conservatory last night to avoid any more problems.'

Sonia leant back in the green leather chair and looked down at her desk. 'Well, I hold her bank book so she doesn't have access to cash unless . . .'

'Unless she's pinched some off somebody.'

'Yes, though she was living rough when she was on the run, she seemed to manage well enough. I must say I didn't expect this to happen; not after the time she's been with us.'

Mike shuffled uneasily in the chair. 'Look, I did nothing to encourage her. I've behaved no differently towards her than I have to anyone else. She just seems to to '

'Quite!' cut in Sonia, regarding him without any hint of emotion. 'Perhaps she felt that having eaten of the forbidden fruit, she could take from any tree whether it was hers to take from or not. She was a thief after all, wasn't she?'

'Look Sonia, I feel guilty about this. If I'd realised how she really felt, maybe I could have – well, I don't know maybe I could have been a bit easier with her.'

'Perhaps you could, Mike,' she replied, looking him in the eye. 'Does it make you feel good to think that she has probably run away because of you?'

He stared intently back at her. In all the years he had known Sonia, she had never looked at him quite like this. She was a beautiful woman. He had always thought so. But her feelings towards everyone, himself included, were hidden behind a façade of polite correctness and pre-formulated friendliness. She was totally beyond his reach even if he had dared to desire her. At last he answered, 'No, of course it doesn't. I didn't want her to go away. I like her a lot. She was hemming me in a bit, that's all.'

'Well, I've already spoken to Inspector Gautier. His relationship with some of the people here has been, shall we say a little involved, so I expect some cooperation from that quarter at least. The only problem could be if she gets picked up too far afield and says too much. We'll have to see, won't we?

* * *

'I thought you were working this afternoon,' said Kim, pushing a tuna fish salad across the bar.

'I was,' replied Angela. 'Annette too, but Hot Roddy got too hot this morning by the pool and took to his room feeling sick.'

'Oh well,' said Kim, 'he'll have to do double the time tomorrow to make up for it. By the way, have you seen Jackie or Rose recently?'

'Actually sweetie,' replied Angela, 'I think our Rose has escaped back into the big wide world.'

'What! You mean she's disappeared?'

'Something like that. And I believe Jackie's confined to quarters.'

'Why is that?' asked Kim.

'Oh, you must have noticed,' said Angela. 'She's been trying to hook Rodolfo since they arrived.'

'Carlene doesn't seem to worry too much.'

'No, well she's used to it. And he's far from indispensable. Carlene's got more male admirers than he's had plates of spaghetti!'

'Good thing, too,' retorted Kim. 'It probably makes for a good relationship in their case. Where is she now?'

'Playing tennis with Annette, Val and Rachel. She's left Rodolfo in peace.'

'I wonder if he's snoring,' said Kim.

'He doesn't,' replied Angela. 'So I've heard, that is.'

Rodolfo indeed was not snoring. At the far end of the first-floor corridor, the door opened, slowly and quietly. A face peered around and glanced in both directions. The corridor was deserted. Rodolfo, in a white bathrobe, emerged from the room and eased the door shut silently behind him. He moved with haste past Cheryl's door on his right, until he reached the next archway, where he hesitated and looked over his shoulder before trying the ornate brass handle. The door opened and he disappeared inside.

The blinds were closed across the windows, and even though the room was in semi-darkness, it was obvious that

113

she was not waiting for him as they had arranged. Ahead lay the entrance to the bathroom. That door was open. At right angles to it was another door only slightly ajar. Rodolfo listened. There was a radio playing. He walked the few steps over to the door, tapped and said in a low voice, 'Signorina.'

'Roddy!' came the reply, and a face appeared in the gap. 'Roddy, I thought she'd locked my door. I didn't think you look, Roddy, I can't use my arms   I can't do anything!' She backed away from the door and he slowly pushed it open. The only illumination in the bedroom was from the small pink shaded table lamp by the side of the bed. The windows were covered by curtains as well as blinds, and for all Rodolfo could see, it might have been twilight outside.

Jackie stood between the three quarter bed and the chest of drawers. About her slim waist was fastened a heavy black leather belt fifteen centimetres in width. Riveted to each side of this, a thick leather cuff held each of her wrists hard against her body. Her hands were enclosed in semi-rigid leather mittens which were joined by a steel link at the front of the belt. Apart from the restraint, she was quite naked.

Rodolfo moved closer, his eyes fixed on her middle. 'Why do they do this thing to you?'

'To stop me from going out,' replied Jackie. 'It could have been worse. At least I can walk about and see. When Pauline was here she used to   '

'I will take it from you,' cut in Rodolfo reaching towards the restraint.

'You can't. It's locked.'

Jackie turned slowly about. Rodolfo, his eyes becoming accustomed to the dim light, could see quite well the brass padlocks at her wrists and at the rear of the belt. His eyes moved down over the cleft of her behind for the few moments it was in view.

'*Afortunata ragazza*,' he breathed, placing his hands on the sides of her face and gazing into her eyes. 'Always they are doing this to you, I know. Sometimes to me as well, for the movies. It is their way.'

114

Jackie stood looking up at him and said nothing, but her lips parted a little and she closed her eyes. When he kissed her, she returned his kiss with passion. He placed his hands about her shoulders and pulled her tightly against him, feeling the warm softness of her body and tasting the perfume of her breath as it caressed his face and neck. She in turn trembled with the awareness of his arousal, hard against her even through the thick material of the bathrobe. Had her hands and arms been free, she would have reached inside the bathrobe to take the precious entity which stirred beneath.

He moved her towards the bed until she stopped with the mattress against her legs.

'I can't lie down,' she said. 'The locks on the belt; they'll dig into me.'

'Oh, then we will sit,' he replied.

They moved over to an upholstered, upright chair standing by the chest of drawers. Rodolfo pulled the chair out and, with his back to Jackie, slipped the belt from his bathrobe. When he turned to face her, his ample erection freed and brandished before him, Jackie sank to her knees. As enthusiastically and spontaneously as she had kissed him seconds before, she slid her mouth over the head of his penis. So quickly did she do it that Rodolfo almost drew back in surprise. But the electric burning spread through his loins as her lips moved down the shaft until she could take no more. He breathed in sharply and placed his hands upon her head as she moved back and forth. She had done this with him before, in their pre-planned recordings, but never in private, when time was their own. For two minutes she continued her voluptuous play and his urge intensified. But feeling himself beginning to lose control, he withdrew from her and pulled her to her feet.

'Now I will do the same for you,' he whispered.

Kneeling before Jackie, he lifted up her leg and placed her foot upon the chair. With one hand under her behind and the other beneath her uplifted thigh, he had full access to what he most desired and could allow his tongue to enter and incite her further. He quickly found the clitoris, already moist and swollen. Teasing it within its tiny theatre of lust first, he then entered deeper to taste the nectar of her passion.

She was beginning to moan and to quiver when he stopped. But his hesitation was only a change in tactic, for even in the heat of their intimacy, he recognised the conflict of needs. Whilst both craved fulfilment, each wanted to prolong the ecstasy for as long as possible. As he turned her around, she tugged hopelessly on the restraints, knowing that it would intensify her arousal even more if she reminded herself of her situation. His hands closed over her breasts and squeezed the hardened nipples. At the same instant, the head of his engorged lance butted and chafed between her legs from the rear, coursing back and forth against her maddening heat. He expected her to struggle, she always had, for it was her way as the crisis approached. Moving backward, he felt the chair against his knees. Arching his pelvis back, he pulled her twisting body about until she faced him. At once he was down on the chair and forcing her astride him. Only for a moment did she hover above the glistening shaft before being impaled fully upon it with a murmuring cry to compliment his soft moan. With their mouths pressed together, he hooked an arm under each of her thighs and lifted them up until her legs swung over his elbows. His hands grasped her upper arms to hold her steady and the joust of love entered its final phase. Each worked their pelvis with the other and the burning tide began to quickly rise. Their bodies trembled hard and Jackie's high-pitched moans became louder and longer.

Suddenly the bedroom door swung open and the form of Cheryl appeared. The main light blazed on to her exclamation of, 'Jesus Christ!'

But it was too late, for though Jackie and Rodolfo knew she had entered, the tides of lust erupted through their bodies, sweeping away the flimsy chattels of self control. Rodolfo groaned loudly but Jackie threw back her head and cried out as though pierced by glowing needles.

When their senses returned, Rodolfo lowered her legs to

the sides of his own, opened his eyes and sighed, 'Ah, *maledizione!*'

'Rodolfo!' came the voice from the doorway. 'I'll be back in one minute! If you're still around I'll let Carlene take over, understand?'

'*Si – capisco,*' he groaned.

'And you!' continued Cheryl, glaring at Jackie. 'If your arse isn't in that bidet when I get back, I'm going to thrash a layer of skin off it!'

As Cheryl disappeared, Rodolfo eased Jackie up from him. She closed her eyes, feeling regret at his need to withdraw from her.

'Tell her, Roddy,' she sighed. 'Tell her we're in love. Tell her and it will be all right.'

'Oh, *mia bella,*' he replied kissing her, 'this is much – much *pericoloso,* how do you say, unsafe!'

'You mean dangerous, Roddy. Why?'

'I cannot say more now. Soon she will return and it will be not so good.' He gathered up the bathrobe and pulled it about him. She wanted to prevent him from leaving but the complete restraint of her hands and arms dashed all hoped of that. He kissed her and left without another word or a backward glance. She jerked in frustration at the mittens and straps, let out an exasperated, 'Oh, shit!' and walked to the bathroom.

'No wonder Pauline went over the top!' remarked Cheryl as she rinsed the soap from between Jackie's legs. 'She could have been in the Salvation Army before she met up with you and that other one!'

'What's happened to Rosie?'

'She's been caught; she got no further than Toulouse. They let me phone her at the police station this morning.'

'What are they going to do with her?'

'She's coming back here,' answered Cheryl, patting Jackie dry with the large pink towel. 'Officially she's being delivered to our own Inspector Gautier. You know him rather well don't you my love! Gautier will, of course, allow me to collect her tomorrow. I suppose you know she left because she was as besotted by Mike as you are with Rodolfo. But I think she found the outside world is not what she really wants any more.'

'I'm not besotted,' said Jackie as they left the bathroom. 'Roddy and I feel a lot for each other.'

'You stupid girl!' retorted Cheryl. 'You ought to know better than that – you've got enough experience of men!'

Jackie did not reply. Cheryl moved her towards the bed and Jackie saw lying upon it a garment in black leather which she was not at first able to identify as it had been left folded.

'Lie down,' ordered Cheryl, picking the garment up. Jackie lay down on her front.

'I came in here originally to release you,' continued Cheryl, 'but you can keep the restraints on until supper time now, and you'll wear this as well.'

Cheryl slipped the leather over her feet and pulled the long sheath up her legs, tugging and easing it up until it reached the belt about her waist. Returning to Jackie's ankles, she began to edge up the heavy duty zip, tightening the sheath about Jackie's legs as she went. In less than a minute the zipper was up to her waist and secured to the belt by another small brass padlock. Jackie rolled aside and looked down at the sleek leather sheath; it fitted her like a glove and allowed for no more than the slight bending of her knees.

'It goes better with the straitjacket really,' remarked Cheryl, regarding the helpless form on the bed, 'but I suppose it will do for now and it's certainly enough to keep out the likes of Rodolfo!'

Cheryl left her. Jackie listened until she heard the outside door close. Then she squirmed about for a few moments before burying her face into the pillow with a loud, 'Oooh!'

118

6

Unexpected Role

'Karen, I'm going in ten minutes. Is there anything you want to see me about?'

Karen turned away from the word processor with her fingers poised over the keyboard. Framed in the doorway stood Sonia, her black hair pushed back into its old-fashioned bun, her dark eyes intense but not hard. She wore a dark brown biker's jacket and loose, black satin trousers tucked into her ankle boots.

'No, I'll be OK,' said Karen, getting up from the desk. 'You're still back by tomorrow evening aren't you?'

'Yes my dear, I am,' replied Sonia, stepping into the small room.

'I hope you have a good time in Paris.'

'I won't have time to see much of it, I'm afraid; it's all business and interviews. You will next week, though, if you're still looking forward to doing the fashion shots.'

'Oh, yes,' replied Karen cheerfully, 'I'm quite looking forward to it.'

'But remember, you are under no obligation to do any of these things; this afternoon, I mean.'

'I know, but when I offered to help out I was doing more than just that. I think I'm still trying to shake off old hang-ups. Anyway, I'm only there to make up the numbers.'

'As long as you don't feel you have to be the same as everyone else,' said Sonia, moving closer and putting an arm on Karen's shoulder. 'I wouldn't want that because you are not the same. You are special. Very special.'

Karen felt her reassuring warmth. She knew Sonia was .

going to kiss her and closed her eyes, feeling herself stir within even before their lips met. 'Don't worry about me,' she breathed. 'I'm not about to do Rose's disappearing act.'

'No, I dare say you're not,' she said. 'By the way, you can expect Cheryl back before lunch. She's returning with Rose. That little problem has all been sorted out, I'm relieved to say.'

'From what I've heard she might well have come back under her own steam, if she'd had the chance.'

'Yes, well perhaps she got things into perspective when she was out on her own.' Sonia held Karen by the shoulders and glanced down at her chest. 'By the way, the silver locket – I see you wear it outside now.'

'I know we agreed I'd be discreet about it, but I feel – well, I don't see why anymore. Everyone must have guessed, and they're far less likely to pass judgement on me than I used to on them.'

'They won't pass judgement on you at all, my dear. You know that as well as I do.'

'Right,' said Karen putting her fingers on the locket. 'Then as you gave it to me I think it would be wrong now for me to hide it away.'

'If that's the way you feel, then I'm happy too.'

She followed Sonia out of her room, through the main office and to the door. Sonia turned and said, 'Look, close up shop after you've finished the typing. Go out and enjoy the sun until lunch time.'

There was nobody to be seen in the ground floor corridor. They kissed again and Sonia was gone.

'You're a lucky girl you know,' said Cheryl. 'If it hadn't been for Inspector Gautier, you'd have been appearing in court by now.'

'It's nice to have the coppers on your side for once,' remarked Rose, gazing out at the rolling, drifting landscape.

They turned from the main highway and on to the winding road. On each side, the vineyards spread away under the blue sky and harsh light of the midday sun.

'Not far to go now,' said Cheryl.

Rose peered through the windows at a small, seemingly deserted hamlet of stone houses with its ancient church standing solid in the heat of the day. As they passed through, Rose turned to her and said, 'Cheryl, thanks for coming all the way to pick me up. I'm sorry for all the trouble I've caused.'

'Well, if you decide to do it again, it really would make sense to tell Sonia – not just for our sake but for yours as well. There's your bank book for a start. I'm amazed you, of all people, never thought of that. And Sonia would have arranged a cab to Béziers railway station for you. You could have gone all the way to Paris on the high-speed train then back through the tunnel to London. Instead, you just cleared off on foot. Rather silly, don't you think?'

'I know,' replied Rose, watching the fields drift by, 'but at the time I was mad; not just with Mike but with myself. I suppose it looks stupid now, but I wanted to shove everything out of my mind and pick up where I'd left off – you know, pretend it had all never happened. Cheryl, I really feel embarrassed. I don't know what I'm going to say to them all.'

'I understand Rose, but don't worry; they all want you back.'

'I bet Mike doesn't!'

'Rose, you have to understand Mike. The last thing he wanted to do was hurt you. And it isn't as though he doesn't think the world of you. That's the trouble, he thinks the world of all the girls. If he had to choose one and only one of them for a partnership he'd probably have a decision crisis and blow a fuse!'

Rose looked at Cheryl for a moment, then smiled for the first time since she had left Toulouse. She could not deny her own contentment at the prospect of returning.

'The best thing you can do,' continued Cheryl, 'is wait for a convenient opportunity to go and say you're sorry to Mike. Believe me, he'll be so embarrassed he'll be convinced it was all his fault.'

'I'll go straight to see Sonia first; she must have been mad at me.'

'Well she isn't mad at you now Rose, but you won't be able to talk to her, not for a couple of days. She left for Paris this morning whilst I was collecting you.'

The car slowed. They approached the old stone gateway, standing dark against the blue sky, its forever-open iron gates standing in the embrace of green shoots and creepers. Rose sighed as they turned into the drive. 'I can't wait to see everyone and get back to the swimming pool and the lovely gardens.'

'Rose,' said Cheryl, a little ominously, slowing down the car and turning to her. 'You and Jackie are to keep out of the way for a couple of days. Jackie has been particularly badly behaved and needs to be kept under control until Carlene and Rodolfo have gone, if you see what I mean.'

'Yes,' answered Rose, looking straight ahead and feeling the dark currents flowing through her body.

'I'm sure,' continued Cheryl, 'you won't mind keeping her company during that time. I know how well you both get on.'

Rose looked down at her hands. 'Em, I – yes, whatever you say, Cheryl.'

They passed between the trees on the curving driveway. Rose glanced from the corner of her eye at the chalet to her right. On her left there was the swimming pool, calm, familiar and inviting but quite deserted, and ahead, the house. Rose hoped that Cheryl did not perceive her trembling. 'Out of the way.' 'Under control.' That's what Cheryl had said. Through Rose's mind passed the images of Jackie and of what might be.

'Well, she didn't drop in to say hello,' remarked Kim, trying to manipulate an olive and a slice of tomato on to the end of her fork.

'I doubt if we'll see her or Jackie for a bit,' said Valerie, across the little table.

'Not until the show's over,' added Annette, peering through the conservatory window and hesitating with a sandwich half raised to her mouth.

They watched Cheryl emerge from the porch and return

to the car. In a moment, she was moving away, out of sight along the front of the house; she drove around the small annexe to the parking spaces at the rear.

Cheryl glanced at the single-storey annexe and saw that the Venetian blinds were closed. She could see in her mind's eye, the gaunt and heavily spectacled James, sitting in his swivel chair, surrounded by his screens and consoles, gathering together, processing and mixing the information from the multitude of hidden cameras in the secret rooms. She had always been intrigued at the way human intimacies, the passions, the lusts and the burning abandonment of the climax, could all be converted into a stream of binary numbers, of souless electronic data, and manipulated with such dispassionate ease.

They had been fortunate in having the services of James for, as everyone knew, his job needed the skills of an electronics expert. The fact that the images he saw on the screens might raise the temperature of other people was not a problem. James, as they all knew, was totally uninterested in the female sex, being far more concerned with the instrumentation than the subject of its usage.

Cheryl locked the car and approached the rear of the house. With a rattle of keys she unlocked and swung open the solid oak door, turning only to re-lock it once inside. Then she carried on up the dimly lit and windowless rear stairs to the first floor.

Rose and Jackie would be waiting.

'I take it you're not too apprehensive this time around,' said Angela.

'Why? Do I seem calm and unconcerned?' replied Karen, looking out across the valley towards the distant sea.

'I suppose you do, sweetie,' said Angela, relaxing back on the wooden seat where they so often talked and laughed together. The tree shaded them now from the early afternoon sun. The insects buzzed lazily and intermittently; the breeze caressed their faces, warm and pure.

'Has anyone told you what we're doing?' asked Angela.

'No, I didn't ask either.'

'Oh well,' continued Angela, 'it's going to be a sort of weird hospital scene with '

'Angie!' cut in Karen.

'Oh, sorry,' replied Angela, a gentle smile spreading under her blue-grey eyes.

'Angie,' continued Karen, 'you know what I'm like. If I know all about it in advance, I'll be getting uptight and telling myself I shouldn't take part. All I know is that I'll be standing around as some kind of attendant. I'll imagine I'm in a different world and that all the others are figments of my imagination. I've had a reasonable amount of practice at it since I've been here, you know. It helps me. I'm not by any means the realist you are.'

Angela placed a hand on Karen's. 'But I have to tell you all the same, sweetie, I'm in it with Hot Roddy, if you know what I mean. I don't want you to – to feel awkward with me after.'

Karen stared into her eyes. 'Angie, I don't give a damn what you do. Nothing would ever make me think badly of you – ever.'

Karen could not help but recall the act she had seen Angela perform with two men at the party in the grounds of the house the previous summer. She had watched, hidden amongst the trees, and seen Angela impaled at front and rear by those two men; watched her abandon herself entirely to flagrant lust. And though she might not be aware of it, there was little Angela could do that Karen had not equalled, albeit in private. The difference was that Angela sailed calmer seas and carried no guilt. Karen was beginning to doubt if her own guilt would ever be banished, no matter what she indulged in or with whom. 'Want a smoke?' she asked, smiling at Angela and reaching down to her shoulder bag.

'No, this time have one of mine,' replied Angela, producing the packet and lighter. 'I shouldn't keep pinching yours the way I do.'

Karen breathed out a swirl of smoke into the warm air and looked at her watch.

'I suppose we ought to think of going back in ten or fifteen minutes. It's two thirty already.'

They left the place under the tree which was so special to them and walked slowly back over the rise towards the house. There was nobody to be seen by the swimming pool, though Mike carrying his gardening tools, waved from the direction of the old summer house.

'God, I couldn't do that in this heat,' said Karen, looking beyond the house to the tennis court. There, two figures pranced back and forth with rackets flashing.

'You can do anything, anytime, if it gives you enough pleasure,' observed Angela.

They reached the driveway and strolled towards the main entrance of the house. As they reached the portico, Angela hesitated and passed a hand over her eyes; closing them tightly for a moment she pushed aside her blonde hair.

'Are you OK, Angie?' asked Karen.

'Yes, I'm all right.' Angela smiled.

But Karen saw her squeeze her eyes shut twice more before they reached the stairs up to their rooms.

Karen remembered her instructions; she knew what to do. Fresh and warm from the shower, she pulled the pink bathrobe about herself and fastened the belt. Beneath the bathrobe all she wore were her small briefs and black hold-up stockings. On her feet were black, patent leather stiletto-heeled sandals, held in place by thin criss-crossed ankle straps. The uniform awaited her downstairs.

It was almost three thirty when she reached the arched doorway on the first floor. This was the room where she had acted out the first fantasy with Sophie and Danielle. She did not recall anything in the room to give her cause for concern, though the hanging circle of black curtain was a nagging puzzle. Perhaps she should have asked about that, but the matter was out of her mind for most of the time, and when it did for some reason present itself, the occasion was never appropriate.

She pushed open the door and entered the ante-room. It was well lit but unoccupied. Various items of clothing were arrayed about the chairs. When she entered the main room there were three people seated in the chrome and leather chairs. The large dining table had gone and where it had stood was a small coffee table upon which rested an opened bottle of amontillado sherry and several glasses. Annette and Valerie looked up, and Cheryl, with her back to Karen, glanced around the side of the chair.

'Hi!' greeted Annette. 'Hope you've learned your lines properly!'

Karen stopped before them. 'Er – lines? What lines?'

'Don't tease her,' said Valerie, looking from Annette to Karen. 'There aren't any lines. The sound is dubbed later.'

All three wore uniforms suggesting the nursing profession. The uniforms were of soft vinyl with white, cotton-edged short sleeves and open collars. They were, as Karen observed, considerably shorter than regulation length and closer fitting, but had a white trimmed pocket at each breast to dispel any doubt as to what the uniforms were intended to represent. Annette's and Valerie's uniforms were of mid-blue, Cheryl's of a darker tone. On her left side breast pocket was clipped a large silver stopwatch. Their stockings and shoes were identical to Karen's.

'Your uniform is outside,' said Cheryl. 'By the way, you haven't seen Angela, have you?'

'Not since we came back from our walk, no. I thought she would be here.'

'Oh,' continued Cheryl. 'She's usually dead on time. I can't imagine she's forgotten.'

'Look, I'll pop back upstairs if you like,' offered Karen. 'It'll only take a minute.'

'All right,' agreed Cheryl. 'Tell her everyone else is ready.'

Karen passed back through the ante-room, and saw the blue uniform folded and waiting for her on one of the chairs. On another chair, just beyond, lay something of a more sinister nature.

Stepping into the second-floor corridor she hesitated.

126

The corridor was silent and deserted. Reaching Angela's door, Karen raised her hand and knocked. There was no reply. She knocked again a little harder.

'Come in,' came the voice at last. The voice sounded weak and distant. Karen opened the door and entered. The apartment was in semi-darkness, for the blinds were closed. Angela half lay, half sat upon a two-seater by the window, her head pushed into two large cushions.

'Angie, what's up? Are you OK?'

'Oh, Karen, sweetie,' sighed Angela, 'I've had a bloody migraine. I thought it would have gone by now. I suppose they're all waiting for me, are they?'

Karen leant forwards and placed an arm around her shoulder. Even in this light, Angela appeared pale. 'Poor Angie. I didn't know you suffered with those. You've never said anything.'

'No,' replied Angela, pressing her hands against her face, 'they're very rare nowadays, fortunately. It would have to be this afternoon, though, wouldn't it?'

'Well they'll have to do without you, won't they?'

Angela lowered her hands and smiled weakly. 'It's really stupid, isn't it?'

'No, of course it isn't stupid. Why say that?'

Angela placed her hand on Karen's, forced a weak smile and looked into her eyes. 'What I mean is – well, I just fancied Roddy this afternoon, even if it was all fixed up in advance. Do you understand?'

'Of course I do,' she whispered, squeezing Angela affectionately. She kissed her cheek and imagined the vain but appealing features of Rodolfo with his steel-blue eyes and sensual mouth. 'But it can't be helped. I'll go back and let them know. You go to bed and rest until you feel better, OK?'

She left Angela and closed the door quietly. She was almost at the top of the stairs when Valerie appeared around the corner, and stopped before her with questioning eyes.

'She's not well,' said Karen. 'It's a migraine.'

'Oh, poor kid,' replied Valerie. 'I suppose we'll have to call it off in that case. That's a damned nuisance.'

Valerie swung around to head back down the stairs.

'Val, what about, er – what about someone else?'

Valerie stopped and turned to face her. 'There's no one available, deary. Kim and Rachel were on the tennis court last time I saw them and Lorna's away. I could suggest Jackie or even Rose. Jackie would be in like a shot but Cheryl doesn't want either of them involved with Rodolfo.'

Valerie was about to continue on down when Karen drew her breath in sharply and said, 'Val, what if . . .?'

'If what?' Valerie faced about once more and regarded her with dark gypsy eyes. Karen swallowed hard and hesitated. 'Val, what if – I mean if I . . .'

'He's a good lover, deary.' Valerie smiled, putting a hand on Karen's cheek.

Karen caught her breath, felt herself shaking and gripped the stair rail. Valerie, her eyes glistening and intense, put her arms about Karen's shoulders. 'You're a very passionate girl, Karen; I know that.'

Karen sighed and put her cheek softly against Valerie's. 'Sometimes I just want to behave like a slut and let anyone do what they want. But I'm not like Jackie. I get all twisted up inside. I'm so bloody scared!'

Valerie stroked her hair and kissed her cheek. 'Just pretend you're in the beauty parlour, lovey and we're going to relieve those pent up tensions, right?'

'It's O.K. if you help, Val. I don't want to say anything to the others. You deal with what happens, yes?'

'Of course I will, deary. What we're going to do is -'

'Val! No!' cut in Karen. 'I don't want to know what's going to happen. I don't care! If you tell me, I'll more than likely change my mind. I know I will.'

Inside the ante-room, Karen sat on a small stool. Valerie walked around her and said, 'I'll tell them I've begged you into standing in for Angela. How's that?'

'It's OK, Val. But don't be long.'

'No, I'll only be a minute.'

'And Val, before anything else, I'll have a drink please. The sherry I saw in there will do.'

Within a short time, Valerie had returned. She held two glasses and the half full bottle of amontillado. She placed them on the small circular table and poured. 'Say when,' she said.

Karen said nothing. The glass was filled until it was almost brimming.

Valerie watched her drink the sherry nervously, and sipped her own. Karen uttered nothing until the glass was empty and Valerie said, 'Have a little more if you want.'

Karen took up the bottle, refilled the glass and breathed, 'I think I better had.'

When the second glass was finished, Valerie stood up and walked behind her. Karen felt the hands resting on her shoulders for a few moments before the bathrobe was pulled away. She raised herself from the stool to allow Valerie to drag it from beneath her, then sat and waited with her hands on her knees. She heard the swish of the garment, as Valerie lifted it from the chair, and the chink of metal buckles. She caught the smell of the leather in her nostrils before she saw the source.

'I think you know what this is,' said Valerie, passing the restraint in front of her and pulling it high about her waist. Karen stood whilst the wide belt was tightened and buckled at the rear. Valerie worked quickly, enclosing each wrist within its felt-lined leather cuff so that her arms were held securely against her sides and she could just bring together her fingertips.

Karen had expected the gag and made no effort to resist as Valerie positioned something before her face. She closed her eyes, allowing the smooth rubber plug to slip into her mouth and keep it opened. Around the plug was a soft ring which squeezed and sealed the outside of her mouth. The black rubber pad upon which both were mounted was fitted over her lower face and under her chin. It took little time to fasten this lesser-sized restraint. It's tight web of straps ran over and about her head in various directions, forming a triangular aperture for her nose and leaving her eyes free.

'Perfect for the part,' said Valerie, moving around into

Karen's field of vision. 'Now you have to appear reluctant, deary OK?'

Karen glanced aside at her and managed a barely audible grunt by way of response.

'It's the only bit of acting skill you'll need. Just make as though you really are a prisoner trying to resist. Struggle for all you're worth. You'll know when and where.'

As Valerie eased her to her feet, Karen's imagination began to run riot. What was going to happen to her?

As they passed into the main room, Karen knew how it must feel before a first parachute jump. She had of course expected to see the faces of Cheryl and Annette, and indeed there they stood, by the chairs, waiting. But what of Rodolfo? She had expected him too, but he was not to be seen. In the room, now very well lit indeed by the clusters of spotlights, Annette's face bore a smile which carried more than a hint of mischief. Cheryl exhibited only cool impassivity. If reassurance was of any value at this point, which Karen much doubted, then it was more likely to be found in Annette's expression than in Cheryl's.

Karen stood facing them with Valerie behind. Cheryl and Annette stood and regarded her for a time with hands resting on hips, as if to express satisfaction at what they saw. Annette walked over to join them and stood at Karen's right side. Valerie moved to her left. Each placed a hand on her shoulders and they moved her forward.

It was at this point that real apprehension beset her, for Cheryl stepped over to the black circular curtain and disappeared inside. Annette and Valerie brought Karen to a standstill before the curtain and held her there. Above the curtain, the ceiling lit up with bright light from within the enclosed space. There was an electric hum and at once the curtains began to open, the gap widening before them and spilling light out on to the rich maroon carpet. Karen's protest remained stifled behind the gag and though she twisted about against the restraint, her attempt to back away was halted before it began.

The chair glittered under the lights. Its glaring chromium fittings formed a counterpoint of light and complexity against the smooth sheen of the black leather back support. Its small semi-circular seat had a cut-out front, and an array of hanging straps. This chair was more elaborate and more clinical than the one in the beauty parlour where Valerie and Kim had removed her pubic hair. It was more threatening because it stood alone and out of context; it was not in warm and intimate privacy, but was like the pillory in a town square awaiting its unwilling victim to be displayed and seen by all. And unwilling Karen stared wide-eyed, first at the chair and then at the smiling figures of Carlene and Rodolfo who stood waiting at each side of it in white surgical gowns and sleek, translucent pink rubber gloves. Behind the chair stood Cheryl.

'Just what the doctor ordered,' came Annette's voice as they propelled her forward. Squirming and jerking with futility against the restraints, she twisted frantically about, her eyes darting wide from one to the other.

'That's it,' remarked Annette, 'we'll make a star of you yet!'

Once before the chair, they hesitated only to remove her small blue briefs before turning Karen about and half lifting, half pushing her writhing form down on to the padded seat. They held her ankles to prevent her kicking. Her heart beat against her ribs and the sensation in her belly was akin to that of descending in an express lift. She felt herself burning with shame as the straps were passed around and secured quickly about her neck, chest and waist, to finish about the lower part of the wide belt. She knew well the hopelessness of struggle but still resisted as each of her legs was taken by the gloved hands and lifted outward and upward. Each knee was fitted and secured into the padded rest at the end of the chrome extension bars which sprang up from the sides of the chair. The ankles were secured likewise at the other end of the rests, leaving her stiletto heels protruding horizontally. Carlene and Rodolfo stepped back and Cheryl moved about the chair, adjusting and tightening wheels and levers, in order to tilt the prisoner rearward a little and bring her knees back further and wider until she was openly displayed before all.

'Oh baby, do you look sweet!' Carlene smiled as Cheryl moved back.

'*Belissimo*,' breathed Rodolfo, his eyes feasting hard upon her helpless body.

'Look Roddy,' said Carlene, 'the kid's shaved clean and slick, the way we like it!'

Carlene ran her latex finger slowly between Karen's buttocks, over her anus and between the lips of her sex. Karen stiffened involuntarily as the sensation passed through her body in a sharp, electric ripple. She could no longer see Cheryl, Annette or Valerie. There was only Carlene and Rodolfo in the pool of light, and herself. She was spread out before them in the most lascivious manner, her most secret and intimate places open to their gaze and the play of their fingers.

Carlene knelt down before the chair and circled her arms about Karen's thighs, bringing her full and sensual lips close to the vulva. Karen felt the tongue flicker into her for a moment then course about the pink labia. A murmuring arose within her loins.

'Time we got rid of these coats, Roddy. Time for the oral examination. I think this baby is ready for it!'

Each undid the tapes at the rear of the other's gown, and the gowns were cast aside. Carlene had on a plain black vinyl mini-dress; it was sleeveless with a low-cut square neckline. Rodolfo wore a white T-shirt and pale blue trousers, which Carlene at once helped him to remove. His only item of clothing was a pair of bikini briefs in white satin lycra which did little to disguise his state of arousal. Rodolfo took Carlene's place before the chair, but whereas Carlene had merely breathed upon the flame of Karen's lust, Rodolfo now began fuelling it to full measure. His tongue darted and played about inside her, summoning the clitoris to full arousal and then circling about it. Then defying its needs, it tormented the anus with its fickle and exquisite meanderings. For a time, Carlene attended to her breasts, circling and squeezing the swollen nipples with her fingers.

Karen quivered and moaned softly through the rubber gag. Carlene ran a hand down her body and placed a finger either side of Karen's sex to squeeze and pull back the moist flesh of the labia, as Rodolfo tasted the nectar of her growing passion.

'The kid's going to come any time now, Roddy. It's time for the lucky strike,' breathed Carlene. She reached out and pulled down the briefs, releasing his burgeoning erection. Karen was inflamed and glistening with excitement. Rodolfo would have struck home at once for his own need was pressingly urgent. But Carlene took the reddened and ample shaft in her hand and allowed him to enter Karen only a short way. 'Easy does it now,' she said. 'Let's make it so you're both taking the same elevator!'

Rodolfo closed his eyes and groaned. Carlene stroked and caressed the swollen head between the equally reddened lips of Karen's sex. At last she released him and he at once speared deeply. He gasped loudly and arched his back, moving his pelvis back and forth with rapid motions. Karen wanted him to thrust and penetrate her deeper still, to spread into every part of her body, for the smouldering within was becoming a blaze, running out of control and about to consume her entirely. She closed her eyes, and wanted to cry out but could only bite into the rubber plug; she wanted to scream but only a stifled moan came through. She was about to burst asunder with lust and felt her body seized by the flames of orgasm. Rodolfo lost control at the same time. He fell forward to grasp the back of the chair, heaving and crying out as Karen's body too became rigid and the flames seared through them as one, in blazing torrents.

She was still moaning quietly, and still had her eyes closed tightly when he withdrew the glistening lance.

Cheryl reappeared and, with the help of Carlene, quickly released the straps. As the gag came off, Karen gasped as though the heat of passion still ravaged her. Carlene looked into her eyes with a broad grin and said, 'Sure beats the shit out of running the company accounts, doesn't it?'

Karen hurried with head down, up the back stairs, her hands clutching tightly on to the lapels of her bathrobe. At

133

the second-floor landing she stopped and leant against the wall, letting forth a loud sigh and pressing the back of her hand hard against her part-opened mouth. Her body felt different, as though it had in some manner been taken apart and reconstituted so that nothing was quite in its accustomed place anymore. The effects of the stringent bondage might account for it, or perhaps the attentions of Rodolfo. She did not feel entirely convinced on either account. The strong odour of leather still hung about her. It would not be gone until she showered. She closed her eyes and breathed deeply, wondering if she might soon awaken to find it had been yet another dream in this gamut of sexual fantasies.

'Karen, are you all right?' came a voice out of the darkness.

She opened her eyes and there stood Angela, her face shaded with concern.

'Oh God, Angie,' she sighed.

Angela took her arm and peered into her face. 'What's the matter, sweetie?'

'Angie I – I need a drink!'

'Well, come on down to the bar. That's where I was going.'

'I couldn't, not like this.'

'Then let's go in my room. I've got some gin stashed away and we can have a quiet chat.'

'Want to talk about it?' asked Angela, adding a measure of tonic to each of the glasses.

'I – I daren't,' replied Karen. 'I just daren't.'

'Let me make a guess,' said Angela. 'You volunteered to help out by taking my place in the show.'

Karen looked down at the carpet and did not reply. She sensed Angela's eyes fixed on her. 'Yes, I did,' she muttered finally.

Angela too was silent for a time. Then she began to laugh. Karen glanced up in surprise. Falling back into the chair, Angela shook her head and laughed louder still. 'Oh, Karen! Karen! You're so funny, you really are!'

'Well I'm glad somebody thinks so!' retorted Karen, finding herself unable to suppress a smile.

'Oh dear,' said Angela, wiping her eyes with the back of her hand. 'I hope you're getting paid the going rate for this appearance! It is above and beyond the call of duty!'

'God yes. Sonia's going to find out, isn't she? And – oh, I just thought.'

'Thought what?'

'James! How can I ever look him in the face again?'

'Easy, sweetie, just stare straight at those big thick spectacles and smile. Annette's got the best technique; she manages to pull a face at the same time.'

'How does he react?' asked Karen.

'He doesn't. He doesn't care in the least. He's not interested in us; you know that. The only time anyone got through to him was a bit before you arrived here. Carlene had done a show and bumped into James the following day in the bar. She grabbed hold of him in front of everyone and said out loud, "Have I really got spots all over my arse, honey?" '

'Oh no!' Karen grinned. 'What happened?'

'Well, I was nearly in hysterics. Val almost choked on a piece of toast! Poor James had a coughing fit. We all thought he was going to die! That's why you won't see him around when Carlene's here. He simply daren't come out.'

'Oh, Angie, as usual you've cheered me up again. You always see the lighter side of everything, and I'm glad you're feeling better, too.'

'I shouldn't be,' replied Angela. 'Not after you pinched my place with Hot Roddy!'

'Well now,' said Cheryl, closing the door behind her. 'I hope you have both been behaving yourselves during my absence.'

She regarded the two figures leaning upon the brightly coloured cushions within the circular steel pen. They looked up at her, without speaking. The pen, some two metres in diameter, occupied an area in the middle of the room. Beyond it, on the opposite side, the TV screen danced with life and colour. Music blared from it, alternating with frantic dialogue and sound effects as two cartoon characters rocketed back and forth.

135

'It's a pity,' she continued, looking up at the screen with undisguised disapproval, 'that you can't find something better than this to occupy your minds with.' Walking around the pen, she stooped and reached through the steel bars to retrieve the remote controller from where it lay close to Rose. She placed the unit on top of the television and switched off the set. At once the silence asserted itself. She turned and placed her hands on the edge of the pen. 'I have a few notes to write up for the next half hour. I can't work with that din going on so you'll have to put up with a little silence until I've finished. Unless, of course, you prefer to listen to some Chopin. Well?'

The two pairs of eyes looked at each other then back to Cheryl. Both heads shook from side to side.

'All right, have it your way. But don't blame me if you get bored.'

Rose and Jackie adjusted their positions against the cushions. Neither of them had spoken for some time. Not since Cheryl had confined them to the pen before leaving earlier in the afternoon in order to oversee the proceedings in the games room.

Not only had they not spoken, but they had done very little else other than, in the case of Rose, to alter the television channels. Even that facility was unavailable to Jackie. She was cocooned from neck to waist in burnished, metallic grey vinyl with her arms enclosed and folded across her middle. Rose was held in restraint by a pair of bright steel cuffs. These were attached to the front of a thick belt about her waist. Their silence was accounted for by a small, oblong piece of white plastic adhesive tape which held the mouth of each securely shut. At least Rose had limited use of her hands and could struggle to her feet if she so wished. These luxuries were denied Jackie most effectively by the boot-like restraint, in the same material and colour as the straitjacket, which tightly enclosed her feet and legs as far as the knees. Why Cheryl had imposed a much greater degree of restriction upon her had not been explained to either.

The thirty or so minutes which passed by were less

evident to Cheryl, busy at her desk, than they were to the occupants of the pen. At last, Cheryl returned, looked down at Rose and said, 'I'm going to release you. After that, I'm going to shower and change out of this uniform. I expect you to be waiting in your room in fifteen minutes.'

With the prisoner freed, Cheryl swung back the small gate. From Jackie came a stifled grunt as the gate was clicked shut but, though Rose looked at Jackie and Cheryl, and opened her mouth to speak, Cheryl ignored the figure in the pen and said, 'Fifteen minutes, all right?'

Cheryl did not tap on the door but entered unannounced. Rose, wearing a mid-length, white flared skirt and navy blue nylon blouse, sat waiting by the coffee table. Rose said nothing, but watched her close the door. Apart from Sonia, Cheryl was the only other person in the house with whom she had not formed a social relationship. Cheryl gave the impression of cool efficiency a great deal of the time but she was very far from being a stranger to glamour, and Rose now could see how this Nordic beauty presented herself. Cheryl's slim form was clad in a silver sequinned sleeveless dress with a high collar. It fitted perfectly over the curves of her body and, though not conspicuously short, allowed an ample view of her black nylon clad legs with their silver high-heeled sandals.

Cheryl sat down opposite to her and said, 'In the light of our little session today, are you back for the foreseeable future, do you think?'

'Yes,' said Rose, clasping her knees with her hands, 'I think so. There isn't much for me to look forward to anywhere else.'

'And Mike? Have you had enough time to consider this is still going to be a problem?'

'Cheryl, I still like Mike a lot but I don't think it's going to bother me the way it did before.'

'Good. But you know as well as everybody else; this isn't a free for all. Trust and discretion are - well, you know about that; you've been told often enough. So we'll try to behave a little more responsibly from now on, shall we?'

'I will Cheryl, honest.'

'And if you and Jackie are going to get up to anything, you'd better make sure I don't catch you out again!'

'What's going to happen to Jackie?' asked Rose, feeling her face redden.

'She is going to remain under control until Carlene and Rodolfo are gone in two days time. We do not want any more problems. She is also going to be taught a rather graphic lesson. It will kill two birds with one stone.'

'What do you mean?'

'Yes, I wondered if you'd be curious. It wouldn't do you any harm to be in on it. You're a big girl, now.'

'Will Jackie be kept away from everyone?'

'Not quite,' replied Cheryl. 'She will be obliged to remain upstairs. You can keep an eye on her; especially at night. You can take in her meals as well. And we all know her other needs. I'm sure she isn't going to miss out there. Not if I know you!'

Rose tried to remain expressionless. Cheryl watched her and smiled.

138

7

Sideshows

'It's not fair!' shouted Jackie.

'Well, you've only yourself to blame, love. You shouldn't have got caught!'

'Look Rosie, you got caught and then buggered off! She hasn't kept you like this, has she?'

'That's different. I was going to come back and I didn't say anything to anybody. And I know she caught me at it too, but at least I'd gone somewhere out of the way. She had to follow me to find out, didn't she?'

Jackie remained silently seated on the edge of the bed, her knees pressed together and her head lowered.

'Anyway,' continued Rose, 'nobody outside here cares a sod about me, whereas your old man pays them a packet to keep an eye on you. The last thing they want is you running off with Rodolfo, whereas me having it off with Mike upset them less than it did me!'

'It's still not fair!' retorted Jackie, rocking back and forth. 'Roddy wants me and I want him! I can make my own mind up. I don't care who bloody well pays what!'

'Well Sonia does - that's why Cheryl's kept you in the straitjacket.'

'The rest of today and all day tomorrow!' yelled Jackie, twisting from side to side against the restraint. 'Nearly two bloody days!'

'No it isn't,' Rose consoled her. 'Mealtimes and bed-times she'll come and undo you. I'd undo you myself but we'd both end up in dead trouble and neither of us wants that.'

'It's still not fair!' cried Jackie with tears welling up in her eyes. With that, she threw herself aside on to the bed with an exasperated, 'Oh!' and, jerking her folded arms up and down inside the vinyl cocoon, kicked her legs wildly about and cried out repeatedly in hopeless frustration.

Rose sat down on the bed beside her and placed a comforting arm about her shoulder.

'Look love, he's not worth getting upset over, is he? There's hundreds of blokes out there at least as good as him.'

'It's all right for you to talk,' said the tearful Jackie. 'At least you can still see Mike.'

'Well I'm not going to make any more of it,' replied Rose. 'Cheryl said I'd meet plenty of others if I stayed here; all of them with bags of cash to throw around. And,' she continued, leaning down to kiss Jackie's cheek, 'I want to keep you as my friend, as well. You're my first real pal you are, Jackie; you and Karen.'

She reached over and yanked a paper tissue from the pink box on the bedside table.

'Let's dab your eyes and have a little chat. I won't go and leave you, so don't worry.'

'What do you think?' said Sonia, raising the glass of chablis and regarding Cheryl.

Cheryl relaxed in the green leather chair, drank from her own glass, and considered for a time. 'Yes, I think it would work. It would make a good show and teach the two of them a lesson.'

'And as they're gone after tomorrow it would avoid repercussions,' added Annette, with more than a hint of mischief in her green eyes.

'Then go ahead,' said Sonia in a decisive tone. 'I don't suppose Carlene will have any objections.'

'No,' said Annette, 'I can promise you, Carlene won't mind in the least.'

'Oh, I see,' responded Sonia, 'you've already asked her. I should have realised, shouldn't I? Knowing you.'

'I thought it best,' said Annette. 'In fact, Carlene

140

thought it was immensely funny. She was even more enthusiastic than we were – she just can't wait!'

'And what about Rose?' asked Sonia.

'I think her little escapade has taught her a few truths,' answered Cheryl. 'I get the feeling she'll start to become an asset now, of her own free will. The police don't seem to be as interested as they were when they thought she was directly involved in the robbery.'

'I thought she was in it with them,' said Annette, swirling the wine glass gently.

'She was in the back of the car,' replied Cheryl. 'That's about all. She didn't actually help in any way.'

'That makes life a bit easier,' said Sonia with relief. 'We no longer need worry about who sees her face.' She looked at her watch, then across the room to the smaller office where Karen sat. 'I think it's coffee time.'

Karen was occupied at the keyboard when Sonia's face appeared at the doorway.

'You've shut yourself off from everything today, my dear. I've hardly seen you since I got back from Paris. Leave what you're doing and come out here with us for a bit; I'm putting some coffee on.'

Karen did not move, but looked at her questioningly as though about to speak.

'Is anything the matter?' asked Sonia.

Karen backed the chair away from her desk.

'I needed to have a quick word,' she answered, looking Sonia straight in the eye, 'but you've always been with someone.'

'Is it urgent? Do you want to talk to me now? Cheryl and Annette won't mind waiting.'

'No, no, not right now,' replied Karen. 'When they've gone. And I'll carry on in here for the time being.'

The late afternoon sun reached with golden fingers through the blinds when Cheryl and Annette left the main office. Sonia closed the door and returned to the group of chairs set about the coffee table. Karen now sat nervously in the chair just vacated by Cheryl. Sonia looked at her; the light glittered upon the silver locket where it hung above her breasts. 'We haven't fallen out over anything have we, my dear?'

Karen smiled weakly and pushed back into the chair. 'Em – not yet, no. But I have to tell you, before you see the tape and find out.'

'Go on,' said Sonia, fixing her eyes on Karen's.

'God, I know you're not going to like this but – but, whilst you were away, I – well the show they put on with Rodolfo in it.' Karen tapped her fingers on the chair arm. 'Angie couldn't do it because she wasn't feeling too good, so I went instead.'

She slipped her fingers over the sides of the chair and glanced down, waiting.

'And did you enjoy the experience?' asked Sonia quietly.

Karen looked up sharply. 'Sonia, that's not the point! What I was trying to say was – was, that I . . .'

'Well, you have said it and I'm glad you're so concerned.' Sonia reached over the table and took her hand. 'But why do you so often think I'm going to disapprove and be annoyed with you? Am I so stern and overbearing?'

'I just do, that's all. I don't want it to spoil our relationship.'

'I have told you before,' breathed Sonia, 'we inhabit two different worlds; as different as night and day. When we pass through the looking glass into that other world, we find our fantasies becoming real. It happened in our sacrificial scene. When we were alone together, we had passed through the portal. We were not play-acting. We were real. The outside world was the fantasy, not us. You acted out your role in the real world to feed the images to others. Those images will fuel their fantasies in turn.'

She released Karen's hand and relaxed back in the chair. 'Everything I have, has been acquired through the carnal desires of others. How could I deny those same desires to you?'

Karen closed her eyes. 'Sonia, I'm almost hurt because you aren't annoyed with me. I know it sounds stupid, but I am.'

'My dear,' continued Sonia, 'if I had such control over you in our daylight world that I could predetermine your decisions, then I would have you behave differently. But you are yourself and, to tell the truth, I prefer it that way.'

A smile dispelled the look of concern from Karen's features. 'Oh, I feel stupid now. The last thing I should bother about in this house is doing what I did, I suppose.'

'We all have to be realistic,' said Sonia. 'At least in our day to day world.'

'I'll tidy up in my office,' said Karen, without expression, 'and get out of your way.'

She arose and returned across the room to her own workplace. Outside, the landscape was warmly mellow in the lowering sun. She cleared away a few things from her desk and switched off the computer before closing the blind against the light. When she turned, Sonia stood before her.

'You're never in my way, my dear,' breathed Sonia, placing her hands upon Karen's shoulders. 'You must never think that. Never.'

Karen felt the tremor run through her body, the tremor she always felt when Sonia's hands were laid upon her. She could not help herself. 'I didn't mean it like that,' she said and smiled into the dark, deep eyes.

Sonia drew her closer and Karen placed her arms about Sonia's waist. Her eyes were closed and her mouth already parted when their lips met. Karen felt the dark tide of passion running through her and returned Sonia's kiss with equal intensity.

'Sonia,' she breathed, 'sometimes there are things I want to do. It scares me.'

'What things do you want to do, and why are you scared?'

'When I was in the – when I took part yesterday, I wouldn't have cared in the end if the whole world had seen me, or if that chair had been set up on a stage in front of an audience. Or part of me wouldn't have cared; the other part would have been terrified. It's like being drawn towards a dark, deep abyss. You just have to look. You just have to know, whatever the consequences.'

'And I have frightened you often,' whispered Sonia, her breath very warm on Karen's ear.

'Yes, you have frightened me. But I don't want it to stop.'

She searched into the dark eyes and felt the blood coursing through her veins. 'Sonia, sometimes I wanted to be tormented. I don't know why I'm saying it now, but I'm scaring myself by my own admission.'

'You're shaking,' breathed Sonia. 'Shaking like a kitten.'

'Y - yes, I'm sorry. I know I'm being -'

'My dear,' cut in Sonia. 'You are trying to be in our two worlds at once. We should try to keep them apart you know that.'

'Yes, I know.'

Sonia pushed the hair aside from Karen's cheek. 'I have been away a lot lately and you will soon be off to Paris. We have not had an evening together for some time.'

'No, we haven't, have we?'

'Then why not this evening? Or tomorrow if you were already going somewhere.'

'I wasn't, no I mean tonight, that is. I wasn't going anywhere particularly.'

'Then, perhaps,' suggested Sonia, 'a bottle of champagne?'

'Yes, a bottle of champagne sounds wonderful. And I'm sorry for going on about well, you know.'

'Oh, no my dear, don't be sorry at all. It is the last thing I should want you to keep from me; the very last thing.'

It was a little after seven thirty when, after a sharp tap, the door opened and Cheryl entered. Rose and Jackie sat together on the two-seater before the television set. The window blinds were closed against the setting sun. They turned to look at Cheryl, the colours from the screen dancing upon their faces and in their eyes. Rose picked up the remote controller and cut off the sound.

'It's time for something to eat,' announced Cheryl, handing Rose a small printed menu. 'If you each decide what you want, Rose can go and get it from the bar or the kitchen.'

144

Both conferred for a couple of minutes and then Rose smiled. 'OK, we've decided.'

'Use the back stairs,' said Cheryl. 'We don't want you bumping into anyone with a tray of food.'

Rose, wearing her jeans and T-shirt, left the room and hurried along the first-floor corridor. Going down, she took the main stairs, which would bring her out near the entrance to the bar.

'You had better stand up,' said Cheryl, placing a small package down upon the coffee table.

Jackie looked at her with a look of reproachment crossing her face and did as she was told. The sleeves of the blue and red patterned housecoat swung empty at her side. Cheryl slipped the belt open and pulled the housecoat away, then placed it over the back of the seat.

'I wonder whether I should leave you in that and let Rose feed you,' said Cheryl, eyeing the metallic blue vinyl strait-jacket which still embraced Jackie from neck to waist. 'On second thoughts,' she continued, picking up the small bag, 'you'll need to take a shower so we'll try these instead.'

She knelt down before Jackie and slipped the contents of the bag out on to the carpet with a metallic clink. 'Bring your feet together!'

Jackie obeyed. Almost immediately, she felt the cool, smooth steel encircle her right ankle. The other ankle was similarly enclosed and when Cheryl stood up, Jackie glanced down to see her legs joined by a bright steel chain some ten centimetres long.

'You'll only be able to take short steps in those, as you are well aware,' said Cheryl, moving around behind her, 'so on no account must you leave this room.'

The heavy duty zipper at the rear of the straitjacket be-gan to whirr down and Jackie felt the restraint loosening. 'If you disobey,' continued Cheryl, 'I'll have you hooded until tomorrow morning. That means there'll be no TV and no talking, so think about it, won't you?'

'I won't try to go anywhere,' said Jackie as the vinyl garment was finally pulled away, releasing her arms and leaving her quite naked.

'Good!' replied Cheryl. 'And you had better have Rose help you in and out of the shower. The bracelets will be removed after you've had your breakfast in the morning, but they won't prevent you from getting your beauty sleep.'

She regarded the silent Jackie for a few moments with cool blue eyes, then, with the limp straitjacket over her arm, turned about and left the room.

'So she's confined to quarters until tomorrow?' said Lorna, pushing the tray forward from behind the bar.

''fraid so,' answered Rose with a wide grin.

'It won't make a lot of difference,' said Valerie, topping up a glass of vodka from a small bottle of tonic. 'She'll be just the same once she's let out on the loose.'

'She'll be a loose woman,' joked Kim, sitting next to Valerie.

Valerie, her large gold earrings glittering against her black, gypsy hair, looked from Rose to Lorna with an expression of despair. Turning slowly to the soft-faced Kim, who was drinking through a coloured, spiral straw, she said in a low voice, 'You know, a couple of days out of the way in some sort of restraint would do you a world of good, as well.'

Rose passed carefully down the ground-floor corridor, gripping the ebony handles of the large silver tray with its covered dishes and glasses of cool orange juice. She started up the narrow rear stairs and had almost reached the first-floor corridor when another figure, dressed in pink bathrobe, appeared from the floor above.

'Oh!' exclaimed Karen in surprise as she halted before Rose.

'You off down to the pool?' asked Rose. 'I wouldn't mind an evening swim, if I could get out.'

'Er, no — no, I'm off to the beauty parlour.'

'Then Val must have forgotten.' Rose smiled, turning off the stairs. 'She and Kim are still at the bar!'

* * *

Karen hesitated at the bottom of the stairs. Along the corridor drifted conversation and music from the bar, but there was nobody to be seen. She walked halfway along until she reached the blue door of the beauty parlour on her left. She knew Sonia would have left the door unlocked, but deliberately waited for a moment and then, but only slowly, she pushed down the brass handle and opened the door. On the previous occasion she had passed this way she had been anxious and furtive, not daring to be seen. She was no longer so concerned about secrecy. As with the silver locket, she was becoming less concerned about maintaining the pretence.

It was as she was about to pass inside, with a final glance along the corridor, that a figure pushed through the main doors. He glimpsed her immediately and his face broke into a cheerful grin. 'Hi Karen!' he said, as he raised his hand, and gave her a friendly, passing wave.

'Hello Mike!' She smiled and watched him turn towards the bar before closing the door.

She did not hesitate once inside the beauty parlour. Only the pink cornice lights were on, as she would have expected. The room had an atmosphere of intimate friendliness in the half light. If Valerie and Kim had been there, it would have had a soul.

At the far end, she reached the big cupboard and pulled open the door. How many people knew about this disguised passage? Sonia, Valerie, possibly Kim, and herself of course. She suspected that there was nobody else. Stepping into the secret enclosure, she shut the door on what, to the house, was the ordinary world. The only source of illumination was a small lamp up in the corner behind. As she pushed between the racks of leather and rubber clothing and the hanging restraints, she felt as she had felt before, the strange and compelling fascination of this curious place. When she stopped, the silence would have been as enveloping as the sensual odours had it not been for the beating of her own heart. This was the passage through to the looking-glass world. Once beyond the far door, Sonia would be waiting. Already, the tentacles of desire were stirring within her loins and her belly.

Mike, in white shorts and blue denim shirt, slid up on to the bar stool next to Valerie. 'Hi,' he said. 'Am I butting in?'

'Not at all,' replied Valerie. 'But I thought you'd be in front of the TV tonight. Isn't there a big match of some sort?'

'Yes,' he answered, 'but it's not our lot. We're out of it altogether as usual.'

'Who're our lot?' asked Kim.

'England of course. Why - are you interested?'

'Of course she isn't,' cut in Valerie. 'She wouldn't know one side of a football from the other!'

'It's cricket actually,' replied Mike with a grin.

Kim stuck out her tongue but Valerie turned and said, 'If a doctor sees that, they'll rush you inside!'

Mike looked at her over Valerie's shoulder and winked. Kim finished the remains of the drink and said, 'Well there's something I want to watch in about five minutes, so I'm off now.'

Mike watched her leave the stool. As she passed behind Valerie, she winked knowingly back at him.

'Aren't you having a drink?' asked Valerie, turning her gaze from the mirror behind the bar.

'Not yet,' he replied.

A burst of laughter issued through the archway from the conservatory and Carlene was heard in animated conversation with a number of the other girls.

'You look a bit lost tonight,' observed Valerie.

'No, I'm not really,' he said. 'I was going to ask you if you fancied a stroll around the gardens. It's very quiet and peaceful out there and the sky looks fantastic.'

She brushed a wisp of hair from her temple and turned her face to his. 'Yes Mike, why not? It's a while since we talked together.'

He regarded her for a moment; the sharp points of light reflected in her eyes, the fine black eyebrows, the soft red lips, the black hair tumbled about her shoulders. He slid from the stool and stood aside for her, breathing in her sensual perfume as she went by.

She walked to the door and he followed, his eyes taking in her lithe figure with its white nylon sleeveless top and red, flared cotton skirt which finished just above the knee. On her feet were red leather sandals. He wondered if she wore a suspender belt, for his eyes had caught the sheen of her fine black stockings.

He reached past her to push open the door and she said, 'Were you thinking of anywhere in particular, Mike?'

'Towards the valley maybe?' he suggested.

'That sounds like a good idea.' She smiled at him.

They left the portico and followed the path into the warm night. The lamps were lit along the main drive but the pool to their right was in darkness, the nearby chairs propped at an angle against the tables, the flagstones glistening wet.

'You've done the pool already,' she observed. 'That's a bit early, isn't it?'

'Well, yes, but there was nobody about so I thought I'd get it over with.'

'Very sensible too,' she said, with a subtle hint of irony. 'Leaves you with the rest of the evening free.'

There was a half moon low in the sky, and the sweep of stars above the still air enabled them to easily make out the groups of trees and the rise as they turned off the curving drive. He moved a little closer to her and, feeling her arm brush against his, reached down and took her hand. She made no objection and when he squeezed, she squeezed back, a smile passing briefly across her face.

As they followed the path, he said, 'You seem to work long hours sometimes, Val. Is there really all that much to do in the beauty parlour for you and Kim?'

'We don't just do hair, you know,' she answered. 'There are all sorts of things people need to have done.'

'Oh yes, I'm sure,' he said. 'But it's a part of the house I've never seen, even though it's so familiar to you.'

'What other parts of the house have you never seen?'

'Well, none of the top floor,' he said, 'I'd be for it if Sonia caught me up there. About half of the first floor and

149

a bit more of the ground, if you count the bar and conservatory. Oh, and the cellars I've always fancied poking my nose down there. I've always had a fascination for secret places.'

'And how many people have seen your place from the inside, Mike?'

He looked aside at her and hesitated. 'Er, well, I've had the odd visit from time to time; just for a chat and a drink, you know. Why do you ask? Would you like to?'

Valerie glanced at him, aware of the undertone of nervousness in his voice. 'You're so funny at times, Mike.'

They reached the top of the rise and stood listening to the intermittent chirp of insects. The valley before them was in darkness, but beyond, the sea caught the moonlight and shimmered speckled bronze.

'Funny? Me?' he asked at last, turning to her. 'Why?'

She smiled into his face, the moonlight glistening softly in her eyes.

'I know you arranged for Kim to leave us alone when you arrived in the bar, and I saw you both wink.'

'Ah, well I er . . .'

'Never mind, deary,' she breathed, slipping an arm about his neck. 'It was probably a lot more fun than just asking outright.'

He slipped an arm about her slim waist. 'No, no, it wasn't that, Val. It's because you're always with Kim or somebody else. I've wanted to ask you often but it's difficult.'

'Oh, difficult. So only the difficult ones are left. Let me guess. Apart from me, there's Cheryl and, well, we won't count Sonia for obvious reasons. And Pauline, I bet even you wouldn't have dared that.'

'I did,' he replied weakly. 'Not long before she left.'

'Oh, and what happened?'

'Val, let's not go into that now, and look, if you want to go back I '

'Michael, you haven't schemed and plotted to get me out here alone in the dark for nothing, have you?'

He stared into her eyes for a few seconds, then his face

melted into a smile. 'Well no. Since you put it that way, I haven't.'

Their lips met in burning heat. He breathed in her warmth and perfume and she placed her other arm about his neck, moving her body against his and feeling his arousal.

'You'll have to pay the penalty,' she breathed as he tugged at her top and drew it up over her head.

He thought for a moment about her remark as his fingers circled about her firm breasts and squeezed the dark, prominent nipples. 'I'm used to that, Val; believe me.'

As his hand slipped the button at the rear of her waist-band, Valerie eased her fingers under the brass stud at the front of his shorts. It gave with a dull click. They moved from each other to undress themselves and in a moment, shorts and skirt were cast down together on to the grass. He looked her up and down; she was wearing nylon bikini briefs and garter-top stockings.

'Do I live up to expectations?' she asked.

'God Val,' he breathed, pulling her to him, 'you're a sensation! A dream come true.'

The fact that he had seen her frequently at the pool wearing, as with the other girls, almost nothing, made little difference now. Here they were alone, in altered circumstances, face to face. For the first time, one who had seemed quite outside his reach, stood waiting, evidently quite as willing as he to endulge her desires.

Their lips met but his eyes opened wide and he caught his breath as her fingers slipped down the front of his blue nylon briefs and spread open at either side of his penis. The fingers carried on down, pushing away the elasticised front until the burgeoning erection was nearly freed.

'I can't feel them,' whispered Valerie.

'Wh what?' he gasped.

'The notches,' she replied. 'I can't feel the notches. Or do you mark each conquest off with a felt-tipped pen?'

Her other hand tugged down on the elastic and freed his erection completely so that her cool fingers circled and enclosed the shaft in an exquisite and voluptuous embrace.

Despite the distraction, he attempted to gain the initiative at once and slid his hand down the front of her bikini. His fingers coursed over the smooth flesh and found their goal in the heat of her sex. Her body stiffened and her fingers gripped the back of his neck as their lips came together again. It took but a few heartbeats for each of them to remove the remaining impediment from the other, but it was Valerie who regained the lead and pulled him down to the soft grass.

Once there, she leant back on her hands, drew up her knees and spread her thighs. The invitation was beyond his ability to resist, though he did not go immediately to the focus of his desires. He knelt before her under the stars and allowed his tongue to begin its work about her breasts and stomach, savouring the warmth and softness of her flesh. He gripped the sides of her behind like a precious chalice ready to lift to his lips. Soon the focus of her lust was reached and he found her inflamed and eager with passion. He played her with skill, his tongue like an asp striking blue fire into its willing victim. But aroused as she was, Valerie did not for a moment relinquish control. Instead, she reached out and pulled him up, at the same time twisting over and rising to her knees. For a moment, they stood on all fours side by side but Valerie laughed and pushed hard against him until he rolled over on to his back. At once, she placed a hand either side of him and scrambled over his body.

His mastery of the situation had been usurped. She straddled him and leant forward so that the head of his penis pressed hard against the base of her stomach. 'Right, deary,' she breathed, 'you've been wanting this for a long time. Let's make it all worthwhile!'

'Oh Christ!' he groaned as she raised her behind and allowed the head to course between the lips of her sex. He held her arms, his eyes shut in expectation as she poised herself above him. There she hovered for a moment, feeling his impatient body heave beneath hers, as he held his breath. Then she fell, letting him enter her like a sceptre driven hard into its sheath.

At first she moved with measured slowness, savouring

the act like a bird of prey circling on a rising column of air, wheeling about before the final plunge. The electric pulses were building in his loins and he knew the crucial moment could not be far away. But still she kept control, knowing the pulse of his body, slowing down her movements in time to avert the crisis before it occurred. When she pushed hard against him and began to moan softly, he knew the time was close and began to arch up his pelvis. She quickened her rhythm until both lost all semblance of restraint and plummeted headlong into the blinding vortex of passion, crying out loudly into the fragrant air as though delivering up their souls to the night.

They gathered up their clothes from the grass.

'Into the pool?' he asked, taking her hand.

'Why not?' she answered. 'Unless there's already someone else down there. We still have to be careful.'

They walked back over the rise and the house came into view. There were more people to be seen in the conservatory now. The French windows were open and the light spilt out over the patio. The pool remained in darkness.

'It looks like Carlene's got a full house,' observed Valerie. 'We're OK.'

'Won't they wonder where you are?' asked Mike as they descended towards the pool.

'I don't think so. Jackie won't be there, and probably not Sonia or Rose. It looks like they have a few visitors anyway.'

The pool was still in the calm air, reflecting the stars and the half moon and the light from the conservatory. They walked along the edge to where the tables and sunshades stood and put down their clothes.

'Can't see any sign of Karen in there either,' he remarked.

'I wouldn't worry, Mike,' said Valerie with a knowing glance. 'I'm sure she's perfectly OK, wherever she is.'

Quietly they slipped into the dark water and moved together, breaking the stillness of the reflected stars so that they rose and fell like myriad fireflies on the ripples.

* * *

In the warm half light of the secret room, a figure moved slowly and purposefully about the object which had been positioned close to its centre. The bench was narrow and supported by four splayed legs; it had the form of a vaulting horse except that it's surface was not hard but made of soft, padded black leather. Upon this sinister piece of furniture was mounted, face down, a naked figure, its limbs strapped securely to each of the legs of the horse. The head, twisting from side to side at one end, was contained in a web of thick leather straps which held a black rubber ball firmly in the opened mouth. The body tensed as Sonia ran a finger slowly down the spine and into the cleft of the behind. The strap which passed so tightly over her sex and anus, to the waistband, was not for concealment, but held in position the two objects of smooth black latex which penetrated her deeply and voluptuously.

Sonia moved about as a shadow, for she was clothed from head to foot in a catsuit of black synthetic skin. Her hand reached out in silence to a small circular table upon which lay the waiting instrument. Holding this at her side she walked up behind Karen and passed her hand over the smooth orbs of her subject's behind, letting her finger move down over the strap and apply a little pressure to it where it passed over the anus. She raised the cat-of-nine tails and stepped back.

The first stroke brought a tensing of the whole body and a short, muffled, 'Mmm!'

Sonia knew how much it had surprised and stung her. She knew too how the lubricated objects within her most sensitive places would make their presence felt as Karen squirmed with each application of the whip. She watched carefully the reaction to the second stroke, judging carefully the balance between pain and pleasure, for her victim had set out upon a journey of discovery; a journey to find the dark and secret passions which were haunting her. And Sonia was to be her guide and her mentor, now she had passed half willingly through the mirror.

The strokes which followed were measured and deliberate. Even in the warm, subdued glow of the pink cornice

lights, the weals were becoming visible. But the body writhing against the straps was not doing so merely from pain
and discomfort. For the sounds which followed each hiss
of the whip were of passion as much as anguish, and as
time passed by the twisting of her pelvis became continu-
ous, and her moans longer. It was not yet time to stop.

8

The Goddess Speaks

The most remarkable feature of the bar and conservatory on the occasion of breakfast time was the scarcity of people. Not that it was entirely empty, for Karen sat with Angela by the French windows and Mike chatted with Lorna over coffee at the bar, sharing their conversation with Kim who was on bar duty that morning. It was Kim who saw Rodolfo enter. He was dressed in deep pink denim trousers and a pale chamois shirt, which was open almost to the waist to display the large silver Egyptian ankh which gleamed out from amongst the copious black hairs of his chest. His face broke into a broad grin as he caught Rose's eye. 'Ah, *buongiorno!*' he greeted, gesturing theatrically towards her with his hand.

Lorna turned , smiled and said, 'Hello Roddy!'

Mike said nothing. He had never actually spoken to Rodolfo, and though he kept it to himself, his feelings about the Italian were not sympathetic. He regarded Rodolfo as a gigolo, which Rodolfo was not. Had he cared to admit it, his own situation spoke more of dependency than did that of the Italian, for Rodolfo was a man of independent means and free to come and go as he pleased. If anything was motivation for Mike's misgivings, it was plain, old-fashioned envy.

'I have not seen Carlene since we arose this morning,' Rodolfo said. 'Has she gone from the house?'

'Carlene and some of the others have gone for a walk,' answered Lorna.

'Then perhaps I will find them. *Ciao!*' He smiled and

walked towards the conservatory archway with a flourish of his hand.

'Bet he doesn't find anyone,' said Kim as Rodolfo disappeared.

'Oh? Why?' asked Lorna.

'Because I don't think they want him to,' replied Kim with a hint of mischief crossing her soft features and blue eyes.

'You mean they're up to something,' said Mike.

'Wouldn't be at all surprised,' replied Kim.

Rodolfo, with his hands pushed down into his trouser pockets, strolled casually along the main drive until he reached the swimming pool. There he stopped and cast his gaze over the calm, deserted water, and across to the tables and chairs standing empty under their colourful sunshades in the morning light. As far as the tennis court there was nobody to be seen. He turned and looked along the grassy pathway which led towards the rise and the valley. Thinking that he might be able to observe them from a higher vantage point, he set off up the gentle slope, with its scattering of trees and wildflowers, breathing deeply the perfumed morning air.

'Careful in case he looks this way!' hissed Annette.

Four pairs of eyes watched from the shade of the summerhouse as Rodolfo ambled by some fifty metres away.

'Well, there goes old tight pants,' joked Carlene. 'Stepping out along the path to his fate.'

'Are we going to wait until he comes back this way?' asked Valerie.

'I think that's probably the best idea,' added Cheryl.

'Let's see how far he goes,' said Annette. 'I don't want it to look as though I've been waiting.'

In a short time, Rodolfo had disappeared from view, obscured by the trees between himself and the summerhouse. Reaching the crest of the rise he turned back towards the house and shaded his eyes. Two figures moved away from the house towards the pool. He watched Mike

157

and Lorna as they reached the tables and chairs, then turned back to gaze across the sunlit valley, towards the bright but distant sea. To his right stood the deserted wooden seat, waiting under its pine tree and, to his left, the old stone bridge basked in the warm distance. He stood motionless for a time, feeling the sun on his face and chest, his eyes half closed against the intense light.

'Hello, what brings you out here?' came the voice from behind.

Rodolfo spun around. Annette stood not four metres away, arms folded; the sun glinted in her green eyes and a wisp of auburn hair swayed across her cheek and sensual lips in the soft breeze. The white nylon, long-sleeved blouse was opened low enough to expose the full cleavage of her breasts and tucked into the wide black belt of her blue denim mini-skirt.

'Ah, *signorina* Annette, *che bellezza*! What are you doing here?'

'I'm just taking a little walk, Roddy,' she said. 'And you? Out listening to the birds, are you?'

'I was looking for Carlene,' he replied, walking towards her and holding out his hand. 'But she is not here.'

Annette raised her hand. Rodolfo took it and lifted it to his lips, keeping his eyes all the time on hers. 'Instead *signorina*, you I have found. This I think is better than listening to the birds.'

'Well,' replied Annette, indicating towards the bench, 'shall we go and sit down?'

They moved to the wooden bench and sat.

'I think I see all you ladies smoke. Would you like to have a cigarette?' asked Rodolfo, reaching into his shirt pocket.

'I thought that was usually afterwards, dear.' Annette smiled.

'Please – I do not understand,' replied Rodolfo, holding out the packet.

'I said, I don't smoke any more. Thanks all the same.'

'Oh, then I will not smoke either,' he said. Replacing the packet, he moved closer to her and placed his hand across the back of the seat behind her shoulders. Annette showed no sign of objection. 'I think we should know each other a little better,' he suggested. 'You are so different from the other ladies,' he continued, letting his arm rest against her shoulders and his gaze fall upon her thighs as she slowly crossed her legs. 'Ah, yes! So special, so beautiful.'

Annette did not reply but looked across the valley with the hint of a smile upon her lips. Rodolfo's hand had closed about her shoulder and he leant closer still. 'You must come one day to Italia, to Milano and stay at my house for your holiday. I will show you many things. We will go to the best *ristoranti* in town. Just you and I.'

'That would be nice,' replied Annette, turning her gaze to meet his and placing her fingers upon the silver ankh.

The hand on her shoulder tightened and their lips met. 'Ah, *bello, bello,*' he breathed. Letting his free hand find her neck, he ran his fingers down over the softness of her full breasts. 'I think, you and I, we will make love. I desire this very much.'

Their lips met again and his fingers pushed inside the blouse to find and play with her nipple.

'Not here, Roddy,' she said.

'But here we are alone,' he answered. 'This is perfect.'

'No Roddy!' she responded, pushing his hand away with gentle firmness.

'*Signorina,* I think perhaps you do not find me attractive,' he breathed with the look of a child who has been denied the use of a favourite toy.

'Of course I find you attractive   *molto attraente,*' she said. 'But I don't want to get into trouble, Roddy. So we should go indoors, yes?'

'OK, if that is what you wish, indoors,' he replied with more than a hint of impatience.

On the way down from the rise, Annette glanced towards the summerhouse, unnoticed by Rodolfo. She observed a movement behind the glass.

'Looks like he's hooked, babes!' Carlene giggled as the two figures moved hand in hand across the open grass.

159

'Good and proper,' agreed Valerie. 'Still, it's all in a good cause!'

'I hope he thinks so,' put in Cheryl.

'Well, if he doesn't,' said Carlene, 'he can always take his arse off somewhere else.'

At the pool they stopped to watch Mike and Lorna circling about in the crystal water. Annette turned and said, 'Roddy, hang around here for a while. I'll go first. It might be better, OK?'

'OK,' he replied. 'I will wait.'

'Then in twenty minutes come up to the first floor,' she continued, 'and go to the third room on the right. Just let yourself in if there's nobody around. *Capisce?*'

'*Capisco!*' he returned with a smile.

She walked back towards the house and Rodolfo found himself a chair in which to relax for a time. Time was something Rodolfo usually had in abundance.

Rodolfo showed no concern on entering the first-floor corridor, for the small apartment at its far end was allotted to himself and Carlene for the duration of their stay. He only hesitated to glance about when he stopped at the door before this, noting that Cheryl's door opposite was closed.

When he entered, the pink cornice lights showed Annette, seated in one of the chrome and black leather chairs before the coffee table in the centre of the room. As she got up to greet him, he saw that she had changed. The blouse and skirt were replaced by a short, form-fitting dress in gleaming black vinyl; it was sleeveless but had a high collar which fitted snugly about her long neck. Her shapely legs were emphasised by their skin of sheer, black, seamed nylon and the black vinyl, high-heeled sandals fixed by slim straps about her ankles.

'So glad you could make it, dear,' she said, walking towards him. Rodolfo remained facing her and quietly pushed the door shut. Annette moved up to him and gazed into his eyes. Rodolfo said nothing, but took her in his arms and kissed her passionately. Annette returned his attentions with equal enthusiasm, but feeling his hands seek the zip fastener at the rear of her neck, caught his arms and pulled them away. 'No, Roddy! I have something to show you first.'

She turned and gestured towards the archway at the far side of the room with its heavy black curtain concealing the inner chamber. 'In there.'

'But ' protested Rodolfo.

'But what?' responded Annette.

'But, I am here to be only with you. This is not for a movie show!'

Annette appreciated Rodolfo's familiarity with this and the other rooms on the first floor, and had considered the possibility that resistance might be encountered at this point. She faced him, pushed the abundant auburn hair back from her shoulders and passed her hands, with fingers splayed out, slowly down over the sides of her breasts, over her slim waist and over her thighs to the hem of her dress. 'No film show, Roddy. But if you don't want to bother, I'll go.'

'Ah, *per piacere*,' he breathed. 'I will go where you say.'

Cheryl glanced at her watch. 'I think that's time enough,' she said, looking at Jackie.

Jackie sat within the steel enclosure, leaning against the cushions, waiting. Cheryl had dealt with her in the manner to which both had become accustomed only some ten minutes previously. Until then Jackie had at least enjoyed the use of her arms and the facility of speech. Now she possessed neither.

Cheryl unlatched and pulled open the gate in the circular pen. Two eyes regarded her from the open part of the rubber hood. Apart from the small area about her eyes, her entire head was encased in shining black latex. Beneath the breathing holes at her nostrils there swung the short tube with its rubber inflation bulb. The hood continued down into the smooth cocoon of heavy rubber which held her arms enclosed and folded across her middle. From her waist to the tops of her thighs Jackie was naked; the nakedness was accentuated further by the absence of any trace of hair about her sex.

'Up we come!' said Cheryl, hauling Jackie upright from behind.

Even with Cheryl's determined assistance, Jackie gained a standing position with difficulty. The heavy black latex boots enclosing her legs allowed only minimal bending of her knees, and the towering stiletto heels were not calculated to make the struggle any easier. Nor was the fifteen centimetres of strapping which joined her ankles and added to the precariousness of her walking. Fortunately for Jackie, walking for any great distance was not a part of Cheryl's plans, though what those plans were had not so far been revealed to her.

'Well, my sweet,' said Cheryl, placing her hands on Jackie's shoulders and looking into her eyes. 'I'm not altogether sure if these restraints were made for you or you were made for them! Nobody suits them better than you. And you'll be glad to know Sonia has some rather interesting and novel designs coming through from Germany in the near future. I'm sure you'll be the first to try them out.'

Cheryl guided her towards the door. Jackie had seen her pick up the three-tailed strap but had long since learnt that any form of disobedience or resistance was pointless. Indeed she was well aware that any refusal to comply would lead to prolonged or even stricter restraint and punishment, though the prospect of this had not always proved to be the deterrent it should have been.

They crossed the corridor and entered the room opposite. Jackie noted, though was unable to comment on the fact, that the door was already unlocked. She had expected Cheryl to take her through the curtained archway and had begun to move with short, measured steps in that direction. But instead, she was guided to the left, moving past the kitchenette and on towards the bathroom. Had not Cheryl already given her an enema, she might have regarded this as the reason for their present course. But the feel of the rubber nozzle and the rush of the warm solution into her rectum were still fresh in her mind as they entered the warmly lit, blue tiled room with its luxurious rugs and fittings. They moved past the blue porcelain sink and the low-level bowl with its sinister fittings and stopped before the walk-in cupboard.

'Now then,' said Cheryl, pulling open the cupboard door. 'Despite your familiarity with these rooms, there is something here even you don't know about. You shouldn't know about it either, but now you are going to have to. Follow me and be careful.'

Cheryl entered the cupboard and Jackie followed. The cupboard was not deep and contained the anticipated hanging bathrobes, folded towels and mundane bathroom items. There was barely enough room to accommodate the two of them but, once inside, Cheryl reached past the anxious Jackie and pulled the door shut. In the darkness Jackie heard a click. A dim light appeared at her right and she observed the side of the cupboard open outward to reveal a narrow, carpeted corridor beyond.

'Surprise, surprise,' breathed Cheryl. 'Off you go.'

Jackie glanced at her, the rubber bulb swinging from side to side like a black pendulum, and moved into the corridor with short steps. After a moment, she found herself before what seemed to be a large window. It took her some moments to realise where she was, for she found herself looking into the chamber beyond the archway, into a room familiar to her with its functionally sinister furniture. But she knew that this room had no windows. It suddenly dawned on her that she was behind one of the large mirrors, several of which were spaced about the room. The corridor went onward and turned abruptly right, some five metres from its entrance.

'This area is not fully soundproofed,' said Cheryl in a low voice. 'That is why you must be kept silent.'

Jackie turned her head back to the glass. Beyond the glass she observed Annette and Rodolfo. They stood kissing not three metres from the mirror in the brightly lit room. Rodolfo, in his bare feet, was still a little taller than Annette in her high heels.

'I've brought you here to prove one thing,' said Cheryl.

'And that is something that ought to have been apparent to you in the first place. You are listening to me Jackie, aren't you?'

Jackie glanced at her; emitting a barely audible grunt she nodded her head. The rubber bulb pranced up and down before her chin.

'You have to understand,' she continued, 'that your Rodolfo is a playboy and a philanderer. It feeds his ego when silly girls like you dote over him. As far as he is concerned, you're just another easy screw. He thinks no more of you than he does of Annette or anyone else here. He only sticks with Carlene because neither of them depends on the other for anything. She uses him even more than he uses her. They might be two of a kind except that Carlene is nowhere near as selfish.'

Annette was undoing the lower buttons of Rodolfo's shirt and pulling it out from the waist of his pink denims. She proceeded to remove the shirt and, with a mischievous smile, draped it over a nearby chair. Rodolfo attempted to undo her dress, but Annette rapped his hand and pushed it away. Cheryl and Jackie could not hear what Annette said to him, but both of them were seen to grin and Rodolfo gave a little laugh.

'He thinks he's got another conquest,' whispered Cheryl, 'but he's walked into this one good and proper.'

Annette was pulling at Rodolfo's belt and soon had this undone. She quickly knelt before him, and within a few seconds had his trousers wide open and was pulling them down over his thighs. Rodolfo's unmistakable state of arousal was barely contained within his vivid, turquoise blue, silk bikini briefs. Annette ran her fingers over the distended bulge and squeezed it. Rodolfo, running his fingers through her auburn hair, closed his eyes and groaned.

'You're such a hunk, Roddy,' she said smiling up at him. 'Just look at yourself in that mirror. You ought to be a pin-up.'

He regarded them both in the nearby mirror, and had

the added pleasure of seeing as well as feeling as Annette ran the fingers of both hands down each side of the swollen pouch.

'I think we'll have these off!' She grinned at him via the mirror and tugged hard on the briefs. They skimmed down to his feet, releasing the coiled spring of his ample penis, which at once leapt up before her like a snake about to strike its prey. Annette gave him but a moment to kick off the briefs before taking hold of his thighs and running her tongue about the head of the distended organ, feeling it twitch uncontrollably at her touch. Rodolfo grasped her head and pushed his pelvis forward in order to enter her mouth but Annette resisted and rose quickly to her feet. 'Roddy,' she sighed, kissing him, 'I'm going to do fellatio with you, properly, all the way.'

'Oh, Madonna,' he groaned as her hand closed with electric coolness about the inflamed shaft. 'You would do this for me?'

'I'm going to show you how we do it the English way. Give me your hands.'

She lifted up his right arm and pushed it towards the bright steel cuffs which hung on their chain above his head. Seeing these, Rodolfo stopped short with a puzzled expression. 'But how can we make love if I am not able to hold you?'

'Don't worry, Roddy,' she answered, 'you don't need your arms for this.'

He looked into her mischievous green eyes and relaxed for a moment. That moment was enough. Annette took one of the bracelets and with a final pull, had it closed about his wrist. Her smile broadened further as he lifted the other hand obligingly into position and the second bracelet was secured with a final, unambiguous click.

'Aren't you a good boy?' she whispered.

'Your English way,' he said. 'I have never heard of this before. It is, how you say, *popolare*?'

'Oh, *molto popalare*,' replied Annette. 'Many of our top people wouldn't have it any other way, and I should know!'

'This is good,' he breathed as she dropped back to her knees.

'Turn around, this way,' ordered Annette, pulling on his ankle.

Rodolfo had spotted the steel cuffs at the ends of their short chains, spaced out at either side on the floor, and offered no resistance as she pulled out and secured first one leg and then the other.

'There we are!' she said. 'And you can see everything that happens in the big mirror, Roddy. Doesn't that make it all the more exciting?' She regarded the reflected image of his slim, sun-tanned body, stretched out helplessly before her with the swaggering penis already glistening with anticipation at its bulbous tip. She stood up and kissed him, stroking the shaft lightly with her fingers. Rodolfo closed his eyes and did not see the black curtain across the archway to his left, pulled aside.

'Well, hi, Annette!' sang out the voice. 'My, oh my! What do have we here?'

Rodolfo's eyes started wide open.

'Oh, goodness me!' exclaimed Annette with a look of wonderment. 'Here's Carlene. Isn't that a surprise?'

'Oh *Gesù*!' groaned Rodolfo as he caught sight of her in the mirror. '*Pronto! La chiave!*'

'The key is in the other room,' replied Annette. 'I'll go and look for it whilst you talk to Carlene.'

'No, no,' replied Carlene, moving up to the side of the chained figure, 'leave the guy where he is! He's doing just fine!'

Rodolfo looked into her large brown eyes and at her body, dressed from head to foot in its crimson red, form-fitting catsuit of soft leather and the stiletto-heeled ankle boots in shining black.

'I take it, honey, we were going to have some kind of lesson here,' she said.

'Yes,' replied Annette. 'English lessons actually.'

They stood facing each other, at either side of Rodolfo, ensuring that his form was not obscured from the direction of the mirror.

'Full English?' asked Carlene. 'The way some of those old guys in London like it?'

'Well I hadn't really thought,' answered Annette. 'But if you want. You know what he likes.'

Carlene looked him up and down, and noted his flagging erection.

'Oh, Christ, what a shame, Roddy,' she said with a look of concern. 'You've gone off the boil. Maybe I can do something to sweeten you up a little. You bastard!'

'Oh, Carlene!' he blurted out. 'This is not fair. I am *sedurro*. I am compelled by this woman! She is misleading me here!'

'You talk much too much!' responded Carlene. 'Even when you don't say a lot!'

Carlene strode to a small table by the wall. Upon it lay several items, placed there by Annette but unnoticed by Rodolfo. She returned and Rodolfo watched her position herself behind him, unaware of what she held in her hands. Annette smiled into his face and raised a finger close to his nose. Rodolfo focused his eyes upon the finger and was about to speak when the red rubber ball was planted firmly into his open mouth. Just as quickly, with Annette's finger keeping it in place, Carlene tightened and buckled the strap behind his head.

'Nnnnnnng!' came the cry of protest. Carlene stepped back.

'Isn't that incredible?' said Annette. 'It's exactly the same in Italian as it is in our language!'

'And here's something else that's the same!' added Carlene, picking up the three-tailed leather strap from the floor behind Rodolfo. She raised her arm up and swung. A sharp crack rang about the room and the wide-eyed Rodolfo jerked hard with shock as the leather fell hard across his small, firm buttocks.

'There!' exclaimed Carlene. 'And I didn't even notice any accent!'

'None at all,' agreed Annette. 'Perhaps if I have a go.'

'Why not, honey,' agreed Carlene. 'There's another strap just like this one over on that table, by sheer coincidence!'

A look of despair crossed Rodolfo's features as Annette returned with the second strap. Carlene stood with legs

167

astride, hands on hips, full, sensual lips parted and eyes flashing. 'Have you heard what this bastard's been up to?' she called. 'You wouldn't believe! He took advantage of young Jackie when she was helpless and in her own room!'

'Oh no! In her own room?' repeated Annette with a look of astonishment. 'That's awful, Carlene! He insisted on me doing this, so I could give him – you know. I realise now how much he deserves to be punished!'

Annette brought her strap up and swung it with a crack against his thigh. Carlene did likewise with the other. '*Bastardo!*' she yelled as each of them swung in turn and the strokes began to fall in rapid succession. '*Stronzo! Stronzo grande!*'

Rodolfo let out anguished cries through the gag, his body jerking and twisting frantically in hopeless attempts to avoid the biting sting of the two implements of torment being applied with undiminishing vigour to his behind and legs. The semi-flaccid penis bobbed about with each crack. Carlene glanced at it and exclaimed, 'Watch his jewels! Without those he'd be a zombie!'

Within five excruciating minutes, Rodolfo's behind and thighs were distinctly reddened and glowing. With a final resounding crack against his left buttock, Carlene laid aside the strap, took a step backward and with hands on hips once more, cast her eyes over his body. Annette leant against the back of a chair with her aching arms folded.

'Boy!' declared Carlene. 'You can almost feel the heat! This guy could keep your room warm in winter if he got a daily dose!'

'Yes,' agreed Annette, 'but there's always the other.'

Carlene moved around to the front of the outstretched figure and they both observed his penis, now showing signs of a regenerating erection.

'It's the only part of him that ever does any work!' remarked Carlene. 'I suppose we'd better give it it's exercise. What d'you say, honey?'

'I agree,' replied Annette. 'Wait a second.'

She moved away to the small table and pulled open the drawer beneath it. Carlene could not see what she was about, but in the intervening time she retrieved the strap and stood dragging the tails slowly along Rodolfo's quivering erection. Annette returned and held up the small diaphragm of translucent pink latex with rolled edges and protruding teat.

'Oh babe!' Carlene grinned. 'That will save us a bit of trouble.'

'It certainly will. And we have to take care of the carpets.'

Annette knelt down by the side of the chained and gagged figure, glancing momentarily at the mirror to ensure all concerned had an unhindered view of the proceedings. With the teat pinched between her fingers, she held the condom over the glistening head of his penis and, with deliberate slowness, rolled it little by little along the engorged shaft.

'He's a Catholic,' said Carlene. 'Did you know? He'll go to purgatory for using one of those – with a bit of luck!'

'Oh,' replied Annette, 'that means we'll have him as company down there, too.'

'Christ, that's all I need!' replied Carlene in despair. 'In that case I'm going to sign up as a nun!'

'Perhaps he'll get remission,' suggested Annette, working the shaft vigorously back and forth with her hand. Rodolfo tensed and began to groan.

'Pretty soon too, I'd say,' remarked Carlene, seeing his pelvis begin to shake and his head fall back.

'Ooooh! Geronimo!' sang Annette, gripping the pulsating shaft and seeing his body tense rigid as the rubber teat sprang up hard.

Rodolfo sagged in the chains with his eyes shut. Annette straightened up. 'One more thing needs to be done,' she said, looking from Rodolfo to Carlene. 'It will only take a few seconds. If you want to get the keys, they're on the coffee table outside.'

When Carlene reappeared through the curtain, Annette was occupied with the ankh which still hung about Rodolfo's neck. She had removed the condom and passed the open end through the loop at the top of the ankh and was busy manipulating the sheath into a knot. Carlene watched her tighten, then release it to hang down and wobble about his chest.

'Oh, that's great!' laughed Carlene. 'Everyone should see him wearing that!'

'It's got a name,' said Annette.

'It has? Tell me!' said Carlene.

They looked at each other. Annette grinned, 'It's called a wankh!'

'That wasn't fair,' said Jackie as Cheryl closed the gate on the steel pen.

'It wasn't fair of him to creep into your room on the sly,' responded Cheryl. 'And it wasn't fair of you to tempt him into it. You both know the rules!'

'You just did it to spite me!' protested Jackie.

Cheryl looked at her with cool Nordic eyes, the helmet and inflatable gag hanging from one hand, the heavy latex boots gripped in the other. 'If I wanted to spite you I would have left these on.'

'Then what about this?' said Jackie, looking down at the smooth black cocoon which still enclosed her upper body and contained her folded arms.

'You know perfectly well why that is staying on,' replied Cheryl. 'Carlene and Rodolfo leave here in three hours for Lyon. Before then, Valerie will be calling in to take you down to the beauty parlour. You are very tense, my darling. A session down there will help you a lot. After that you'll be released and you can join the others as normal and have a late lunch if you want. Meanwhile, you can sit and watch TV.'

Cheryl walked around the pen saying, 'I'm going to wash and powder these.'

'Cheryl!' called Jackie.

Cheryl stopped short of the bathroom door. 'Yes?'

'When are they coming back?'

'When? Well, Carlene will be here for the autumn fashion show. Whether or not she still has lover boy in tow is a different matter. She's overdue for a change of partner.' Cheryl stepped back towards her. 'Look Jackie, nobody is trying to spoil your life. If you want to chase after Rodolfo, you go ahead. But you have to leave here first! Sonia cannot be held responsible. Now, if you want his address in Milan, you shall have it on the day you go. I'll get it from him before they leave if that's what you want! God knows what your father will have to say about it!'

Cheryl continued on into the bathroom and there remained for some ten minutes. Jackie listened to the faint sounds of running water and the opening and closing of cupboard doors.

When Cheryl returned, Jackie watched her pass by carrying the newly dried and powdered items. She was about to leave the room to take them across the corridor when Jackie called after her again. She turned in the doorway.

'Cheryl – don't. I mean, don't say anything to him. I don't want to go from here – not yet.'

Cheryl looked at her for a moment then nodded. 'Very sensible you are, my sweet.'

She had pulled out the key and was in the act of opening the playroom door when a sound to her left caused her to hesitate. The door of the spare apartment swung open and a sullen looking Rodolfo appeared. He walked past Cheryl with a nod and a weak smile, followed by Carlene in a purple two-piece, lightweight suit with gold trimmings. As she passed Cheryl, her face broke into a broad grin and she winked one of her large brown eyes.

Cheryl switched on the soft cornice lights, and closing the door behind her, breathed, 'One down, one more to go.'

It was just past eight o'clock in the morning and he stood before the bathroom mirror, face covered in shaving foam, razor in hand. Working carefully with the razor, he listened intently to the BBC world news from a small radio resting on the window sill close by. The telephone rang.

It seldom rang, but when it did, it was usually at an inconvenient time. He knew it would be someone from the house, probably Sonia, for he did not have a line to the outside world. He wiped the foam away with his face cloth and hurried from the bathroom into the lounge.

'Hello . . . Oh, Cheryl, yes . . . Yes, I'll be over for breakfast in quarter of an hour or so . . . Yes, OK, I'll come up to your office straight after   is it anything important? You sound serious . . . You can't - oh, all right, I'll see you soon.'

He returned to the bathroom and re-lathered his chin. As he continued with the razor, he smiled at his reflection, seeing in his mind's eye the cool and enticingly sensual features of Cheryl. She was the greatest challenge of all, the south pole of his lustful endeavours, and he was determined to be an Amundsen rather than end up a Scott.

He sat by the Yucca plant in the conservatory, sipping coffee. As he nibbled on a croissant, he thought of Cheryl.

'Morning Mike!' came the voice.

'Oh, hi Angie!' he said, looking up into the blue-grey eyes.

'You're looking unnaturally smart for a working day,' she observed.

He looked down at his dark blue chino shirt and newly pressed fawn trousers.

'He's drenched himself in aftershave too,' came Annette's voice from a table nearby. 'It's turning my eggs black!'

'Where are you off to?' asked Angela over her shoulder as she walked over to Annette's table.

'Oh, er, just a meeting, that's all,' he answered sheepishly.

At that moment, Kim entered with a plate of food and a glass of orange juice, followed by Valerie. 'God, what's that smell?' she queried, looking about the conservatory.

'It's him,' replied Annette, pointing with her knife at the subdued figure. 'People will think this is a brothel with that stuff wafting around!'

'I thought it was!' exclaimed Kim.

'God! She's hit the jackpot again,' breathed Valerie, with mock exasperation.

172

'Take no notice of them, Mike,' said Angela, seating herself opposite Annette.

He looked about the conservatory with a puzzled expression.

'What's up?' asked Kim.

'I'm sure that's not my aftershave,' he replied.

'Well it's certainly not ours!' put in Valerie.

He finished the small breakfast and was about to leave the table when his foot tapped against something. Pushing back the chair, he peered beneath the table, sniffing loudly. 'Oh, I see!' he exclaimed. 'And I wonder who that belongs to!'

On the floor, up against the wall, stood a small bowl. The bowl contained a loosely screwed up paper tissue, doused in a liquid which exuded the powerful aroma of musk. He looked about the room. The only person not smiling at him was Annette, who gazed nonchalantly into space and continued to eat.

'I might have known,' he breathed, narrowing his eyes at her.

Annette's green eyes at once switched to him and she protruded her tongue for an instant. Mike could not help a fleeting smile.

The last time he had approached this doorway had been after a summons from Pauline. He recalled with distinct misgiving his ill-fated attempt to win her over and the humiliating scenario she had manoeuvred him into afterward. But what did he expect from Cheryl? Being truthful to himself, he had no idea other than the impression that she was less physically sadistic than her predecessor. She was certainly more sensual; he had received her attentions directly, the previous year, when Annette's machinations had led to the loin-tingling and well-planned episode in which his plight had been first recorded.

But events had changed since that time. Cheryl had been a visitor to the house then, and took part as a member of the cast. Now, she was in a situation of authority and might well behave very differently towards him. Like it or not, he was what some people might describe as a bag of nerves.

He tapped on the door; not too hard, not too softly.

From inside a voice called, 'Come in!'

He pushed open the door and entered. She was sat where he expected her to be. In the same place where Pauline had once held sway. It gave him meagre confidence that so little appeared to have changed in the room and he could stride without hesitation or uncertainty to the empty seat before her desk. To the steel pen, now empty, he gave only a fleeting glance. But Cheryl was standing. So he remained standing. They eyed each other for a moment, both without expression.

'Sit down, Mike,' she said.

On her desk were a number of papers which she began to clear away. He sat still and watched her intently, taking in her eyes, bluer than his own, her full, red and very sensual lips and the lightly permed blonde hair framing her soft features. Her dress was of plain, black, satin lycra. She wore it off the shoulder but with a high, close-fitting collar so that it flowed smoothly over her well-defined breasts and every curve of her slim body. The hem finished half way down her thighs and his gaze fell upon the part of her legs not hidden by the desk. Her black stockings were sheer, seamed, and held an elusive reflection. Her perfume was heady.

As she turned to sit down, she smoothed her hands down the sides of her body; not so slowly as to appear deliberate, not so casually as to have been an unconscious act. His partial erection was proving uncomfortable. He squirmed as discreetly as he could in the chair to adjust himself. He was convinced she was manipulating him with every nuance of her behaviour.

'You're wondering why I asked you up to my office, Mike – yes?'

'Er – well, yes, of course I am.'

'Right, of course you are.'

His nervousness had increased to the point where his mouth was beginning to dry out.

'You like it at this house, Mike, don't you?' she continued. 'It suits you. It's taken the place of your life in England and we know you can't go back there even if you wanted to.' She stared at him for a few moments with her lips slightly parted. He wondered if she expected a response to what she had said but he remained silent. 'But your role here,' she went on. 'It doesn't quite fit in the way it should. You are in a sort of uncertain orbit, never quite touching the ground, never being quite in or out of things, grabbing what you want, or should I say who you want, when the opportunity arises. Isn't that so, Mike?'

He cleared his throat and pushed himself back into the chair in an attempt to convince her, if not himself, that he felt quite relaxed. 'Sonia pays me to do my job. I look after things outdoors the way she wants; the gardens, the pool, other things. And I get involved sometimes in – in . . .'

'I know perfectly well what you're involved in, Mike. It would be remarkable if I did not! And that is part of the problem. You have become involved by default, because of your little affairs with Annette and the others. You have, in effect, set yourself up as a branch office with its own policies, haven't you?'

Again he thought it better to allow her to go on uninterrupted.

'Do you know what this house is all about, Mike? It is, in case you had forgotten, or never realised, about domination and submission. It is not about opportunism. Of course it comes in degrees; shades of grey rather than black and white. We have Jackie at one extreme, let us say white, with Angela, Lorna and Rachel in the pale grey area. We had Pauline at the opposite end, the black end – over the top if you like – with Annette and Valerie still over that side but within reasonable limits.'

'I appreciate what you're telling me, if not why, but they don't all fit so nicely into your scheme, do they? What about Rose, Kim and, if you like, Karen?'

'We thought Rose was another Jackie at first. But that was because of the role Pauline forced her into. She really isn't that at all. Kim is very adaptable in her own quiet way

175

but hovers towards the paler side of centre. As for Karen, she is Sonia's affair, if you'll pardon the use of the word, but I would place her close to Jackie on our little scale of shades.'

Cheryl stood up and walked around the desk to lean against the front, just to the left of him. He felt obliged to push back his chair in order to look up and converse with her properly. He considered getting up to face her but something told him she did not wish him to do so.

She folded her arms and kept her eyes upon him. But despite her gaze he could not help his eyes running up and down the curves of her body, from her almost daunting red lips down to the black, patent leather sandals with their intimidating, long and slender heels which dug into the carpet. Even her perfume threatened to envelop him in the manner of some invisible ectoplasm combining and conspiring with the aura of her personality.

'Do you like this, Mike?' she asked, running a hand slowly, very slowly, down the top of her thigh, over the hem of her dress and over the sheer, glossy smoothness of her stocking.

For a moment he remained speechless. 'Er, well – I mean, you wouldn't want me to tell a lie, would you? Tell you the truth, Cheryl,' he breathed, 'I'm breaking out into a sweat!'

'Then you can touch me if you wish, Mike,' she said softly, bending over and placing a hand on his shoulder.

He stared momentarily at her pelvis and thighs, then reached out a trembling hand to touch her leg. It was as smooth as glass, cool and soft. The electric sensation passed from his fingers and down his spine to his loins.

'Be honest, Mike,' she said quietly, 'it's the image, isn't it? Would it matter who was wearing these things? Or what if it was me in a pair of old jeans? It wouldn't be the same, would it?'

She leant closer to his face so that their eyes were staring into each others. He held his breath, overwhelmed and speechless. 'You want to serve me don't you, Mike?' she whispered. 'I mean serve me completely; be under my control.'

'Jesus Christ,' he groaned, closing his eyes. Secret, private images passed through his whirling mind. He could do nothing to prevent his face reddening. He wondered if she knew his thoughts.

'It will be your role in this house if you agree, Mike. We'll set aside a day, just one special day. On that day you will be your alter ego but, be warned, everyone else will get to know. It won't be a secret, except when we are alone in here for our private rituals.'

'But – but why? Why must anyone else know?'

'It's the penalty you must pay,' she breathed. 'True subservience must be seen in order to be. And there will be worse.'

'Worse?' he croaked. 'Wh – what do you mean?'

'There's only one way to find out,' she whispered, kissing him on the forehead. 'Once you have agreed, there will be no turning back. You cannot go on as you are. It simply will not do.'

'Wait!' he declared, straightening up in the chair. 'This is impossible! How can you expect me to –?'

Cheryl stepped back and her face hardened. 'If you want me to be businesslike, I will. There's no room for any more problems to be created here; not with Rose, Annette nor anyone else. It's up to you, Mike.'

He stared into her eyes. 'What if I go along with this?'

Cheryl's features softened into a wry smile. 'It's Thursday, today Mike. Be here at two o'clock. Thursday can be the day. Even though it will be half over, it can be the first day.'

'The day for what? What am I meant to do?'

She leant back towards him until he felt the warm perfume of her breath stroke his cheek. He felt his penis straining. He dared not look down to see how much his erection showed through the thin cotton trousers, nor could he adjust himself in the chair to try and conceal it. He knew she could see it. How could she not, looking down at him so closely?

'The image, Mike,' she breathed, 'the image you so like to see; the image which so excites you and people like you. You're seeing those images now as I talk, aren't you?'

She touched his cheek with her fingers. Her eyes were on him, unblinking. Yes, she was right, he could see those things in his mind; the sensual and the bizarre. And as if reading his thoughts, she spoke softly. 'The sleek latex dresses; black gossamer stretched over the skin; little black straps and laces on everything. You know all about them, Mike. You know. And they form the image you are going to become.'

He opened his mouth to speak but no sound emerged. His erection craved release from its confinement. He wondered if she could hear his heart thumping.

Cheryl moved away and sat facing him on her desk. With a tantalising swish of nylon, she slowly crossed her legs. He made no attempt to ignore them.

'Two o'clock,' she said calmly, the tranquillity of her voice contrasting with the turbulence inside his mind and body. 'Two o'clock,' she repeated as he arose awkward and shaking, from the chair. 'We'll need a little time to prepare you.'

'W – we?' he whispered.

'Don't be late, Mike,' she said in a low, grave voice.

'A large cold beer, please!' he said hoarsely as Lorna stared at him over the bar.

'Are you all right, Mike?' she asked wide-eyed as he settled on to the bar stool.

'All right? Me? Of course I am. Why shouldn't I be?'

'You look flushed.' She smiled and shook the smooth raven hair back over her shoulder.

He scrutinised her slim face with its delicate features for a moment, then turned towards the archway leading into the conservatory. Inside, he could see the auburn head of Annette, hear her voice and hear Angela talking to her. There were other voices too. 'We,' Cheryl had said. It must be one of them. One of them knew; maybe more than one of them. Who?

'There!' came the voice, cutting into his thoughts.

'What?'

'Your drink, Mike! Careful, you almost knocked it over. I've never seen you so nervous!'

'Oh sorry,' he said lamely, 'I was daydreaming.'

'Well at least you don't look quite as hot and bothered as you did when you first walked in.'

He drank the cold liquid deeply and observed her face as she busied herself arranging the glasses. She was like a pre-Raphaelite painting: cool and composed, just the way he wished himself to be.

She looked up and said, 'You're not in trouble over something, are you?'

'Not me,' he replied, feeling marginally more certain of his composure. But was he in trouble? What was Cheryl proposing to do? Should he see it as punishment, pleasure or both? He'd had a taste of it the previous year, when Annette had obliged him as his side of their wager, when he had fallen into her and Cheryl's trap and, all too late, realised that the whole episode was being recorded. He had protested. He could not have done otherwise. He had told himself he had no wish to take part in such a thing. But, underneath, he had found the experience strangely and deeply sensual. Annette! It was obvious. He had assumed it was the work of Cheryl, but why? Who else but Annette would be devious enough to arrange all this?

Annette and Angela were still seated at the table when he passed through the conservatory and made for the French windows. Both glanced at him and smiled as he went by, but neither showed anything faintly untoward in their expressions. Annette was a good actress all right, he thought.

Fortunately, the jobs which occupied him until lunch time needed little concentration. He could not rid himself of her face. Her eyes seemed to be with him everywhere and he did not attempt to count the number of times her words replayed through his mind. Even so, moving about under the open blue sky, feeling the warmth of the sun on his back and hearing the birds overhead, the interview seemed unreal, the echo of a different world. Angela and Kim sat by the pool. They waved as he strolled by.

'Mike looks preoccupied,' remarked Angela, squeezing the tube of sun cream.

'Yes,' agreed Kim, 'his eyes looked odd to me. Lorna said he had a funny turn this morning at the bar. D'you think he's off colour?'

'Perhaps he's getting bored with all us women about.'

'Yes,' answered Kim, slipping off the cotton bathrobe to reveal her near-naked body to the warm air, 'it could well be that. Hand us the cream, will you?'

'A Scotch?' said Jackie. 'That's not like you, Mike; drinking whisky at lunch time.'

'Make it a large — no, a very large one,' he answered, taking a bite out of the cheese roll. 'Incidentally, where have you been? I haven't seen you around since I don't know when.'

'Oh, I've been tied up with other things. Nothing important.'

She lifted out the bottle of whisky and placed a small tumbler before him. 'Say when!'

He had not spoken when the glass was almost filled and Jackie stopped pouring. 'Are you sure about all that?' she asked. 'You'll end up pissed!'

'Yes, I'm sure' he replied, picking up the tumbler.

Over half of the drink was gone when he felt a touch on his arm. Turning around, he met Valerie's gaze. Her brown gypsy eyes looked into his, deep and searching.

'Hi Val,' he said.

'You seem nervous, Mike,' she said, looking at the tumbler close to his hand. 'I saw how much of the whisky, Jackie poured.'

He glanced at it and replied, 'Stresses of the job, Val.'

Valerie reached out and moved the tumbler away from his reach. 'No more now, Mike.'

Her eyes took his thoughts from everything. Her hand squeezed gently on his arm and she breathed, close to him, 'Don't be late,' before walking out through the bar room door and into the main corridor. He felt a tingling in his spine and his heartbeat quickened. When he turned his attention back to the bar, the half-finished drink was gone.

A little later, when Lorna had her back to him, he slipped away without a word.

By the time he had reached the door, Cheryl's door, he had made a decision. It was not the one he had started out with when he left the bar. For bravado, bluffing it all out, facing them down and making light of what they were proposing to do had been his intention. Standing before the doorway with his arm raised, ready to knock, all of that had dissolved away. He could never maintain the façade before Cheryl. The thought of her, the way she looked at him, stirred the currents within and his resolve, no more than a house of cards, had fallen and already seemed a fleeting memory.

There were still misgivings when he knocked on the door, for the prospect of his being recorded he found utterly distasteful. But a moment later his concern, in that respect at least, was alleviated, for the room was in partial darkness.

For a moment he remained still, unable to ascertain the whereabouts of the voice which had bade him enter. He had seen at once that the green blinds were closed but there was no light switched on to compensate for the restful glow filtering through from outside. The playing of a jazz pianist reached his ears.

'Please close the door!' came the voice.

It was directed from the group of green leather easy chairs on the opposite side of the room by the covered windows. Its owner was seated and partly obscured by one of the chairs. He pushed the door shut and moved slowly forward. A perfume hung in the warm air; close, sensual and inviting. It blended with the rich aroma from the chairs and spoke of quiet relaxation. A figure arose from the chair, silhouetted black against the green blind. Cheryl stepped quietly towards him. Another figure, which had been hidden entirely by the back of the chair in which it sat, also appeared. His eyes gradually adjusted to the subdued light and he saw that both Cheryl and Valerie were dressed alike; each had on a black lycra catsuit with a wide red vinyl belt and red, stiletto-heeled ankle boots. If they intended to present an intimidating image, as far as he was concerned, they had entirely succeeded. The steel pen had disappeared. What the significance of that had been was unclear but at least it was to play no part in what they had planned.

There were words racing through his mind, sentences forming and reforming to express the comments he felt he ought to make but did not because they seemed inappropriate or foolish. But the need for dialogue receded as Cheryl said, 'Kick off your shoes,' and Valerie began to unbutton his shirt from the top down.

'Look, I can –'

'Don't argue!' cut in Cheryl.

He stood in his white cotton shorts. For the time being, the condition of his nerves had forestalled any manifestation of physical excitement. Valerie folded his clothes into a small heap and placed the shoes on top. Cheryl said, 'In the bathroom you'll find a tube of depilatory cream. I think you know where you have to use it. Just say if you don't. Follow the instructions on the side and make sure you don't leave a mess. There is also your other duty: you'll see the bottle hanging up ready, and the syringe. Do I need to explain Mike, or is it all quite clear?'

'Wh – what are you trying to do? I mean . . .?'

'Do you think he needs help?' asked Cheryl, turning to Valerie.

'No, he's a bit nervous, aren't you, deary? He'll manage,' answered Valerie, squeezing Mike's arm. 'We don't want to treat him entirely like Jackie. Not unless we have to!'

'All right,' agreed Cheryl, turning back to him, 'do what is required then take your shower. Leave the shorts by the door. There will be something to put on when you're finished.'

He dried himself with the soft pink towel. The deep blue wall tiles glistened in the bright light and he saw his reflection in the large mirror opposite the low-level bowl, above which still hung the now deflated rubber bottle. The smooth flesh about his penis and groin still tingled from the effects of the cream but there was another sensation; one of nervous but enticing anticipation. The humiliation they were subjecting him to made the blood course through his veins. He was hot; his body prickled with an exhilaration no pretence could hide, for his penis stood flushed and firm though his conscious thoughts willed it to do otherwise. He waited, concentrating hard upon all the unpleasantries his mind could summon until his excitement, at least in part, subsided.

By the door, where he had left the shorts, there lay something else. He put it on with some difficulty, fastening the clips at the sides of the waistband but finding his regenerating erection awkward to accommodate inside the thin strip of elasticated, sheer black nylon which ran down the front. At last the problem was overcome and the small garment held that part of him, if not concealed from view, at least under firm control.

They were waiting by the door when he emerged. Once again it took him a little time to adjust to the subdued light of the main room, but when he did, he saw the things arranged on the small table by the wall. They led him over to this, his mixture of anticipation and misgiving quite undiminished, his face feeling as though the sun had been beating upon it.

'Better lean against the table,' said Cheryl.

He did so. Valerie busied herself behind him whilst Cheryl let her eyes and her hand move down his body as far as his stomach. 'Hmm,' she breathed, 'it would be much better without any of this hair but I suppose he'd feel awkward at the pool.'

'It won't matter,' replied Valerie. 'His hair is almost blond.' She bent down by his side and said, 'Lift your feet.'

He watched her pull the stocking over his toes, and felt the fine nylon brush and caress his skin as it whispered about his ankle.

'Now the other,' ordered Cheryl.

They eased up the stockings, straightening the seams and adjusting the elasticated garter tops. As Cheryl lifted the next item from the table, Valerie's fingers brushed delicately up the skin-like nylon pouch, causing him to twitch. He saw a fleeting smile cross her face. The heavy aroma of latex was already evident when they held the black dress before him.

'Step into the skirt,' said Cheryl.

They eased the heavy rubber up his legs until the hem was little more than ten centimetres above the knee. The skirt was tight and constricting but the rest of the dress was loose as he fed his arms through the short sleeves and they pulled it about his body, snapping shut the brass stud on the high collar. The rest of the dress they laced down the back through brass eyelets, alternately pulling the threads so that it embraced and stretched about his body with a strangely comforting snugness.

'It's as well he's not a big man,' remarked Cheryl.

'Nor scrawny,' added Valerie.

'No,' continued Cheryl, 'his features are rather soft for a male. I noticed that before, you know, when he first took part in one of our little events. Did you see the tape?'

'No, I don't see most of them,' answered Valerie as they tugged very hard about his waist, causing him to sway.

'Steady on,' he breathed, as the dress constricted further.

Neither of them reacted to his remark but Cheryl said, 'A bit more, Val, before both sides meet,' and they renewed their efforts.

'There!' breathed Valerie as the laces were knotted. 'It pulls him in nicely. I think shoes next?'

The shoes were of black patent leather and fastened with small straps and miniature locks about the ankles. The heels were high but not exaggerated.

'God,' remarked Valerie, 'his feet aren't much bigger than mine.'

'Nor his hands,' observed Cheryl. 'Annette once said he'd had an easy life. You can tell, can't you?'

'You certainly can,' replied Valerie, handing her the drooping form of the long rubber glove.

'Arms out!' ordered Cheryl.

He raised his arms and said, 'Pardon me for asking, but –'

184

'Shut up!' snapped Cheryl.

'The maids must not speak until they are addressed by someone in charge,' added Valerie.

He breathed softly and looked from one to the other as they pulled on the latex gloves, coaxing, tugging and snapping them up his arms, all the way up to the top like a sleek, black skin.

'Almost there,' said Cheryl, reaching back to the table.

The not unfamiliar chink of metal buckles reached his ears. The belt they fitted about his waist was of black patent leather, like the shoes, and some ten centimetres in width. From its sides and rear dangled smaller straps fitted, like the large belt itself, with small brass padlocks. It was quickly tightened high on his waist and three soft clicks confirmed that it was secured in place until Cheryl and Valerie decided otherwise. The same applied to his arms, for the smaller straps at the sides were passed about them, just above the elbow, then tightened and locked.

He had not seen Cheryl pick up the wig and so attempted to turn his head when she began to fit it over him.

'Stay still,' said Valerie, assisting her from the front until it was in place, with the long blonde hair spilling down over the black latex.

'Good,' breathed Cheryl, moving around to study him from the front. 'He wouldn't even recognise himself. Let's open the blinds.'

Whilst the room had been dim, he had felt compliant and his earlier apprehension had turned to a state of erotic tension. When the room was flooded with daylight he felt vulnerable and suddenly wished he had not allowed them to do this to him. He flexed against the restraint, quickly realising that not only did it hold his arms in a slightly awkward position, but it would prevent him from removing anything other than the wig.

Cheryl and Valerie returned to him, Cheryl holding something small in her hand. They stood before him and Cheryl ordered, 'Open your mouth a little and stay absolutely still!'

He obeyed until she raised up her hand to reveal the pink lipstick.

'Hey, no!' he objected, pulling away and almost stumbling on the high heels. Cheryl switched the lipstick to her other hand and slapped him across the mouth. He stopped moving and looked at her in disbelief.

'What did I say?' scolded Cheryl, her blue eyes staring into his. She thrust her arm out towards the table. 'See that! Well? Go on, look!'

He turned. On the table remained one thing only. The short, braided black whip lay coiled, meaningful and menacing.

'Further disobedience and you will get five strokes of that! If you have not experienced it before, I can assure you that you won't quickly forget it!'

She moved closer and raised up the lipstick. 'Shall we try again?'

'Your duties, on this occasion, will be confined to this apartment,' said Cheryl. 'You will be alone for about an hour and a half. The cleaning materials are in the small room about half way down this side of the corridor. If you're quick you probably won't be seen.' They moved towards the door and Cheryl looked over her shoulder. 'We're going down to the gym. When we get back I will expect to find that you have done a complete and thorough job in here and in the bathroom. If you have not, the restraint will be kept on for as long as necessary!'

He stood unmoving for some minutes after the door had closed, almost in a state of incomprehension. He looked about the room, planning how to go about doing what he knew had to be done. But there was something he had to do first. He walked to the bathroom. As he moved, he was very much aware of how the rubber stretched and tensed about his body, and how it caressed with almost life-like insistence against his swollen, yearning, yet confined organ. They were right. Turning before the large mirror, he found it difficult to believe, at first, that the erotically bizarre image which confronted him and mimicked his every move, was indeed himself. The disturbing sensuality he had earlier begun to feel was becoming intensified. He more

186

than ever suspected that there lay deep within him, something which they had awakened.

'Has he done a reasonable job of it?' asked Valerie.

Cheryl walked about the room, running her finger over desk and tabletop, scrutinising the carpeted floor and making a detour into the bathroom. She emerged and looked him up and down. Turning to Valerie, she remarked, 'It's passable.'

'It can't have been too easy to reach the electrical sockets,' said Valerie.

'A bit easier than it would be now,' replied Cheryl.

The remark was an understatement, for the first thing they had done upon entering the room was to seize and twist his lower arms across his back, and there to secure them with the remaining two straps and locks which hung from the belt at the rear of his waist.

'As he gets used to doing it,' continued Cheryl, 'we can add wrist and ankle cuffs. It will be more of a challenge for him.'

'And perhaps we could try a few masks,' added Valerie.

'Yes,' agreed Cheryl, 'that sounds like fun. Shall we close the blinds?'

With the room once more in semi-darkness and their prisoner ordered to stand by the desk, Valerie left and Cheryl vanished into the bathroom. He listened to the splashing of the shower and wished that he too could enjoy the luxury, for his body was hot and damp with perspiration where the latex enclosed it. When Cheryl reappeared the catsuit was gone and had been replaced by a bathrobe.

He watched her cross the room in silence and, once at the group of chairs, slip off the bathrobe and sit down with her back to him, out of sight. Had he not observed her cross the room, he would have been quite unaware of her presence. He lapsed into a mood of introspection. There was little alternative.

After what seemed like an eternity, her voice broke the silence. 'Come here, please!'

He caught his breath and started towards the chair. She was almost naked and would have been entirely so but for

187

the small black suspender belt, fine blue-grey stockings and black high-heeled shoes. She sat with her legs crossed and regarded him with her wide blue eyes as he stood before her. 'You've been less of a problem that I expected,' she breathed. 'You have taken to it rather well, I think.' She uncrossed her legs and leant towards him. 'And you see, our little ritual is going to be quite private, just as I said.'

'And what about all this?' he asked, turning half towards her and tugging against the restraints.

'What about it?' she answered.

'Well, you'll have to undo me if we're . . .'

'Oh, have to? No! No, I don't have to do anything,' she said rising to her feet. 'I thought you understood. You are here to serve, not to make demands. Now, my love, let's see how well you continue your duties.' She placed a hand on his shoulder and ordered, 'Down!'

For a moment, he hesitated, and his objections remained unvoiced. He lowered himself slowly, his face passing close to her breasts with their prominent pink nipples. He felt the heat of her body upon his face and the currents passing through his loins. On his knees, he faced her stomach and the soft, neat down of the fair hair above her sex. She lowered herself back into the sighing leather of the chair and lifted a foot to his face, saying, 'Begin here. And take your time!'

He kissed the shoe several times, and her ankle, moving forward little by little, turning his attentions from one leg to the other as she spread herself and allowed him to approach the sanctum of her own pleasures. Barely had he reached her knee when he saw the black whip, clutched in her hand at the side of the chair. To hurry, he knew, would have meant the taste of its cruel sting. He brushed against the top of her cool, smooth stocking when she let the whip down, reached forward and placed her hands upon his head. 'There, my sweet,' she breathed. 'If you do well, you will find how many different ways you can become the person you are now, and how many ways you can serve myself and others.'

She drew him closer to the cockpit of her lusts, and there to the place where his tongue could enact its drama of sensuality; swaggering and gesturing, darting and teasing, inducing then revelling in the climax that its performance must bring. But he knew he must not show haste here either, but play her slowly, for she wished to savour the journey as much as the destination. And the tongue found her secret rhythm, felt her stiffen and tremble to its salacious music, felt her body rise on a tide of silent lust. She heaved and cried out, the nails of her fingers pushing into his neck.

After the act was finished, she pulled on the bathrobe and took him to the door. She had not forbidden him to speak but did not speak herself. And so he remained silent. She glanced along the corridor before they left and walked to the door opposite. He had little option but to follow.

He had walked almost willingly into her trap. And now he was ensnared, not just physically but emotionally. She might remove the restraints from him and allow him to dress in the clothes of his own gender, but they both knew that his position and his future at the house depended on his obedience to her and the fulfilling of her needs. Pauline had never made such demands. Would he have been as compliant if she had?

Pauline had behaved as a tyrant. Cheryl was a goddess who demanded from her chief acolyte the abrogation of his own gender in the service of her carnality.

They crossed the deep maroon carpet and skirted the chrome and black leather furniture, all bathed in warm, pink light. She reached the heavy black curtain hanging behind the big arch and pulled it aside for him to enter. He glanced only briefly at the array of sinister furniture and equipment, for she led him to the far side of the room where stood, a metre away from the wall, the big wooden structure in the form of a letter X.

'We both know you have a choice,' she said quietly, withdrawing a small key from the pocket of her bathrobe. 'But I think you will make the correct one. It will only be for a short time and I somehow doubt that you will be disappointed.'

The straps were released and soon he felt the tightly laced dress begin to loosen. Cheryl pulled away the wig, stood back and said, 'Take everything off except the briefs.'

He struggled out of the dress, finding it difficult to pull away wet from his skin, then the stockings and shoes. She took them away in turn and placed them upon a nearby bench. When she took his wrist, he resisted momentarily and said, 'The shower: I mean, I'm all damp.'

'After!' she answered decisively.

He looked at her questioningly. Surely he had done what she had intended him to do. What more did she want? She looked closely into his eyes and whispered, 'It's for your own good. Don't disappoint me now.'

She worked quickly and efficiently, to the swish of leather through metal buckles until he was spread out and mounted on the cross with two straps about each limb. Standing before him, she placed a hand gently on his cheek and said, 'Rewards and punishments; give and take; that is what we are going to be about.'

She moved her lips closer to his and the furnace of her breath burned his soul. 'When you begin to love me, you will want to do everything I ask; everything to please me. You will want me to do more; more to control and transform you as you were today. Sometimes I'll be kind. Other times strict. I can be very strict. But your devotion will overcome it all, until you accept everything I have to give you.'

Her lips touched his, and his body tensed as the current flowed between them. Had he been able, he would have paid carnal homage to her again, on whatever terms she demanded. She smiled and ran a finger down his chest as far as his lower abdomen, causing him to close his eyes and draw in his breath sharply. When he opened his eyes, he caught a fleeting glimpse of her passing through the curtain and she was gone.

How long he remained in the silence he could not say, for his mind could not divest itself of her image and her voice, and the words she had spoken to him. His eyes must have been closed for a time because he had no recollection of anyone entering the chamber until a voice said, 'Hi Mike!'

She stood before him smiling, in her white T-shirt and denim mini-skirt with its designer frayed hem.

'Jackie!' he exclaimed, twisting against the straps. 'Why are you — what do you think you're . . .?'

She folded her arms and tilted her head to one side. Looking him up and down, her eyes came to rest upon the strip of elasticated nylon which held his erection in limbo. 'You have got yourself into a spot, haven't you? It looks to me as though you've been a naughty boy. You certainly pong of rubber and no mistake. I wonder if you're not as bad as me! Maybe we'll end up in the playpen together. I think I'd like that, you know. Anyway, Cheryl said to come and help you out of the mess you're in. That's why I'm here.'

'Well, come on then, undo me!'

'Oh I will,' she replied, walking up to him and putting her arms about his waist, 'in a little while.' She ran her hands to the front, reached under the elastic and squeezed the base of his penis with her thumbs.

'Oh God!' he groaned as her fingers found the small clips at the sides of the waistband.

The little garment jerked up as she released it. Reaching down, she took it from where it swung, on the end of his erection, and cast it aside. A moment later she was on her knees before him and a cool hand slipped under his testicles. Her other hand at once took the inflamed shaft and held it whilst her lips closed over the distended head. In this position, her hand began its devilish act, causing the effervescence to rise up quickly within his loins, whilst she allowed him deeper into her.

During his time with Cheryl, the sexual tensions had built up within him like raging torrents held in check behind a dam. Now that dam was about to burst forth. The crisis was approaching rapidly, surging out of control. making his whole frame sing like a tuning fork. He began to gasp, 'Hey! I'm going to – I'm going to !'

But she paid no heed other than to remove her hand so that he might enter her deeper still as his body quivered and shook in mindless ecstasy before her.

She withdrew him slowly. Twirling her tongue about the head, she made sure that nothing was lost. He kept his eyes closed, and relaxed against the restraints. Jackie got to her feet and moved behind the wooden cross. Soon he was released. All she said before leaving was, 'Your things are in the bathroom. Cheryl said to make sure you leave everything ultra-tidy!'

He stood for a minute or so, quite bemused.

'Look, he's back again,' said Annette.

Angela looked over her shoulder at the figure seated in front of the bar.

'God, what's he got there? It must be a litre of beer! I haven't seen him doing enough hard work today to get that thirsty.'

'And he's just staring into space, totally oblivious,' put in Annette. 'I wonder if he's still thinking of Carlene.'

'He's definitely got something on his mind,' said Angela. 'It could be he's been smitten.'

'What here? He wouldn't be! I mean who?'

'I don't know. We could ask.'

'I'll get his attention,' announced Annette, picking up a pea from her plate and positioning it on the end of her knife. She pulled back the blade and took careful aim.

9
Sybaris

Sonia had taken her to Béziers on that morning, the morning when she was to take the high-speed train to Paris. And even though she was to be away for only a few days, Karen had felt a little sad as they approached the junction of the main road and the house disappeared behind the trees.

At the railway station, they had kissed with overt passion, not caring who went by. Their private intimacies had reached an intensity which glowed like a furnace, giving forth its heat even in a place where all might see the burning. And burning deep in her loins Karen had been, when she boarded the train. Even the excitement of her trip to Paris had been dulled at the sight of Sonia watching her from the platform as the train slid with remorseless acceleration, ever onward, leaving one abandoned, the other in flight. If Sonia had said to her, 'Don't go now. Not now. Perhaps another time,' she would have willingly relinquished the journey. But Sonia had not asked her and that too had made her sad.

She knew she was to be met at the *Gare de Lyon*. She thought that it would be Armand, for Armand had been there to greet her on the first occasion. She put down her fawn case and gazed about the crowded, bustling concourse, expecting to see his round, smiling face and alert brown eyes. But the voice which called her name was not that of Armand, but of another whose presence was equally welcome. Karen turned to see laughing, dark eyes, and smiling sensual lips. Josephine, in a long-sleeved satin blouse with a swirling pattern of jade, black lycra leggings and red spike-heeled shoes, looked as striking as Karen remembered from the time they last met.

'Karen! Karen! *Ma cherie!*' she cried, throwing her arms around Karen's neck with open enthusiasm, and planting kisses about her cheeks as though they had been parted by years rather than months. 'It is wonderful that you are here! I am so happy to see you again!'

When Josephine hesitated to push back the long, raven hair from her cheeks, Karen replied, 'Oh, Josephine, it's lovely to see you again as well. Have you brought Armand? Is he here?'

'No, no!' she answered, wide-eyed. 'He is at his office in St. Germain-des-Prés. He helps to plan many of the fashion photographs you will do. He will be with us soon after six o'clock.'

She took hold of Karen's case and said, 'We will take a taxi now, and soon you can freshen up at our little shop.'

'Josephine,' she said as they set off towards the exit, 'give me the case, please. I don't want you carrying things for me.'

Karen thought it incongruous that someone not quite her own height should be carrying her luggage.

'Oh, no! I will keep it!' replied Josephine, pulling the small case away. 'You are our guest once more and everything we shall do for you!'

Everything, thought Karen as they stepped outside, everything. Indeed, what they, Josephine and Armand, had done for her and with her, ought, she felt, to have made her blush. But it did not. Not now. With Josephine and Armand, the erotic was fun, a mischievous adventure, an erotic play acted out between friends. With Sonia, it was much more intense, and more discreet. As they got into the taxi, and Josephine smiled at her, Karen wondered if she was a relation of Sonia's for there was a resemblance. Josephine might have been a younger sister.

Breaking into her thoughts, Josephine said, 'You have been at the house for well over a year. Do you think you will stay with Sonia?'

'Stay?' asked Karen. The question came almost as a surprise. 'I have no plans to leave. I'll stay as long as Sonia wants me to do my job there. Why do you ask?'

'Well,' replied Josephine, 'I have known Sonia for many years. She has not had many very close friends in that time because of her business. I know she would be very unhappy if you leave the house. I can tell these things, you see.'

'Is that what she said to you?' asked Karen, as the taxi pulled into the busy traffic, thinking how very little Josephine could really know.

'Oh, no, no. She does not have a busy mouth like me. I just know, that is all. When you have known someone for a long time, you can sense these things.'

Their cab turned off the Avenue Daumesnil and into the Avenue Ledru Rollin. Crossing the Rue du Faubourg, Josephine said with a hint of excitement, 'Two more turns and we shall be there!'

Soon they turned into the little street with its mix of bars, restaurants, chic boutiques and tiny galleries. At the end of the street, Karen saw it. The shop, with its small double front. It was at once familiar and she read out loud the name, painted in ornate gold letters above the door: SYBARIS.

Although it was not the busy, bustling street she knew it would become later, there was still much going on and, as they emerged from the cab, Karen was at once aware of the multitude of enticing odours which drifted by from the eating houses. One side of the street was still flooded with the warm glow of the evening sun, for it was now a quarter past five.

As the cab departed, Josephine said, 'Your little room, we have this ready for you again. I think you liked it, yes?'

'I couldn't wish for anywhere nicer,' replied Karen.

They entered the shop and those sensual aromas, so familiar from the house, or at least the more discreet parts of it she had come to know, flooded upon her. She gazed about at the displays and racks. Away from the window, situated discreetly against a rear wall, were several mannequins, heavily made up with rouge, eyeshadow and lipstick, and wearing some of the things which immediately brought to mind, in an ambiguous way, her recent encounters with Danielle and Sophie.

'Those are a new addition,' remarked Josephine. 'We have several new things in the shop; some of them are very naughty, I think!' She picked up Karen's case and walked towards the stairs. 'You must look around later, but for now, perhaps you wish to shower and to change. Then we will have coffee and wait for Armand. Unless you prefer that I make the coffee now?'

'I wouldn't mind a coffee first, please. I'll take up my case whilst you get it going.'

'Very well,' replied Josephine. 'I will bring up the tray in five minutes.'

The room was as Karen remembered, with its warm pine furnishings, oriental prints and rugs, and multi-coloured bedspread; friendly and comforting. The pendulum under the little brass clock danced away brightly in its tiny mechanical world as though no time at all had passed since she last looked at it. She set the case down upon the bed and opened it to pull out and arrange a few clothes. Inside the small bathroom, she found the bathrobe Josephine had left for her and, removing her own clothes, she put this on.

Back in the bedroom, she saw the sunlight as it slanted across to the small pine chest set against the wall. The room was one in which to contemplate, to be pleasantly submerged and lost in thought. From the window she looked down into the small courtyard with its colourful arrangements of potted plants, and to the narrow alleyway beyond it which led to another small road, devoid of shops and almost deserted. There was a tapping on the door and a call of, 'Hello!'

Karen stepped over to the door and pulled it open to reveal Josephine in a black satin housecoat, clutching a small brass tray upon which were two cups of coffee. 'I remember, you like cream but no sugar,' she said with a smile.

* * *

They had not finished the coffee when the sound of a telephone ringing in the shop interrupted their conversation. Josephine hurried away to the door saying, 'Excuse me, that must be Armand! Follow me down if you wish!'

Karen, seeing Josephine's coffee only half finished, picked up the tray and followed her downstairs. Josephine was speaking rapidly in her own language, making it impossible for Karen to follow in detail, though she ascertained quickly enough that it was indeed Armand at the other end of the line and that there was a minor problem.

'It is possible Armand will be a little late,' said Josephine, putting down the telephone. 'He says maybe, maybe not, depending upon a call from Amsterdam for which he is waiting.'

Josephine moved over to the windows and pulled down the deep red rollerblinds, cutting them off from the street outside. As she switched on the lights, the interior was transformed. No longer was it a shop, but an Aladdin's cave of glamorous and sensual things; a shadowed world of fetish fantasy. Karen's eyes returned to the mannequins, which stood out in greater detail now that the shop lights were on. 'I don't remember those last time,' she remarked.

'No,' came the reply, 'they arrived here only two days ago from the house. There, they were photographed. You, I think, would not see them there.'

'Well, I – er, I do recall seeing something like them, now you mention it.'

Karen had an uneasy feeling that, at any moment, one of the figures would turn its head and look directly at her.

'Now we are down here,' suggested Josephine, 'perhaps we will choose our things for this evening. Tonight, we go to see a cabaret, so it is not important if Armand is here late. Today is not so busy and we do not need to book the table.'

She followed Josephine to the rear of the shop where there were two doors by the side of the stairs, one leading to the office, the other into the store room. Outside the store room, suspended on a coat hanger by an iron wall-hook, was a black garment of rich, gleaming leather. Karen recognised the straitjacket immediately and would have made a point of ignoring it all together. But this one was different. 'Good God!' she exclaimed, hesitating before the ominous garment.

Josephine stopped and turned, as Karen reached out to touch it. The leather was heavy but still supple. At the collar and waist were heavy straps going all the way around and, in between, at the rear were five smaller straps. All of the straps, as well as the seams, were fixed or reinforced by brass rivets. Each strap ended not in a buckle but with a brass padlock. All the padlocks hung open.

'*Ma cherie*,' asked Josephine, mischievously 'you like that?'

'What? No, no! I was surprised at it. I mean, isn't it a bit of an overkill? All those locks – what's the point?'

'Yes, all the locks,' replied Josephine, still smiling. 'This is for total security. It is very strong and has steel wires inside the lining and the straps, so it cannot be cut. Only the one who has the key may remove it.' She turned her gaze to Karen. 'You should model for this. It has never been photographed because it is a new design.'

'Oh no! No thanks!' responded Karen, backing away from the sinister form. 'I'll be busy enough doing the out-door stuff. Anyway, you have the mannequins. I'm sure they won't mind'

'Yes, of course,' said Josephine, 'we have our manne-quins!'

'Tonight, we can be glamorous,' said Josephine, pulling out a dress from the rack.

She held it up before Karen then turned it away from the light to admire it better. The dress, in deep gold satin, was mid-length and obviously close fitting. Equally obvious was the nature of the bodice, with its wide-set gold shoulder straps and shaped, quarter-cup bra which would leave the breasts exposed.

'This I have in other colours,' announced Josephine. 'We can have different colours but the same style if you like this.'

Karen opened her mouth to say no, but thought for a moment and replied, 'Oh, all right, if you're going to, so will I. But I'm putting a coat over it to get there and back, OK?'

'But of course!' exclaimed Josephine. 'We cannot go out in the street with these. I do not think it would be allowed!'

'Just as well,' remarked Karen. And under her breath, she said, 'I dare say that's where you'd have me end up if it was.'

'OK, so we choose a colour for you, shoes to go with it and some nice things from the shop for the ears and neck. I think,' she continued with eyes flashing, 'we will be the belles of the ball, you and I, and Armand will not have the eyes for anyone else!'

Karen browsed for some time through the dresses, then selected and removed one in deep purple. 'How's that?' she asked.

'Ah! *Merveilleux!*' cooed Josephine. 'It is just right, I think. Just perfect for you!'

As they began their way back up the stairs, carrying the dresses and other items from the shop, Josephine looked at her watch. 'There is plenty of time, I think. We should take our things to my room. There is something else you should see.'

'Oh! What's that?' asked Karen close behind, trying to disguise a ripple of mild apprehension.

'Ah! Just a moment and I will show you.'

They entered Josephine's room and laid out the dresses, shoes and items of adornment carefully on the bed. 'Now,' said Josephine, 'this way.'

Karen followed her into the bathroom. Josephine stood aside and flung out her arm with a grand gesture and a cry of, '*Voila!*'

There was no need for Karen to follow the direction of her arm, for the object of her attention was easily the main feature of the room and more than obvious. Karen folded her arms and laughed. 'Josephine, how on earth did you get a bath that size into this house?'

'*Ce magnifique, oui?*' Josephine laughed, swishing back her long, raven hair.

'It's utterly decadent,' replied Karen. 'And quite wonderful!'

The object of Josephine's pride was deep blue, quadrant shaped, and stood out from the corner of the room to occupy almost half of the floor area. Part of the remainder was taken up by the matching toilet bowl, wash basin and bidet. The walls above and either side of the bath were lined with oblong tiles in mottled shades of red and burnt orange, and the gold taps and shower fittings stood in sparkling elegance against these. The remainder of the walls, as well as the ceiling, were painted a rich cream and the floor was fitted with a rich brown carpet, scattered here and there with thick cream rugs. Large mirrors filled in the remaining spaces.

'They have to take out the window to bring this through,' said Josephine. 'But now, I am very happy with it!'

'I bet you are!' replied Karen. 'If it was mine, I'd probably spend all day in it.'

'You must try it out with me,' offered Josephine. 'It is much too big for one person.'

'Well I – oh, all right. Yes, I will.'

'Good!' said Josephine, stepping over to the bath and closing the plughole. 'I will start the water and put in the crystals. We will have much hot water and lots of foam. We will put up our hair, yes? And keep it from becoming wet.'

Karen had watched the slim, lithe form of Josephine, watched as she eased herself down into the cumulous surfeit of shivering pink foam with a big smile and a bright cry of, 'Ooh la-la!'

Karen laid aside her bathrobe and in a moment they faced one-another with the billowing froth almost up to their chins. 'Oh, this is wonderful!' said Karen laughing. 'God! It's sheer luxury!'

'And plenty of room!' sang Josephine, blowing the top from a peak of foam; it scattered through the air like pink snowflakes. Karen seized an armful of foam and attempted to throw it into the air, but it merely rolled down her arms and landed on her nose and mouth. Josephine burst out laughing and took hold of one of her feet. Karen squealed as she lifted the foot up on to her raised knee. 'I will massage your toes!' exclaimed Josephine. 'It is good for you!'

'What's it supposed to do?' asked Karen.

'Oh, I don't know,' came the reply, 'but it's very sexy!'

Suddenly, from across the room, came a voice. '*Bonjour* ladies!'

Karen and Josephine froze and looked at him wide-eyed.

'Armand, you pig!' called Josephine. 'You should not walk so quietly upon two innocent girls when they are taking their bath! Go away!'

Armand, with his round, sun-tanned face, warm brown eyes and black hair, regarded them with some amusement. 'I have to come and say hello because Mademoiselle Karen is here and I have a little present to welcome her to Paris once more!'

'Armand,' said Karen, 'it's really great to see you again. We'll be out of here soon to come and join you.'

'No, no!' he replied leaning against the door frame. 'The present I have, you will enjoy more if you stay where you are – look!'

He reached outside and produced the object which had stood on the floor, until then out of sight.

'Ah! *Magnifique!*' cooed Josephine as he held it triumphantly aloft.

From the silver bucket, glistening and running with condensation, there protruded a large bottle of champagne.

'Gosh, I'm being spoiled rotten,' said Karen with a huge grin.

Armand carried the ice bucket over to the bath and placed it down by the side. Karen willingly received his kiss, covering her breasts with her hands instinctively even though the pink foam still obscured them. Without another word, he left the room, only to reappear a few seconds later with three wine glasses, which he placed on the side of the bath. 'See,' he said, 'now we have everything for our pleasure!'

He pulled away the foil cap and began to untwist the wire cage as Karen and Josephine watched intently. Then he stopped and looked from one to the other. 'This will be difficult,' he said with an expression of concern. 'You will be embarrassed for me to sit by and watch. It would be better for me to be in the water with you.'

Josephine at once affected a look of startled horror and turned to Karen with staring eyes and raised brows. '*Mon Dieu!* You see how his evil mind works? He has been all the time planning to take away our honour! What do you think of a man like this?'

Armand, mouth agape and eyes darting from one to the other, appeared lost for words. Karen sank deeper into the water and laughed. 'Oh, you're both so funny! I think you're wonderful!'

Josephine's face broke into a smile and she turned to Armand. 'OK, you can join us as long as you behave yourself. But first, remove the cork.'

Armand moved away discreetly from the bath so as to undress. Karen and Josephine continued to talk as though he was not present, until he approached. 'Cover your eyes,' said Josephine, as Armand lowered himself into the water, 'or you will see something terrible!'

Karen could not recall if they had consumed four or five glasses of champagne each. Josephine had let out some of the water from the bath and had risen to her knees in order to operate the tap and add hot water to bring up the level. She faced into the corner with her behind towards Armand and Karen, who leant back against the curving side. Karen could not help but notice what had caught Armand's attention, for the foam was sliding slowly down Josephine's back, between her buttocks and over her sex.

Josephine turned off the tap and was about to manoeuvre herself back into position, when she slipped towards Karen. She at once threw out her arms with a loud cry and caught the sides of the bath with her hands, either side of Karen's shoulders. Karen had instinctively put her arms out too, and with their faces almost touching, found herself holding Josephine's firm breasts in her hands. Josephine did not pull away but steadied herself with her knees on each side of Karen's and brought her lips closer. Karen did not resist as they met, and Josephine closed her eyes. Karen kept one hand on her breast and placed the other about her neck. Josephine bit her lip gently and sighed. Karen bit back.

Armand had arisen to his knees and Karen glimpsed him behind Josephine. His penis shedding pink foam, revealed itself, swaggering and inflamed. She wondered if he would invade Josephine from that position, but he did not. Instead, he placed his hands on her thighs and leant down. Josephine caught her breath sharply, then muttered, 'Oh la-la,' as his tongue found the icon of pleasure nestled within its grotto.

As the tongue continued, so expertly its dialogue of lust, Josephine's kisses became more ardent and Karen sensed the ripples of pleasure spreading through her body and beginning to rise, first to a flow and on to a torrent. Karen held her tightly as she became increasingly animated. Josephine's breathing shortened to a sequence of harsh gasps. It seemed as though she was about to struggle free of their attentions, she had become so animated, but she only wriggled to spread her thighs wider. Suddenly she thrust her cheek hard against Karen's neck and her body tensed. No sound came for a moment, then she let out a long, wailing, 'Aaaaaaaah!'

As she raised her head and lowered her body, she placed her hands on Karen's face and kissed her with sighs of gratitude as though Karen had been the instigator of her climax.

Josephine seemed to relax after a few moments, but eased herself upright and pulled Karen with her. They shuffled themselves around in the water so that Karen was positioned between herself and Armand. Karen realised quickly that she was to become the focus of their attentions and glanced from one to the other with pounding heart.

Josephine began by renewing her attentions and brought her lips once more to close eagerly upon Karen's. With one arm about her waist, Josephine's free hand slipped down beneath the foam. Armand's hand slipped around from behind and cupped Karen's breast. But it was not that which caused her to start and draw in her breath. Not only had Josephine's fingers coursed snake-like down over the smooth flesh of her vulva to find those other lips which held the key to Karen's lust, but Armand's fingers had, with equal agility, slipped under the cleft of her behind. There they moved for a time, fuelling her with carnal passion, entering at front and rear, withdrawing and teasing. But, before her arousal had gone too far, Josephine grasped her by the arms and pulled her to her feet. Karen glanced down, confused for the moment, and watched the pink foam rise and fall against the sides of the bath. Josephine at once pulled up one of Karen's legs and brought the foot down to rest on the edge of the bath, kissed her and fell back to her knees without a word.

Karen let out a sharp moan, for at once, the game which they had played with their fingers was now resumed with exquisite torment by their tongues. Josephine darted about the moist and reddened lips of her sex, finding and teasing the pearl which lay within. Armand's tongue caressed her anus like an electrode, sending effervescent fire up her spine and into her belly. She splayed her fingers out across her face and moaned in ecstasy as the flames burned into her. They continued for some time to play her aching body like a living instrument. But Armand and Josephine knew how close the orgasm was. Much longer and the tide of lust would overwhelm her. They had to cease for a moment. And in that moment, Armand arose from the water to position himself on the edge of the bath. Josephine arose too and eased Karen back towards him. Armand grasped her thighs and Karen, intoxicated by much more than the champagne, felt herself pulled down over the rearing and inflamed shaft which burned to enter her as she burned to take it inside. Only for the briefest of moments did the swollen head slip eel-like against her before she thrust herself with abandon down upon it.

Whilst Armand held her from behind, Josephine coursed

her lips down Karen's stomach until they reached the very place where she was so intimately joined and penetrated by him. Once more, Josephine's tongue resumed its game, darting from the clitoris to the base of the shaft as it appeared and disappeared like a piston into its natural haven, moving to the rhythm of their beating hearts.

Within Karen, the fires were beginning to blaze out of control and she felt the moment of exquisite release was closing upon her. But once more she was forestalled, for Armand, in an act which declared almost miraculous command of his own urges, withdrew the glistening lance from her. Both he and Josephine lifted her clear and Karen, mouth agape in bewildered frustration breathed, 'Oh, no! Don't – no!'

But she was not to be forsaken, for they moved her forward a little before allowing her slowly down again. This time, however, the eager shaft sought a new playroom, for the head butted urgently and hotly against her anus, forcing its passage, lubricated abundantly by her own excitement. Josephine, kneeling as before, held the shaft steady with one hand whilst gripping Karen's thigh with the other. Karen, feeling the head move up inside, pushing towards her rectum with firm insistence, gulped and repeated hoarsely, 'Oh, Armand, Armand!'

Within seconds, she was speared to the hilt from the rear and spread in full view of Josephine who regarded her shame and smiled. 'Ah, *c'est magnifique*!' she breathed.

The movement back and forth began once more in this hot and sensitive part of her body. But her sex, so recently the arena of attention, was not to remain an abandoned temple, for it quickly acquired a new and very active worshipper with the return of Josephine's tongue.

With the strangely ecstatic movement inside, and the sensually electrifying attention she was receiving from the front, Karen felt the tentacles of fire spreading through her loins and limbs with even greater intensity. She was not going to let them stop again, they must not! She wouldn't let them, but it had to go on and on! She grasped Josephine's head lest she tried to back away and would have corkscrewed herself further on to Armand had he not already entered her up to the root. She wanted them both deeper inside, to become one with her singing nerves and trembling body.

When the burning torrent surged through, she could barely catch her breath, for her cries were almost screams and burst forth again and again until they became sobs of gratification. Only a distant echo of Armand's groans reached her ears, though she had felt him quivering within her as she was taken and consumed by her own orgasm.

'I think that it was your first time like that,' said Josephine as they lay back in the water.

Karen, her head resting against Josephine's shoulder, answered, 'God, what does it matter? There's a first time for everything.'

'You must blame it on her new bathtub,' said Armand. 'Without this, we would all behave ourselves.'

'Oh, no, not you two,' breathed Karen. 'I know only too well. You wouldn't know how to behave yourselves if your lives depended on it.'

'*Ma cherie*,' said Josephine, affecting a look of deep concern which Karen at once believed to be genuine. 'If we have made you unhappy . . .'

'No,' returned Karen, 'you haven't made me unhappy. Don't think that, please. Perhaps I ought to be more prepared for these things by now.'

'Then,' said Armand with a grin, 'we should get out of this water and arrange for our taxi. We must not be very late this evening because we have the photography tomorrow morning and must not have an overhang!'

If Karen had anticipated bright lights and a busy atmosphere that evening then her expectations were not to be fulfilled. The Club Marat was located in an inconspicuous side street some distance from the Boulevard de Clichy. When they disembarked from the taxi, Karen and Josephine wore light coats, buttoned up to conceal what their dresses were designed to reveal. Armand wore a lightweight mid-tan suit and left his shirt collar open, for the evening was warm.

The entrance to the club was small and unassuming. Nevertheless, once inside, having climbed the narrow staircase up to the first floor, Karen realised that this place was not intended for the casual passer-by or tourist.

The girl who waited in the dim reception, with its starlike cluster of small, multi-coloured lights was adorned with a sleeveless, high-collared dress in gold satin lycra. It gave her slim body a snake-like appearance. Her abundant platinum blonde hair, Karen concluded, must be a wig.

Josephine removed her coat and handed it to the girl, who ignored her naked breasts. Karen did likewise, wondering if, had Josephine not already done so, she would have been as willing to expose herself in front of a stranger in an unknown place. Through the black lace curtains she could see lights and shadowy movement, but otherwise, all was indistinct.

'You should know,' said Armand in a low voice, close to her ear, 'that Mademoiselle Sonia has a financial interest in this club.'

Perhaps Armand had sensed her nervousness and felt that to mention Sonia's connection with the Club Marat might offer some small reassurance. It did. Josephine pushed through the curtain first, followed by Karen and Armand.

There were some nine or ten circular tables spaced in an arc about a small stage. To the right of the stage, in a small pool of illumination, a white-suited pianist sat at his keyboard. The notes drifted easily through the warm, intimate room. The general illumination came from two sources, a scattering of multi-coloured lights hanging like jewels from the dark ceiling, and a small bronze lamp placed at the centre of each table, which cast amber light on to its little domain of black lace tablecloth and bronze cutlery. Most of the tables were occupied by two or four people but Armand gestured towards one standing empty to the left of the stage and said, 'That one can be ours.'

They had taken but a step, when a figure approached

from the direction of the small bar to their right. She was young and slim, her hair adorned with a blonde wig in the same style as that of the receptionist. There the resemblance ended. 'Monsieur Laguerre,' she said with polite familiarity, '*Comment allez-vous?*'

Karen regarded her as she turned and led them to the table. About her body she wore a harness of sequins, shimmering in all the colours of the lights. The outfit left her breasts bare but passed between her legs and concealed her sex. From the waistband downward, she was clad in fine, black net hose and had on her feet open high-heeled sandals in gold vinyl with thong fastenings about the ankles. As they seated themselves at the table, Karen saw others dressed in a similar manner and concluded that this was the house uniform.

There was no such uniformity with the diners, except that like Karen and Josephine, the majority of the females present were bare breasted and the males more formally attired.

'Tell me about tomorrow,' asked Karen after the girl had taken their order.

'Ah, yes, tomorrow,' replied Armand. 'Tomorrow we must begin early. I will call for you at seven thirty. First we begin at Montmatre, whilst the morning is still cool and before the tourists begin to arrive. You will change your things and freshen up here, for we are only a short walk away from the hill of Montmatre. Both you and Josephine will grace the little streets and become immortalised in the camera!'

'And what about the shop?' asked Karen.

'Oh, I have someone to take care of this whilst we are away,' answered Josephine.

'And after Montmatre,' continued Armand, 'we go on to the Jardin du Luxembourg. Here it is pleasant and not so many people as Montmatre. And then, we can ...' Armand stopped and turned, for the pianist began to play what sounded like a fanfare and a round of applause broke out from the small audience. They looked to the deminutive stage as the two girls stood smiling and began to sing.

Karen looked at them intently, even as the two waitresses in their sequinned harnesses placed the food and wine before them on the table.

Each of the singers wore a long, sleeveless satin dress with a high collar and splits up the thigh. The shimmering jade green of their dresses, with their subtle, zig-zag patterns in muted gold, was complemented by the gold, shoulder-length gloves in stretch-vinyl and the stiletto-heeled shoes of matching colour. They sang to each other as much as to the audience. Softly, almost intimately, their voices drifted through the hushed room. Karen regarded the light brown hair, much like her own, and soft features of one, and the dark hair framing the sharper features of the other.

'A little wine?' asked Armand, breaking into her thoughts.

'I think you know those two girls,' added Josephine. 'They have been to the house, yes?'

'Er – yes, we have met,' answered Karen.

'Then maybe we will go and see Danielle and Sophie after, and you can meet again,' said Armand.

'No,' responded Karen. 'No, I won't if you don't mind.'

'I do not mind at all,' replied Josephine. 'They have never time for anyone. They think only of themselves. But Armand, I think is having a – what do you say – a fantasy about them, yes?'

'*Mon Dieu!*' breathed Armand. 'I am insulted! How could I think of any other women in the presence of such beautiful visions as yourselves?' He looked soulfully at Karen. 'Oh, I am so misunderstood.'

'Poor Armand,' mused Karen. 'Life can be difficult at times.'

'Quite so,' agreed Josephine, eyeing him with amusement. 'I think tonight I will wear the little spurs and teach him a lesson.'

'Never!' said Armand defiantly. 'I shall escape to my own apartment until you lock them away!'

The evening passed pleasantly, and as is the case with all evenings which progress this way, time was the enemy.

Karen was glad that Danielle and Sophie had confined themselves to the stage and had not seen fit to mingle with the audience. 'Are those two here often?' she asked.

'One, maybe two days each week,' replied Armand.

'And what do they show here on other days?'

'Well,' continued Armand, 'cabaret and, sometimes, a special show for invited guests only. Very special! Perhaps we will bring you to see this in a few days, unless you do not wish it?'

'It is very good,' put in Josephine, 'but very naughty. You should see it.'

'I don't mind at all,' answered Karen, looking from side to side at their attentive faces. She glanced at the stage, which was now empty, and wondered what it would be like to perform some outrageous sexual act upon it in front of all these people. She felt an odd, warm sensation pass through her.

'Our taxi will be here in fifteen minutes,' said Armand, glancing at his watch. 'The night is still young here, but we have tomorrow to think of. It's a pity, I know.'

They shuffled their chairs closer to Karen's and each placed an arm about her shoulder.

'You have enjoyed our little evening?' asked Josephine.

'Yes, of course I – I . . .'

A hand slipped coolly under each of her breasts and squeezed gently. Before she could protest, two pairs of lips descended to join them and began to suck hard upon the nipples.

'Hey! Look!' she protested pushing at them. 'Behave you two. Not in here! Not in front of all these people!'

But after only a few moments, the teats were reddened and hard, though Armand and Josephine desisted before they attracted anyone's attention and prepared to leave the table.

Even after Armand had signed for the account and they waited for their coats in the small reception, Karen's arousal was still evident and she knew that the brief attention they had given her had reawakened the desires she had experienced at Josephine's apartment earlier that day. She wondered if the receptionist would notice her arousal.

Karen almost hoped she would look and keep looking, but she did not.

When they stepped out into the evening air, the cab stood waiting. Before getting inside, Armand had a few words with the driver and then, instead of climbing into the front seat, as he had for their journey to the club, he ushered Karen into the back, slipped in beside her and was joined at his other side by Josephine. He placed an arm about each of their shoulders and said, 'Karen has seen little of Paris by night. We will go on a little tour before we return home. It will not be much over half an hour but you will see some famous sights.'

They turned on to the brightly lit Boulevard de Clichy and drove on. Crossing the Place de Clichy, they headed along the Boulevard des Batignolles. Karen, her face turned to the window was only distracted when she felt Armand's hand twitch and heard Josephine laugh mischievously. She turned to see Josephine pressing kisses about his ear and cheek, and pushing her hand into his open jacket.

Josephine saw Karen's amused expression and grinned. 'He is very, what do you say, cuddly. He is very cuddly this evening.'

'Yes he is,' agreed Karen. 'Very cuddly.' She too turned her attentions to him and pressed kisses on his cheek and mouth.

'*Mon dieu!*' he sighed. 'What have I done to deserve this?'

'You don't deserve it at all,' replied Josephine. 'You are just lucky today.'

It was whilst his lips were united hotly with Karen's that she felt his body tense and heard the metallic rattle. Glancing down, she observed Josephine's fingers busy at the front of Armand's trousers. She looked up at Josephine, whose face had taken on an expression of serious concentration as her hand continued its progress to the accompanying whirr of the zip fastener.

'Josephine,' she hissed, 'what are you –? The driver – what about the driver?'

211

'He sees nothing.' Josephine grinned.

Hearing Armand groan, Karen looked down once more. His penis was rigid and upright, freed from the confines of his clothing. It was held lightly by the smiling Josephine, whose fingers slowly but steadily worked the foreskin with unmistakable intent.

'Oh, you take advantage of me,' he sighed. 'I will complain about this.'

Josephine did not reply, but, despite the cramped space which all three occupied, lowered her head down to his lap and took the straining shaft into her mouth. Karen continued to kiss him but it was obvious that he was being distracted and stirred by the attention he was receiving below. She therefore manoeuvred herself down from the seat and placed herself face to face with Josephine. She was well aware of the effect the drink they had consumed over dinner was having on her behaviour. Nevertheless, she concluded that as Josephine and Armand had never hesitated to involve her physically, even on the occasion of their first meeting at the house, there was no reason why she should not play her part now. Perhaps a little initiative on her behalf, for once, would not go unappreciated.

Josephine withdrew the glistening and quivering shaft from her mouth and smiled at Karen with a downward nod. The silent message was understood. At once, Karen leant forward and took the head into her mouth. It felt hot and tense as though it posessed a life of its own. She twirled her tongue about it as Josephine's fingers continued to work the shaft back and forth with increased vigour.

To the sound of the engine and the feel of the vehicle, as it weaved its way through the bright lights of the city, Karen was quite oblivious. Only Josephine distracted her when a hand caressed her head, and lips touched her ear. She attempted to take more of the engorged penis into her mouth and Josephine moved her hand down to allow this, although her fingers continued their work as before. Each felt the grip of Armand's fingers upon her shoulder as Karen went about her business; she could sense the urgent straining within his loins, and knew his climax was not far

212

away. She heard his groans, and felt the fingers tighten on her shoulder. As he tensed, Josephine removed her hand from the shaft and placed it against Karen's cheek, and Karen bore down further still on to him. Suddenly, the pelvis jerked and the organ pulsed within her mouth as he ejaculated. She accepted the repeated spurts with almost frenzied enthusiasm, treating the salty flow as a precious nectar not to be wasted at any cost.

When the taxi arrived outside Sybaris, the street was alive with the lights of the restaurants and bars, and the bustle of people. Karen and Josephine kissed Armand as they left the vehicle, then stood and watched as it took him off into the living night. Josephine turned her key in the lock and they entered the shop, leaving behind the glitter, the intrigue, the talk and the laughter.

Josephine did not switch on the lights. Inside was stillness. The air was heavy with sensual aromas; the atmosphere was quiet and brooding.

213

10

The Vengeance of Pauline

The photographic schedule proved more demanding than Karen had anticipated, though she soon found herself enjoying the experience as much as Josephine. Also, there was time enough during the day to see those parts of Paris which she had looked forward to visiting but had not had time to see during her first stay. The photographer occasionally showed signs of exasperation but Armand was always there to ensure smooth progress.

Thursday afternoon was free. After lunch, Karen and Josephine had walked down to the Seine and crossed over the Pont Neuf to the Square du Vert-Galant at the tip of the Ile de la Cité. There, they boarded the small pleasure boat to spend the next hour in the relaxed enjoyment of a river cruise.

With the light of the early afternoon sun blessing the water, and the splendour of Notre-Dame slipping by in stately majesty, Karen's thoughts returned for a moment to the house in Languedoc; to Sonia, to her friends. With them, with Josephine and Armand, the world was somehow a better place.

'I think soon you will love Paris,' said Josephine squeezing her hand. 'And here we have good weather. In the south I think it is not as good as this, for once.'

'It probably will be when I get back.' Karen smiled, turning the silver locket slowly in her fingers.

'Listen to the rain against the windows,' she breathed. 'Even the birds have stopped singing.'

She sat down close to him and two pairs of blue eyes looked into each other.

'It's so much more private, so much more personal with the grey sky outside and the blinds shut. I like it. Don't you?'

'I suppose I do in a way,' he answered quietly. 'It stops me from working at least.'

'From working?' she asked. 'If that's all that matters to you, then you will have work to do, believe me.'

'No, no,' he answered nervously, 'I didn't mean –'

'I know what you meant, Mike,' she interrupted.

No smile crossed her lips when she placed a hand on the side of his face and ran her fingers down his cheek, and under the collar of his denim shirt. They moved closer on the small couch until their lips were only a soft breath apart. Her breath, warm and perfumed, held him like a magnetic field. It induced within him currents of ardour which spread through his body and stirred about his loins. Yet such had become her authority over him that he dared not move without her consent. Even if she had been unknown to him, her appearance would have inspired caution, for the vinyl catsuit with its high collar and long sleeves made her slim, lithe body gleam like a panther. The cruel, spike-heeled boots, fitted so closely about her lower legs, glistened like lethal weapons. 'I think it's time we transformed you,' she breathed. 'But you may kiss me first.'

Their lips met and he wanted to devour her with passion. His body and limbs sang like steel wires played by a strong breeze. She was irresistible. She was burning him. Cheryl pushed away his arms and stood up without speaking. The vinyl suit creaked softly. He knew he was expected to undertake the ritual in the bathroom and he would do it without question. He turned to leave her, hesitating only for a moment. But in that moment, his eyes encompassed all that had been laid out upon the green leather chair, and the small table which stood at its side. There was no dress to be seen, but lingerie in black and red lace and sheer nylon was set out with the stiletto-heeled shoes, and a number of rubber masks. The restraints in bright steel and black leather lay close by, sinister, purposeful, waiting. He would never have dared admit to the arousal which coursed through his body. He felt blushing shame in admitting it to himself.

'Did you get through OK?' asked Josephine.

'Yes,' replied Karen, putting down the coffee cup and seeing a young couple hesitate to peer in through the shop window. 'I spoke to Sonia straight away.'

'And how is she?'

'Oh, she's fine, and she sends her love to you and Armand. I think she's got a few problems at the London end though.'

'What kind of problems?' asked Josephine, placing the empty china cups and saucers on to the small brass tray.

'She didn't want to go into too much detail, but Annette flew from Montpellier to Gatwick the day after I left. I offered to go back but she said there was nothing anyone could do at the house.'

'No, well,' said Josephine, 'do not spoil your time with us. Armand and I would be unhappy if you leave us too soon. Already we must leave you alone this evening for we have a meeting with our printers and agents at St. Germain-des-Prés. You must come with us if you do not want to stay here, but perhaps it will not for you be very interesting.'

'That's OK,' said Karen. 'I think I could do with a rest anyway. I've got a few things to read and I can watch your television if that's all right.'

'But of course,' replied Josephine. 'I feel bad about leaving you, but we cannot cancel this meeting. Press deadlines are press deadlines. I hate them.' She looked about the shop and continued with a hint of mischief in her eyes, 'On Saturday we will go to a club where people wear the most outrageous clothes, like the party at the house where you first met Armand and me. You can take part or you can stay in the audience if you prefer. Whilst we are away this evening, you go around all the things in the shop or in the back. Find something exciting to wear, yes?'

'Well what about you two?' asked Karen. 'I'll do whatever you think.'

'Ah, no. The evening is for you to enjoy the way you wish. If you prefer an ordinary dress then we too will be ordinary. We can go whenever we like because it is not so far away. For you it will be a special visit.' Josephine's eyes glittered as she laughed.

'Josephine, I've really never been spoiled and pampered so much in my life. I can never repay you.'

'*Ma cherie*,' said Josephine, kissing her gently on the lips, 'it is not a question of repayment. You belong with us. I knew that when we first met you, long before you understood it yourself. And now you are with us, you must share all we have.

It was seven o'clock and they had shared a light meal and a glass of wine in Josephine's room. A car horn sounded outside and Josephine, now in a black two-piece suit and blue satin blouse, said, 'That will be Armand. He will drive around to the back where he can park, so I will leave that way.'

She held Karen by the shoulders for a moment and kissed her. 'Please, *ma cherie*, do not waste the wine now it is opened. We may return inside two hours but it may be four, or even midnight, so do not stay up for us unless you wish to.'

'Don't fuss. I'll see you later.' And with that Karen kissed her goodbye.

For a time, Karen sat reading, occasionally refilling the wine glass until the bottle of chablis was empty. Only an hour and ten minutes had gone by when she decided to take a shower.

With her body warm and tingling fresh, she pulled the bathrobe about her and headed for the shop. She did not at first switch on the shop lights but stood at the bottom of the stairs, listening, and feeling utterly at ease with the effects of the alcohol. It was now dark outside, for the only light which gained access to the secret enclave of the shop

217

was the occasional stab of a car headlight through a gap at the top of the blinds. Little of the street sounds percolated through, and what did only served to emphasise the quiet intimacy within. She reached out to the light switch and the shadows retreated in the warm illumination.

She felt a little guilty about exploring Josephine's shop on her own, the way she had been uneasy in the beauty parlour back at the house when Valerie and Kim were not there. But she realised that Josephine would find it odd if she did not take her at her word. So she moved quietly about the shop for some minutes, examining clothes and other items hanging on the racks, all the time aware of the all too life-like mannequins eyeing her dumbly from the other side of the stairs. It was quite illogical for her to find their presence so disconcerting, but she did. At length she walked into the store room and switched on the light. It was even more private, despite the brighter illumination. She felt at ease, even though the rich odour of that sinister garment of restraint hanging outside still lingered in her nostrils.

One of the dresses on the rack caught her eye. She lifted it out and held it out in front of her to examine it. It was made of a deep pink latex, and was very short. It was obviously not intended to be worn in public. She slipped off the bathrobe and stood naked, seeing herself reflected in the tall mirror at the end of the room. Perusing the little dress further, she decided that a garment of such delicate elasticity might need the help of another to put it on without the risk of damage to the material. She carefully replaced it. Turning to the drawers beneath the racks, she pulled open the one nearest to her and regarded the contents. Most, if not all of the items within appeared to be designed for the studio, for erotic photography or for the stage of some private nightclub, perhaps the Club Marat. She was about to close the drawer when curiosity prompted her to look further inside.

Some of the items were not wrapped up, though none appeared to have been used. Perhaps they had at some time been displayed on the mannequins. She had taken only a passing notice of them during her stay, but was aware that Josephine liked to vary some of the things in the shop on almost a daily basis. What next attracted her was a pair of stockings, different to any she had seen or worn before. She decided to try them on, knowing that she would feel obliged to pay Josephine and keep for herself any such delicate items afterwards.

The stockings required no suspender belt but stayed up by virtue of their elasticated lace tops. So sheer were they, that they would have been all but invisible had it not been for the fine, black pinstripe pattern running down their length from the lace tops to the shadow toe. Regarding her image in the mirror, she saw how they flattered her legs in a way that made her determined to keep them for the special night out.

The next item she laid her hand upon brought a smile to her face. At first glance, she had thought it to be a thin garter in black, ruffled lace. When fully withdrawn, she saw it was not. It resembled the tiny garment she had been given to wear by Sophie and Danielle for her excursion into the labyrinthine domain of the mannequins. That had been brief enough. This was utterly frivolous. She began to laugh and heard herself say, 'God, I have to see what this looks like.'

The black satin ruffle passed snugly down under the cheeks of her behind and nestled against the warmth of her sex, then passed up over the silky smooth flesh above it to join the waistband. Karen walked up and down the room, feeling the elasticated material pull intimately against her with each step. She watched her own reflection and imagined with a slight shiver, the faces of Armand and Josephine if they were to discover her like this. Had she not been devoid of hair, it would have been unsightly. There was something missing; something without which the image she had created for herself would not be complete. The shoes. It wouldn't matter about those. She could choose anything, any style. No one would know. The silver sandals, with their glitter finish, were not for practical wear. The stiletto heels were too high, too precarious to do anything other than to be simply seen in. Nevertheless, she wanted to do just that whilst the mood was upon her and the effects of the wine were still inhibiting her natural caution. She had to sit down on the small stool in order to fasten the thin silver straps about her ankles. To have made the attempt whilst standing would have been at least risky, and probably impossible. And, once more in front of the mirror, she posed, turned about and posed again, imagining the cameras, the ogling faces, the desirous stares. She practised walking with the correct poise in the shoes, and found them not quite as difficult as she had feared initially. She realised that some of the footwear she had worn at the house had helped prepare her for these.

Suddenly in the office next to the store room, a door closed. There were voices.

There was not enough time to remove the things she had put on. Any moment, Armand and Josephine would come through and find her. So she reached out and took the bathrobe, hastily pulling it on and doing up the belt. Having opened the door, she looked out into the shop. They were still in the office, for she heard drawers open and close and then a thud, as though someone had carelessly pushed aside a chair. The voices were subdued and sounded not at all happy. Perhaps Armand and Josephine had not had a good meeting. Perhaps they would not wish her to interrupt. The office door swung open unexpectedly and Karen's face broke into a smile. The smile froze. She found herself face to face with a total stranger.

She felt, rather than heard herself cry out. His hand darted inside his jacket and produced a small, black pistol which he pointed directly at her.

'What do you want? Who are you?' she demanded, clutching defensively at the belt of the bathrobe.

'Oh, you are English,' he replied with a heavy accent. He was aged about thirty, swarthy in appearance and had thick black hair. His jeans and black shirt gave him the aspect of a Sicilian bandit.

'Pierre!' came a girl's voice from behind him. '*Qui est-ce?*'

'What do you want here?' demanded Karen again as the girl looked over his shoulder.

She was perhaps a little younger than Karen herself, round-faced, attractive and slim, with short brown hair. She too wore jeans but with a dark blue jumper.

They began a rapid dialogue with each other in French. Karen could only follow in outline but it seemed they were deciding how to deal with her. Behind them she could see the small office in a state of disarray, with papers strewn about on the desk and files lying open on the floor.

'We – we don't keep money here!' offered Karen, having no idea whether there was any cash on the premises or not.

'It is not money we wish to find,' replied the girl in good English as she moved to the side of her companion. She looked at him for a moment, her face wearing an expression of uncertainty.

He ignored her, waved the pistol and said, gruffly, 'You will come with us now!'

'No, no! I'm not going anywhere!' Karen protested, backing away from them.

'Yes!' shouted the girl. 'You must do as you are told or Pierre will shoot! He does not care!'

The grim smile which crossed Pierre's tight mouth was not by any means a smile of reassurance.

'Wh – where do you want me to . . .?' began Karen.

But the girl was not paying any attention. Instead, her gaze had shifted to the object hanging on its hook next to the store room. 'Ah, yes, I know what this is for!' she pronounced. 'It is very convenient now, I think.'

Pierre glanced at it and scowled. 'Yes, get it on her. Quickly!'

Karen backed away further, staring in trepidation as the sinister black garment was lifted down to the swish of leather and the ominous chink of metal. Pierre levelled the gun at her head and stepped closer. 'Stay still! Do as you are told!'

The girl moved to her side and laid the straitjacket on the end of the counter. At once she tugged hard at the belt on Karen's bathrobe. Pierre, with his free hand, took hold of the collar and wrenched the towelling down over her shoulders. The girl pulled it down her arms and whisked it away from her body. Karen covered her breasts defensively and the girl said, 'Oh, la-la! You are from the stage at the Crazy Horse Saloon, I think!'

She slid the ominous leather garment from the counter and, moving around to face Karen, said, 'Pierre, please! Put that thing down and hold her from behind. I will do this quickly!'

'No!' begged Karen, looking desperately at the garment held open before her. 'Please let me get dressed first!'

'There is not time!' shouted the girl as Pierre's hands gripped Karen's elbows. 'Put your arms into the sleeve. Quickly or Pierre will hurt you! I do not wish for him to do that!'

Karen, her mind reeling, pushed her arms through each end of the internal sleeve until they were crossed over within. Quickly and without a word, the garment was drawn about her shoulders and upper body; it held her arms folded across her stomach as it continued to tighten.

'Ah,' came the girls voice from behind as she changed places with Pierre, 'there are no buckles, only these locks. Well, it will have to do.'

Pierre held her firmly now at the front and kept his narrow eyes fixed upon hers as the girl, working from the collar down to the waist, pulled each strap through its metal slot and secured it firmly with its padlock. There sounded in her ears as many soft clicks as there were letters in the word 'despair'. Pierre released her and the girl moved back into view. 'Good,' she pronounced, touching the front of the black leather cocoon, 'she will be easy to control now she has this on and you will not need the gun.' The girl turned about and regarded the hook which had held the straitjacket. 'Where are the keys?'

'I – I don't know,' answered Karen.

'Forget about the damned keys!' responded Pierre with undisguised irritation. We have no time to look.'

'Very well,' the girl answered, 'but let me put the bathrobe about her and then we can get out of here.'

Karen made no protest until her near nakedness was covered and the belt done up. Then she twisted about and cried, 'Look, just go away and leave me alone! I don't know who you are! I can't call the police, so what does it matter?'

They ignored her pleas and pushed her towards the wrecked office.

'No!' she cried again. 'No, no!'

'*Merde!*' breathed the girl. 'She must be silenced. Hold her for a moment!'

'*Adelle, vite!*' hissed Pierre as the girl hurried back into the shop.

Moments later Adelle returned and said, 'Pierre, make her close her mouth.'

Karen saw him reach into his pocket and raise the pistol. She closed her mouth and eyes, trembling uncontrollably as she heard the small packet being ripped open. Even the possibility of calling for help was to be denied her as the oblong patch of smooth white tape was pressed and sealed securely over her mouth.

They realised she could not move too quickly because of the high heels, but the walk out of the office, across the courtyard and along the alleyway was only a short distance. At the end of the passage, Pierre moved ahead and glanced quickly each way along the street. '*Vite!*' he called, and Adelle forced Karen on. She hoped desperately that they would be spotted by someone, anyone, as they emerged on to the street but saw that, despite a number of parked cars, there was nobody to be seen. A few steps across the pavement and she was confronted by the open rear door of a black saloon car. Adelle climbed inside first and helped Pierre to ease Karen in after her. They pulled quickly away and the car was soon out in the bright lights and moving down the Boulevard de Clichy. That was as much as Karen saw, for Adelle, reaching down into a side pocket, produced a patterned cotton scarf which she wound about their prisoner's eyes.

* * *

She tried to guess how long the journey lasted. She felt the car turn, speed up, slow down and stop several times, presumably at traffic lights. There were other sounds; car horns, police sirens, music from bars and occasionally, people calling. It could have been twenty minutes, perhaps more, perhaps less. Eventually the sounds outside diminished and only the murmur of the engine remained. The car slowed, turned sharply, and continued on for a short way, then stopped.

The scarf was pulled away and Karen could see again. But seeing gave no clue as to where they might be. She hardly knew Paris well enough to even guess which district they had brought her to.

Pierre climbed from the car and opened the rear door to help Adelle ease Karen out. There was little time for her to take in her surroundings, but she saw that they were in a quiet, tree-lined street with elegant old houses, some four or five storeys high. As they approached the front door of one, Adelle glanced over her shoulder as a car passed slowly by. Karen let out a long grunt and tried to pull away. They held her tightly and forced her on. The car disappeared around the end of the street.

Adelle unlocked the front door and they passed inside, closing it before the light was switched on. The hallway was sparsely furnished, though newly decorated, as though the owners had not finished moving in. They passed along to the staircase, a grand affair which swept upward in an elegant curve to the first-floor landing. Karen experienced some difficulty walking up the stairs without the use of her arms and with the extra high heels. She wondered if they might remove the shoes from her but realised that her difficulty in walking quickly would be an asset to them if not to her. At the end of the first-floor landing, directly ahead of them, was a large and imposing door. Karen expected that this was to be their destination, but no, for they stopped at a smaller door on their left and waited whilst Adelle knocked. A voice from beyond called in perfect English, 'Come in!'

The door swung open and they entered. The interior

appeared to be a makeshift office, with nothing standing quite in the right place but up and working nevertheless. A figure was busy at the desk, its face obscured as it leant aside to place some files into a lower drawer. As they approached, it arose and turned to face them.

Karen froze with a look of dismay in her eyes. The face, which regarded her with initial surprise was framed in a pageboy hairstyle of platinum blonde. The eyes were limpid blue and wide, opening wider still as recognition swept across the face. Slowly, the full, red lips curved into an enforced smile and the voice, with more than a hint of irony said, 'Well, if it isn't little Miss Prim-and-bloody-Proper come to pay us a visit!'

'So, Pauline,' said Adelle, glancing at Karen, 'you know who this woman is?'

Pauline, in her long black gown with wide cuffs and gold braiding about the high collar, moved around almost ceremonially from behind her desk and stood before the three. 'I'll say I know her. I know her very well indeed. Why, even in my wildest dreams I never thought ...'

She looked Karen up and down. 'Well, she's obviously wearing a restraint. Let's have a proper look at her and then we can make her feel at home.'

Ignoring the muffled protests, Adelle removed the dressing gown and threw it aside, leaving Karen in full view of the gloating eyes which, at leisure, took in the shoes, pinstripe stockings and thin lace ruffle passing over her vulva. 'Well I never,' declared Pauline with a callous smile; a smile Karen recalled very well was not born out of good humour. 'Fancy seeing this snooty little cow again, and all dressed up like a back street whore! So nicely packaged too. That straitjacket she's wearing looks a real quality job!'

'It has locks,' put in Adelle. 'We have not the keys.'

'Oh dear!' replied Pauline walking around the beleaguered Karen and eyeing the little brass padlocks. 'No keys! Well I don't suppose it matters about that since she'd have to keep it on anyway. It suits her perfectly, don't you think?'

'It is very smart,' commented Adelle with an ambiguous smile.

Pierre occupied himself with checking the pistol before slipping it back inside his pocket. Pauline continued for some time to study their prisoner. At length she addressed Adelle. 'Let's get her into the other room. I want her totally secure. There are some things I want to discuss with her. This really could be a godsend!'

The room at the end of the landing was not large, but was heavily curtained so that Karen's eyes needed a few seconds to adjust to the subdued light. Set about it were items of furniture and pieces of apparatus only too familiar from the playrooms at the house and the secret room between Sonia's apartment and the beauty parlour. And though the designs may have differed in detail, their purpose was unambiguous.

Pauline and Adelle ushered Karen towards one end of the room, with Pierre close behind. They stopped before what appeared for a moment to be a collection of shiny black leather straps hanging from a steel chain which passed over a ceiling pulley. The assemblage of straps began at head level and finished at the red carpeted floor. They turned Karen around and backed her towards it. It occurred to her what they were about to do and she began to struggle, twisting against the straitjacket and kicking out her feet.

'Pierre! Hold her legs!' shouted Pauline.

Karen stopped the futile attempt at resistance as his rough hands closed about her ankles.

They manoeuvred her up to the harness. Pauline held her upper body and Pierre her legs, whilst Adelle secured the lowest of the straps about her feet, and passed them under her shoes and about her ankles. The remainder were tightened and buckled quickly, restraining her entire body in a web of straps from head to foot, with heavier straps running up her sides to join the chain at the top of her head. Adelle was about to complete the enclosure of the harness by passing a strap over Karen's eyes, but Pauline stood back and said, 'No, I want her to see! Pierre, lift her up a bit!'

Pierre disappeared behind Karen and there began a metallic squeaking and rattling. The harness began to pull and constrict further until she felt herself lifted from the floor.

'That's enough!' said Pauline, when some twenty centimetres of space had appeared between the base of the harness and the carpet. 'Adelle, please remove the tape.'

Adelle stepped over to a wall cupboard and returned with a small bottle and a paper tissue. Soaking the tissue with the contents of the bottle, she picked away a corner of the tape which sealed Karen's mouth and squeezed the soaking tissue against it. The smell of methylated spirits was unmistakable; the tape started to come away. At last, Karen could speak. But for the time being, she did not.

'Your arrival at our little den,' said Pauline standing before the suspended figure, 'is quite fortuitous. In fact it's far more useful than anything I ever knew you to be at the house. Chance is an amazing thing, isn't it?'

'Pauline,' said Karen at last, 'you can't keep me in this forever. You have to let me go!'

'You're right,' answered Pauline. 'I'll need the harness for paying customers. But I'm not taking bookings until this place is sorted out so we have plenty of time, believe me. Plenty!'

'Pauline, the police will be looking for me; you know that as well as I do.'

'Yes, well, we may even hear them drive past. But they have no reason to stop here, so I wouldn't hold out too many hopes.' Pauline pulled a small chair over, placed it in front of Karen and sat down. 'Now then,' she said plainly, 'there is something I want to find out. It is very simple, and you will know the answer. Are we ready?'

Karen did not reply. Pauline continued. 'I helped build Sonia's business up to what it is today. I want some of the information which is rightfully mine to use, since I was responsible for putting it there. I know the access codes on your computer system are changed periodically, and I know they were changed when I left. I don't expect for one minute you will have them in your little head, but Josephine will have a record at the shop. Pierre and Adelle didn't find it. They found you instead. All you need to do is ask for the codes as a condition of your release. As soon as we have verified them, you will be taken to the nearest metro station, more suitably attired, that is, and released. What do you say?'

'Pauline, you can go to hell!'

Pauline's expression did not change. She simply looked at Adelle and nodded, saying, 'We need to make ourselves understood properly.'

Adelle evidently did not respond quickly enough in the manner intended, for Pauline's gaze did not change direction. Her eyes opened wider, however, and she said, sharply, 'Now, Adelle! Now!'

Karen was unable to follow Adelle's actions, for the movement of her head was limited. But Pauline arose from the chair and stepped towards the door. As she passed out of sight there was a loud crack. Karen heard the sound before she registered the sharp sting of the strap across her exposed behind. The next stroke fell moments later, causing her to give out a loud cry and to twist about within the restraints. All she achieved was to make her bound body swing around a little on the creaking chain. Adelle continued undeterred. Pierre leant back against the wall and watched, with a grin on his swarthy face and a glint in his narrow eyes. Karen cried out and protested louder and longer with each stroke, but the stinging torment was breaking her resolve and the tears welled up in her eyes.

At that moment, Pauline returned with a small, portable phone held up in her hand. She stood before the hanging figure. 'Are we ready yet? Josephine may be back by now. I'll key in the number as soon as you are prepared to speak!'

'No, no, no!' protested Karen. 'You can do what you like! You'll get nothing out of me, never! And when the police get you, Pauline, you'll be in big bloody trouble for what you've done! Big trouble!'

'I see,' said Pauline, putting down the phone. 'Well, they

have to find out first and you're certainly not going to say anything. Not by the time I've finished with you, you bloody little dyke!' She turned to the pair who waited close by. 'Adelle, set up the bottle, the stand and the steel tray. Pierre, make yourself useful. Set up the cameras, then go and get us all a drink. I'll have a gin and tonic – no ice!' As Pierre and Adelle went about their business, Pauline returned her attention to Karen. 'I really don't mind how long this takes; none of us are, as I say, in any particular hurry.'

Pauline moved out of sight and, for a short time, Karen was able to observe in silence what Pierre and Adelle were doing. The former had positioned what appeared to be three small video cameras on tracks, which also held spotlights. But Karen's fear was not intensified by the sight of the cameras as much as what they were aimed at. For Adelle had removed the cover from what had been a dark and shapeless object at the other side of the room, to reveal the chair. It appeared identical in design and function to that which she had been placed in at the house, when Carlene and Rodolfo had manipulated her body to a crescendo of lust. But pleasure, at least not hers, was not the aim of these people, only distress and degradation. It was very clear what they intended to do. Pierre left on his mission to obtain the drinks which would complement their forthcoming entertainment. Adelle positioned the gleaming metal stand, some two metres high, next to the chair, whose bright chrome and black leather presence became for Karen an object of dread.

Pauline reappeared, a partially filled rubber hot water bottle in one hand, and a coiled black whip in the other. She handed the bottle to Adelle, who hung it from the top of the stand, then proceeded to fix a deep steel tray in position beneath the semi-circular cut-out in the seat of the chair. Stored inside the tray was a coiled length of clear plastic tubing which Adelle removed. She lifted up the rubber bottle to prevent its contents from spilling, and removed the small stopper in order to insert the end of the pipe. Pauline swung about, uncoiled the short whip and said to Karen, 'I hope you don't think I'm out of practice with this. Believe me, it's had more use in London than it ever had at the house, and it's got to know far more high-ranking arses than yours!'

She moved closer to Karen. 'When Pierre gets back, we'll give it a little exercise.' She held the braided whip up to Karen's face and tugged it repeatedly before her eyes. 'Pierre loves anything like this. He'll probably want to have a go himself. He's rather good at it, you know! And by the time we've finished, the chair and the soap solution will seem like light relief.' Her face moved close to Karen's and broke into a scornful smile. 'In fact it will be relief of a sort! And it's all going to be recorded in unpleasant technicolour detail!'

'Pauline!' cried Karen. 'I'm never going to do what you want! Whatever you do to me, I won't help you. I won't betray Sonia and my friends, so please, don't go on with this. Please!'

'Oh, don't go on with this. Please!' mocked Pauline. 'Well, you haven't heard it all yet, you snooty little dyke!' She turned to the girl. 'Adelle, go and get the scissors, hair clippers and shaver. Once she's in the chair, we can begin by removing the lot!' Looking back at Karen, she reached up and fingered her light brown hair. 'You'll still be recognisable without your dainty locks, believe me!'

Karen shivered at her touch. Pauline glanced around. Adelle had not moved. 'What are you waiting for?'

'I – I do not think I wish to.'

Pauline's expression darkened. 'I didn't ask you what you wished! I told you to go and · no! On second thoughts, don't bother. Pierre can do it; he used to be a sheep shearer before his interests broadened into more lucrative operations.' She returned to Karen. 'Yes, it will add a little side-interest to our movie. And do you know what we're going to do with the final tapes? Think about it! There are a number of less scrupulous publications that would take them and,' she continued, the contemptuous smile once more crossing her face, 'before I quitted the house, I took a quiet peep inside your room. Your address book wasn't difficult to find. I dare say your old friends and your parents in their little Shropshire cottage all have video players and would . . .'

'No!' shrieked Karen, writhing hopelessly against the straitjacket and the harness. 'No! You can't do it to me! Not to anyone! You couldn't do that!'

She burst into tears and sobbed uncontrollably. The smile remained on Pauline's face. 'We can avoid all of this, of course. The telephone is over there. Just say the word!'

'No! You can't! You can't!' wailed Karen, and the tears flowed copiously.

'Adelle, is everything ready?' asked Pauline turning about.

'*Certainement!*' replied Adelle with some reservation. 'Now we only await Pierre.

'Yes,' breathed Pauline, 'he's taking his time, isn't he? Never mind,' she continued, swinging the whip at her side, 'we'll get this little bitch warmed up a bit. He'll miss half the fun if he's much longer!' She stood to Karen's left, legs astride to keep a firm balance, and raised the whip high to strike.

'There will be no more fun for you today!' came the voice from behind Pauline.

She stood frozen for a moment, her face bearing a look of puzzled dismay. Slowly she lowered the whip and turned about to face Armand and Josephine.

'Pierre,' growled Armand, pointing the pistol at her, 'will not be coming back. Put down the whip!'

Pauline, her mouth open in an expression of astonished anger, let the instrument of torment fall to the floor. Adelle, knowing there was no way out of the room, moved quietly behind the sinister chair. Josephine at once moved forward and seized the whip. Pauline ignored her and kept her pale blue eyes fixed hard upon Armand. 'You wouldn't dare use that,' she said at last.

'No madam,' replied Armand, 'but you do not know that for sure. It may go off by accident if you do not do as we tell you! If your foot was hit, it would cause you much pain for a very long time!'

231

'Take off the gown!' ordered Josephine.

'What?' responded Pauline.

'Take off the gown!' repeated Josephine raising the whip.

Pauline hesitated and looked from one to the other. Armand raised the pistol up. There was a shattering crack and a blue flash as he discharged it into the ceiling above Pauline's head. 'Do as she says!' he ordered as a thin stream of dust descended on to Pauline's hair.

The helpless Karen gritted her teeth. Adelle sank behind the back of the chair. Pauline, her face expressionless, her eyes glazed, began to slowly undo the gown. Josephine approached the terrified Adelle and said, 'You! Go and undo Karen, quickly!'

Adelle did not hesitate, but arose and hurried over to operate the crank; Karen was lowered to the carpet. Josephine, her eyes darting about the room, saw exactly what was needed, hanging from the wall. Pauline, meanwhile, stood before Armand in a black lace brassière, briefs and a garter belt which served to hold up her sheer black stockings. The patent leather ankle boots with their spiked heels gleamed cruelly.

As Josephine stepped up behind her, Pauline glanced over her shoulder, only to look ahead once more and find the daunting features of Armand looming close to her face. Slipping the gun into his pocket he at once took hold of her arms and pulled them up by the wrists. He held her hands level at either side of her head. As Josephine fitted the padded steel collar about her neck, Pauline's eyes and mouth sprang wide open and she began to struggle and kick. Armand retained his grip and blocked her feet with his own. The collar closed with a solid click.

From either side of the collar there protruded a rigid steel bar, some twenty centimetres long, each ending in a hinged cuff of smaller dimension but also padded. As these were fitted and closed about Pauline's wrists, there was no mistaking the quality and security of the built-in locks which held them fast.

'There,' said Armand. 'Now she must be silenced.'

'This will do,' replied Josephine, stepping over to a small

shelf. 'We do not need anything elaborate for this. It is better that her face is seen.'

Pauline no longer resisted as the red rubber ball was slipped into her mouth. Josephine quickly tightened the thin strap which passed about the back of her head, and buckled it. They left her standing in helpless anger and turned their attentions to Karen, who stood watching with Adelle close behind.

'We told you to undo her!' snapped Josephine, stepping over to them.

'They don't have the keys,' responded Karen, jerking from side to side within the straitjacket. 'They're still at the shop!'

'*Mon Dieu*,' breathed Josephine. 'Then we have no choice; you must keep this on until we get home.'

'What about her?' said Armand, looking at the frightened and trembling Adelle.

'We can secure her in here for the police to find,' replied Josephine. 'They will all be charged together.'

'Oh, no!' begged Adelle. 'You must not leave me with these people! They have been cruel to me! They know things about me which they say they will tell, if I do not do as they say!'

'You mean they blackmail you?' asked Josephine.

'Yes, that is it,' replied Adelle. 'Blackmail. But now I know much about them too and if you protect me, I will tell you about it!'

'What do you think?' asked Josephine.

'We can take her with us,' he answered, 'but she must behave. We must make sure of that.'

'I will find something,' said Josephine. 'Then we can deal with these others.'

Josephine was true to her word, but if Adelle thought she was to be treated leniently, she was mistaken. As Josephine pulled off her blue jumper, Adelle glanced about in trepidation. Armand stood by, keeping an alert eye on her and Pauline, who stood watching intently.

Adelle's brief, shoe-string brassière came off next, to

reveal her small breasts with their firm, pink nipples. She was obviously familiar with the heavy black rubber garment they were about to put on her and looked on with abject fear, from Josephine to Armand.

'We are not going to hurt you,' said Josephine. 'We, at least, can be trusted!'

Adelle, resigned to her fate, slipped her arms into the latex sleeve and stood looking ahead in silence as they pulled the garment about her body and head. To the swish of long laces through metal eyelets, it tightened inexorably about her darkened world.

After little more than a minute, Adelle stood sheathed in a smooth skin of gleaming black rubber from head to waist. The blank face of the helmet was broken only by a small cluster of holes at the mouth and nose. They sat her down in a chair and, with quiet efficiency, went on with their business. Both had taken a good look about the room since their arrival and Armand had devised a plan in his mind, the nature of which Josephine was soon to be made aware.

They took hold of Pauline, whose stifled protest and struggles became all the more acute as it became obvious where she was being directed. Once before the sinister chair, Pauline found hands busy about her body as Josephine wrenched down the lace briefs and Armand tore the straps of her bra away from the stitching in order to remove it completely. The short strap which Josephine secured about her ankles made manoeuvring Pauline into the chair considerably easier than it would have otherwise been.

'Those cuffs we leave on her,' said Josephine, as they passed the straps about her upper body. 'We should have some of them in the shop. They will be popular, I think!'

'I think so too,' agreed Armand, as they pulled her legs up and apart, only to fit them into the supports which sprouted up at each side of the chair.

'Ah, what a pretty picture you make!' Josephine smiled, standing back to regard the unfortunate Pauline who was held spread with her most intimate parts on full display before them. The expression of malignant despair in her eyes told them she did not agree with the sentiment. A streak of saliva had appeared on her chin below the ball gag.

'Now for Pierre,' said Armand, pulling the gun from his pocket and moving towards the door. Karen watched them go and, still in restraint herself, looked from the splayed out Pauline to the cocooned Adelle and wondered if it was all real.

A bumping on the landing outside told her they were returning. A dishevelled Pierre entered the room first, his hands and feet manacled so that his steps were slow and faltering. His mouth fell open and he almost stumbled to the floor when he saw Pauline's situation. Armand did not allow him time to contemplate but pushed the pistol into his back and propelled him towards the hanging harness. Soon the harness was possessed of a new occupant, and with the clicking of the metal ratchet, was hauled up into its former position.

'You bastards will all pay for this!' came the voice from its prisoner.

'I do not think so,' replied Josephine. 'When the police know who you really are, Monsieur Marquand, you will be out of the way for a very long time!'

Pierre's attempted reply never went beyond its first syllable, for Armand quickly rendered him speechless in the same manner they had done with Pauline. Josephine had meanwhile returned to Pauline and was occupied in uncoiling the plastic tube which spiralled down from the hanging rubber bottle.

Armand left the room but returned less than a minute later carrying a ball of string.

'What are you going to do?' asked Josephine.

'You will see in a moment!' he said. 'Let the solution down the pipe as far as the valve, then close it and place it inside her. I will be quick.'

If Karen and Pierre had an interest in common, it was their fascination with what Armand and Josephine were doing. Josephine had allowed the soap solution to speed down the tube, but had let no more than a drop emerge before twisting shut the small valve at the base of the pink rubber nozzle where it terminated. The tube of lubricant was already at hand where Pauline had earlier placed it in readiness to use on Karen. Now, it was applied to the nozzle by the smiling Josephine, who stood between Pauline's thighs, ready to insert into Pauline her own instrument of humiliation.

And insert it she did, the lubricated jelly ensuring its easy passage as it moved in through the anus and up into her rectum. Pauline closed her eyes. Not out of ecstasy but out of despair. Armand, poised on a stool beside the chair which held Pauline, tied one end of a length of string about the neck of the bottle and passed the other through one of the several metal rings which were set into the ceiling. He jumped down and walked over to the door, letting the string out as he went. Once at the exit, he pulled the string over the top of the door and closed it behind him.

Three pairs of eyes watched the string tighten and pull the bottle up until its neck pointed to the ceiling instead of downward. Seconds passed and nothing further happened. Then the door opened partially and Armand reappeared with a smile of satisfaction on his sun-tanned face. 'Now we can go,' he said. 'You take Karen outside the room and I will bring Adelle.'

Josephine located the bathrobe which Karen had worn, and pulled it around her to cover her near nakedness. Karen, still poised on the high heels, was ushered to the door and on to the landing, to be followed by the sightless Adelle, who was guided out carefully by Armand.

Josephine and Karen at once saw what he had done, for the end of the string was tied around a matchbox which was jammed against the narrow gap of the door, just above the top hinge. Armand hurried back inside and straight to Pauline. With a mischievous grin, he opened the valve which protruded between the cheeks of Pauline's behind. The pipe quivered but the bubbles visible in the liquid did not move. Then, almost as an afterthought, he removed the stainless steel tray from beneath the seat and smiled. 'Now madam, you have the carpet to worry about as well!'

'You see,' he said, finally closing the door. 'I now pull out the matchbox. All that stops the string going through is the little knot. When the police arrive, they will never see this. As soon as they open the door, the bottle will be released to fall down and do its work. She will not be able to tell them what is happening and they will not have the time to release her!'

'Ah, *merveilleux*!' responded Josephine. 'But, *mon dieu*,' she continued, turning to Karen, 'is this man not a perverted genius?'

'God, I almost feel sorry for her,' answered the dishevelled Karen.

'Feel sorry?' said Armand incredulously. 'She would have done this thing to you, our friend, and even now we cannot free you because of her!'

'Please,' came the muffled voice of Adelle. 'What is happening?'

'We must go now,' said Armand, ignoring Adelle, except to say, 'This one can go under the hatch and out of sight. You help Karen and I will make the call to the police from the office here.'

'Will she be all right?' asked Karen as the car pulled away.

'Oh yes,' reassured Armand, 'there is plenty of air and I will not drive quickly.'

'Where are we, Armand, and however did you know where they had taken me?'

'We are at Montparnasse, south of the river,' he answered.

'But to find you was not so difficult,' said Josephine, sitting next to her on the back seat. 'When we arrived at the street near to the back of the shop, Armand had only just switched off the lights of the car when we saw them bring you out. That is why they did not see us. But we followed you all they way to the house and entered after them. All the time they held you, we were there. We heard everything they said, all the things they were going to do. But we watched over you, *ma cherie*, because you belong with us and we knew you would not betray Sonia or ourselves unless they hurt you so much that you could no longer bear it.'

'Oh, Josephine,' sighed Karen as their lips met. 'I was afraid they would make me do what they wanted and I would hurt all the people who mean the most to me.'

'But you defied them,' breathed Josephine, pulling Karen closer, 'and they will pay the penalty.'

Josephine held her as the busy streets and the lights passed by. She slipped her hand inside the bathrobe and found the warmth of Karen's body. Their lips were locked together as the fingers moved inexorably down her stomach and under the lace ruffle, to find her sex moist and inflamed with anticipation, and her thighs parted with expectation. The fingers began to massage her pliant flesh and entered her deeply, raising the glow to a bright flame then letting it die down for a time in order to fuel the next surge.

They were crossing the Seine and passing over the Ile de la Cité, with the myriad lights in the water and all about them, when Josephine fuelled the searing torch within Karen's belly to a point where its flames took her beyond the realms of self control. She threw back her head and began to cry out; each cry becoming louder than the one before. She no longer cared if Armand heard, or the rest of Paris for that matter. She was going to come; nothing could stop it, nothing could prevent the flames from devouring her body. She gasped and heaved in the swirling heat, crying out repeatedly to the whole city as though she had been plunged into an abyss of fire.

When they reached Sybaris, Karen was released and hurried to her room. Adelle, secured with straps to a chair in the shop, was left, still restrained and hooded, to contemplate whilst Armand and Josephine put the ransacked office back into a state of order. When Karen rejoined them, the room had been restored to almost its former appearance. She had noted the time as she entered. It was past one o'clock in the morning.

'I shall leave now,' said Armand, 'if you are both happy to deal with Adelle.'

'That's OK,' answered Josephine. 'She will have to answer all of our questions before she is released.'

'Good,' he concluded. 'Then in the morning I shall find out through my own contacts what has happened to our two friends at Montparnasse!'

'So,' said Josephine, 'she was going to set up a rival business, including blackmail, using Sonia's confidential lists of clients and contacts?'

'Yes,' replied the helpless Adelle through the thick rubber helmet. 'If she finds out what I have told you, Pierre will kill me. Please you must not tell them!'

'They will be in the hands of the police,' said Josephine. 'They will not know what has happened to you.'

'Shall we release her?' asked Karen. 'I don't think there's much point in her being like she is much longer.'

'Please,' said Adelle, 'I wish to go to the bathroom.'

Josephine arose and they worked together to release Adelle. She sat naked in the chair, her hands over her eyes to shade them from the glare of the lights, her body glistening wet with perspiration.

'Where will you go now?' asked Karen.

'I do not know,' replied Adelle. 'I have no one in this city. Everything I had is at Pauline's and I cannot return to that place.'

Karen and Josephine glanced at each other and Karen said, 'I'll phone Sonia first thing tomorrow. Perhaps something can be arranged.'

'Yes,' added Josephine, 'and for tonight I will find here a place for her to sleep.'

After Josephine had taken Adelle upstairs, Karen sat alone and silent for a few minutes with closed eyes, considering the events of the evening, wondering what they would do with Adelle. Her thoughts turned to the far away house, the gardens and the seat beneath the tree, with its

239

peaceful view across the sunlit valley. The image seemed to hover before her in the silent room. She could almost smell the flowers and the pine trees, and hear the birdsongs. And Sonia would be waiting for her to return and share their secret delights together. But in Karen was growing, and had been growing for a long time, the desire to submit wholly to all the house had to offer and to be used in whatever manner Sonia and the others saw fit.

In a day or so, she would return.

NEW BOOKS

Coming up from Nexus and Black Lace

Pyramid of Delights by Kendal Grahame
November 1996   Price £4.99   ISBN: 0 352 33112 7
Ancient Egypt. Many lascivious diversions are enjoyed in the court of the pharaoh, and into it stumbles a handsome, libidinous young soldier, Aran, who is all but sated by a beautiful Princess and her handmaidens. Then Aran is drawn to the Pyramid of Delights – a forbidden temple where mysterious and supremely erotic rituals are carried out. He determines to discover its secrets, regardless of the risks involved.

Warrior Women by Yvonne Strickland
November 1996   Price £4.99   ISBN: 0 352 33113 5
The land of Manantia is ruled, with a rod of iron, by the leather-uniformed women of the warrior class. Jennar – a young, athletic blonde, captured from the primitive Outworld – is trained to be a warrior and, with the help of Vargan, her lesbian mentor, fights her way to the upper ranks, discovering a taste for domination in the process.

Madam Lydia by Philippa Masters
December 1996   Price £4.99   ISBN: 0 352 33115 1
Victorian London. Lydia is now a fully-fledged working girl. As she assists an increasingly wealthy and hedonistic clientele – both male and female – with the realisation of its kinkiest fantasies, she comes to enjoy the exhibitionism, ritual and role-play involved – and relishes having her own sexuality tested to its very limits.

Eden Unveiled by Maria del Rey
December 1996   Price £4.99   ISBN: 0 352 33116 X
Sex and discipline form the basis of the alternative lifestyle enjoyed in Eden, a small, hi-tech community deep in the British countryside. When Eden's founders suspect that plans to undermine their control are afoot, they recruit a young couple to spy on its other residents, as they are subjected a programme of bizarre sexual training.

Julie at the Reformatory by Angela Elgar
December 1996   Price £4.99   ISBN: 0 352 33134 8
When Julie is sentenced to three years of bondage, discipline and
corporal punishment at Roughton Hall Reformatory, she discovers
that total submission is demanded by the sadistic mistresses. Behind
closed dormitory doors, however, fellow inmates provide comforting
relief from the daily humiliation, and revolution is soon in the air.

Passion Flowers by Celia Parker
November 1996   Price £4.99   ISBN: 0 352 33118 6

Katherine – a brilliant but stressed-out lawyer – is sent, by her boss, on a well-earned holiday, only to discover that her mystery destination is a revolutionary sex therapy clinic, located on an idyllic Caribbean island. For the first time in her life, Katherine feels free to indulge in the sybaritic pleasures all women deserve. But will she be able to retain this sense of sexual empowerment and liberation when it's time to leave?

Odyssey by Katrina Vincenzi-Thyne
November 1996   Price £4.99   ISBN: 0 352 33111 9

Historian Julia Symonds agrees to join the sexually sophisticated Merise and Rupert in their quest for the lost treasures of Ancient Troy. Using her newly discovered powers of seduction, Julia extracts the necessary information from the leader of a ruthless criminal fraternity, and soon finds herself relishing the ensuing game of sensual deception – as well as the numerous other pleasures to which her new associates introduce her.

Continuum by Portia da Costa
December 1996   Price £4.99   ISBN: 0 352 33120 8

When Joanna takes a well-earned break from work, she also takes her first step into a new continuum of strange experiences and enters a decadent parallel world of pain, perversity and unusual pleasure. Simultaneously exalted and degraded, she explores a secret world of erotic suffering. Will her working life ever be the same again?

The Actress by Vivienne LaFay
December 1996   Price £4.99   ISBN: 0 352 33119 4

1920. Milly Belfort's facade of innocence cannot hide her innate sensuality forever and, when she renounces the life of a bluestocking, in favour of more fleshly pleasures, her adventures in the Jazz Age take her from the risqué fringes of the film industry, to the debauched excesses of the yachting set, to a stint as a Mistress of Correction.

Île de Paradis by Mercedes Kelly
December 1996   Price £4.99   ISBN: 0 352 33121 6
Shipwrecked on a tropical island, the virginal Angeline comes to enjoy the eroticism of local ways. When some of her friends and lovers are captured by a depraved band of pirates and taken to the harem of Jezebel – slave mistress of nearby Dragon Island – she and her handmaidens have a very sensual role to play in the rescue strategy.

NEXUS BACKLIST

All books are priced £4.99 unless another price is given. If a date is supplied, the book in question will not be available until that month in 1996.

CONTEMPORARY EROTICA

THE ACADEMY	Arabella Knight	
BOUND TO OBEY	Amanada Ware	Feb
BOUND TO SERVE	Amanda Ware	Sep
CANDY IN CAPTIVITY	Arabella Knight	Jun
CHALICE OF DELIGHTS	Katrina Young	Mar
THE CHASTE LEGACY	Susanna Hughes	Aug
CHRISTINA WISHED	Gene Craven	Apr
CONDUCT UNBECOMING	Arabella Knight	
CONTOURS OF DARKNESS	Marco Vassi	
DARK DESIRES	Maria del Rey	May
DIFFERENT STROKES	Sarah Veitch	
THE DOMINO TATTOO	Cyrian Amberlake	
THE DOMINO ENIGMA	Cyrian Amberlake	
THE DOMINO QUEEN	Cyrian Amberlake	
ELIANE	Stephen Ferris	
EMMA'S SECRET WORLD	Hilary James	
EMMA ENSLAVED	Hilary James	
EMMA'S SECRET DIARIES	Hilary James	
EMMA'S SUBMISSION	Hilary James	Oct
FALLEN ANGELS	Kendal Grahame	
THE FANTASIES OF JOSEPHINE SCOTT	Josephine Scott	
THE FINISHING SCHOOL	Stephen Ferris	May
THE GENTLE DEGENERATES	Marco Vassi	
HEART OF DESIRE	Maria del Rey	

Please send me the books I have ticked above.

Name ....

Address ....

....

....

.... Post code ....

Send to: **Cash Sales, Nexus Books, 332 Ladbroke Grove, London W10 5AH**

Please enclose a cheque or postal order, made payable to Virgin Publishing, to the value of the books you have ordered plus postage and packing costs as follows:

UK and BFPO – £1.00 for the first book, 50p for each subsequent book.

Overseas (including Republic of Ireland) – £2.00 for the first book, £1.00 for each subsequent book.

If you would prefer to pay by VISA or ACCESS/MASTER-CARD, please write your card number and expiry date here:

....

Please allow up to 28 days for delivery.

Signature ....

Please print on the lines / lines listed above

Send/to: Cash ... Pearson House, ... Aragon Street, Finton W10 5AH

Please enclose a cheque/postal order, made payable to Virgin Publishing ... the books you have ordered, plus postage and packing costs as follows:
UK and BFPO – ... In the destination A copy for each subsequent book.
Overseas (including Republic of Ireland) for the first book, £... for each subsequent book.

If you would prefer to pay by VISA or ACCESS/MASTERCARD, please write your card number and expiry date here:

Please allow up to 28 days for delivery.

Signature ...